BORN BRAVE: GARRICK

A Romantic Suspense

PINE CROSSING COWBOYS

JULIET BRILEE

ACKNOWLEDGMENTS

Thank You

I couldn't write my books without the amazing team of friends, family, and paid professionals who offer their expertise and observations. Special thanks go to the firefighter EMTs, people in law enforcement, military veterans, medical professionals, and ranchers who have advised me. Thanks go to Joshua for his input about navigating the world while visually impaired. And special thanks go to my writing groups. Your feedback and inspiration is invaluable.

For information about Post Traumatic Stress Disorder, visit: https://www.ptsd.va.gov

https://www.psychiatry.org/patients-families/ptsd/what-is-ptsd

For information about domestic violence for yourself or someone you might know: National Domestic Violence Hotline USA https://www.thehotline.org/

For more information about the five love languages and the book by Gary Chapman
https://5lovelanguages.com

CHAPTER ONE

G arrick Stone stared in the direction the trauma team had taken his patient. Double doors closed behind the gurney. Beeping and murmuring voices, the usual late-night hospital sounds, faded into the background as he fought back the images escaping the vault inside him. He finished typing his report and wrapped up his conversation with Janie, the ER nurse.

"I hope that's it for tonight," Janie said, drawing down her brows. "You look how I feel." Despite being busy and hardened, as you had to be to survive in this environment, she noticed the details and showed empathy. She was good people.

"Yeah." He huffed. In the months he'd worked for the Pine Crossing Fire and Rescue District, he'd witnessed a lot—and years working as a combat medic should have prepared him. He'd seen worse. But tonight, it got to him. Tonight, it was a young girl. "Call when you know something?"

"Seriously?"

"If you don't mind." Following up on the sick and injured people he'd transported to Heron Park Mercy wasn't part of the job. Unless he caught the gossip at the feed store or diner, he never even knew if his efforts had paid off.

"Okay." She shrugged. "But it might be a while."

"Thanks." The automatic doors of the emergency room entrance whooshed as he strode through them and over to his rig. His driver, the EMT, had their rescue cleaned and was restocking the cervical collar.

"You ready to heat up the bricks?" Levi drawled.

The corner of his mouth lifted at another one of Levi's odd expressions. "All set." They climbed in, and Levi started it up.

He squeezed his forehead between his thumb and fingers, relieving the tension.

It's not your emergency. It's not your emergency.

His chief had told him to remember that when he'd taken the job. It was true. What might be the absolute worst day for that family wasn't his emergency. But he'd seen a kid like that before, back in Afghanistan.

And he'd seen her again. Last night, in his dream.

A wave of guilt and regret pressed on his chest, and he brought his attention to the city lights giving way to dark landscape outside the window. Long ago, he'd learned to compartmentalize. There were more vaults and catacombs inside him than under Rome and Paris put together. But lately, the hinges on those doors seemed rusty, and memories were slipping out, affecting him more than usual.

Like other veterans, he'd been offered various services when he'd separated from the Army. And like most guys he knew, he'd barely taken advantage of them. He didn't need to talk. He was good. Tough. And he'd wanted to get back to real life. Normal. What was that, exactly? If normal was a place, he couldn't find it if you handed him a map.

It might be time to go back to that group at the Vet Center.

"Did you get a chance to talk to Janie?" Levi asked.

"Not much."

"But you talked to her. How'd she look? Did she ask about me?"

He snorted. Levi had it bad. "She was busy." What was this, grade school? He wouldn't play middleman for Levi and Janie. If Levi wanted to go out with the woman, he'd have to figure it out.

"Did you see Kelsey?" Levi asked.

"I didn't notice."

Levi gave him a skeptical glance.

Kelsey, an ER tech, was Janie's friend, and Levi had it in his head that they should all four go out. They'd run into Janie and Kelsey when they'd stopped for a beer at Turner's Tap, and Levi had fallen hard and fast.

He didn't have that problem.

A quick scan of the ER had revealed no sign of Kelsey, and Garrick had breathed a little easier. After breaking his rule and going out with Kelsey a second time, he'd decided to make a list. Rule number one. Only date tourists. Rule number two. Don't forget rule number one.

Levi continued, "I was thinkin' we'd go to Pete's and dance. Janie likes to dance."

"You're on your own. Things are good the way they are. I'd rather go to Turner's. Less complicated."

True, he'd been agitated lately, not because he needed a woman—something else was happening. When he'd earned his paramedic certification and taken the job offering high-stakes work with a solid team, a legitimate way to help, he'd figured that would do the trick. The job should be a perfect fit. What was wrong with him?

Darkness blanketed the road as their rescue headed toward the independent volunteer fire station in the small town of Pine Crossing, about an hour in from the SW Florida coast. They pulled into the firehouse and unloaded their gear.

Zeke, the fire chief, appeared in the doorway. "I got a call from the ER. Janie wanted me to tell you the girl's still critical but holding on. Same with the mom. And the adult male will be released soon."

"That's what I'm talking about." Levi fist-bumped Zeke. "I need me some coffee." He headed into the lounge.

"Good to hear." Garrick turned away. It'd been a miracle the girl had made it to the ER alive. She'd lost so much blood, and he'd only been able to give her isotonic IV fluid. There was likely internal bleeding, and her spleen was probably involved. Her small arms and face were cut up from glass and metal. The woman was worse, but she'd arrived in a different rig.

Dead on his feet after being up thirty-six hours, dealing with bad news would've been rough, but it was too soon to celebrate. Still, his shoulders relaxed, and he shut the door on the memory of the girl in that village, back in Kandahar.

"Are you staying?" Zeke nodded toward the bunk room.

It was supposed to be his day off, and ranch chores came early. He'd been playing poker when the call came in requesting additional support. As the paramedic on staff, Garrick had stepped up. It had been a bad wreck, and three other rigs had transported injured to Heron Park South.

An image of his own bed came to mind. "I'll stay if you need me."

Zeke waved a hand, dismissing him. "Cody and Walt will be here in a few hours. Levi and I will handle anything else that comes in." Molly, their female firefighter, often worked with Levi, but she was out sick.

The chief lived in the house behind the fire station, supposedly a perk of the job, but it meant Zeke was never entirely off duty. The firehouse had a crew of seven, with two paid staff members on-site at any given time. Others were officially on call, and the others off duty, but along with their fifty or so volunteers, wore pagers in case they were needed. Apps on their phones gave them more details when they got the page, but some of them lived in areas where cell service was spotty.

Zeke cocked his head. "Are you safe to drive? You look..."

He raised his palm. "I've been worse."

His friend nodded slowly. "Okay then." A few years older,

Zeke was his friend and his boss and knew a bit about Garrick's time in the Army.

Garrick hit the john and splashed cold water on his face, then climbed into his Jeep. Before he put it in drive, his phone buzzed with a text.

Avery: *Garrick?*

Avery? Why would his nineteen-year-old niece be texting him at this hour? A lump formed in his throat as he wrote back. His dad had been recovering from a stroke but was almost back to normal—and now pushed himself too hard. But if anything would've happened, wouldn't he have heard the 911 call on the radio? And Zeke would've told him if he'd missed it.

Garrick: *Everything okay?*

He studied the screen, drumming his fingers on his thigh, waiting for the reply. The phone vibrated in his hand. Avery was calling.

"Garrick. Good," Avery slurred her words a little. "I figured you might still be up."

She didn't sound upset. Was she...had she been drinking?

"Where are you?" he demanded. "Are you okay?"

"I'm sleeping over at Emma's and ...well. We just got in from a party."

He ground his teeth. At three-thirty? There'd likely been alcohol there, but he had little room to talk. He'd raised hell when he'd been her age. "I might've been sleeping."

"And I wouldn't have called if you hadn't texted back."

"Fair enough. What's up?"

"Uncle Garrick," Avery's Georgia accent became more pronounced, and her voice filled with honey. "I need a favor." She always used that sweet tone to get what she wanted from his brothers or the other cowboys on the ranch. It wouldn't work on him.

"What?"

"I need you to feed Bambi and Snowy."

"Come again?"

"They still need bottles."

She wasn't seriously asking him to bottle-feed her baby goats. Was she? The first-time mama goat didn't have enough milk for her babies. He knew that, but until now, hadn't seen that intel as relevant.

"They still need to be fed four times a day, and well," Avery's tone lowered, "I shouldn't drive home because...."

"You went to a party and got wasted?"

"Not exactly wasted. But...please. I'll owe you. I fed them early last night. They need to be fed extra early this morning."

He snorted.

"Don't tell my dad or Jack. I promised I'd be responsible."

"I didn't say yes." The vision of his bed was breaking into pieces.

"Please. I'll make you cookies. Peanut butter-oatmeal."

He would've done it anyway, but he wouldn't turn down homemade cookies. "I'm not lying to my brothers for you." His half-brother, Luke, had adopted Avery when he'd married her mom. It still boggled his mind. And Avery called Luke "Dad". How strange was that?

Avery continued, "If you get the goats fed soon, they might never know."

"I'll handle it. And you shouldn't be out there drinking until all hours." He winced hearing himself, sounding so parental, feeling older than his thirty-nine years. But he'd seen the carnage resulting from those back-pasture parties.

"I'm tired, Uncle Gare. I need to get off now."

The call ended, and he stared at the phone. She was tired? He hadn't had eight hours of sleep in years.

He drove the dark seven-mile stretch to Tall Pines and pulled in front of the cottage he called home. Several months ago, his oldest brother married a woman who lived at the ranch. She'd moved in, and Garrick had moved out and taken her empty house.

It's the damnedest thing. When he returned from overseas,

he hated staying at the house with his father and brother. Their bickering brought back all kinds of bad memories. Living with family again was strange enough, but settling in on a different ranch from the one in Montana where he'd been raised was like slipping into someone else's life. It made him feel like some kind of alien body snatcher. Only this body, so achy and scarred, had to be his.

Before setting up a hideout in the abandoned farmhouse next door, he'd enjoyed solitude sleeping outside in a hammock, listening to the birds. Now that he lived in his own house, with as much alone time as he wanted, the quiet got to him, made him miss the camaraderie of Army life.

He changed his clothes and headed over to the small barn he'd helped his brothers build for the goats—an Avery project. One step inside, and the smell engulfed him. Images flooded his mind, taking him back to the outskirts of that village in the desert.

He anchored himself in the present moment. He stared at the hay, the new fridge, the microwave—the orderly system Avery had created. This was new, shiny, and state-of-the-art, thanks to Luke subsidizing Avery's venture. Nothing like the dusty images fighting for space in his head. He focused on the texture of the bottle in his hand and checked the time. Zero four hundred. He was here. Florida. It was early morning. February. Family was nearby. No threats.

He prepared the formula, scooped up the first kid, and leaned back on a bale of hay holding the small creature. It bleated as he positioned the nipple, and the goat greedily drank. Soft and warm, it nestled into him. It was kind of ... nice. Ten percent of his tension drained away. He'd never admit it to anyone else, but goat-feeding didn't suck. When the first goat finished, he moved on to the next one, alert for the sounds of his brothers.

Boots thudded in his direction. His senses sharpened. Who else would be working this early?

Striker, the foreman, entered the small barn, wearing a wary frown.

"Morning." Garrick adjusted the goat in his arms and continued feeding it as though it was the most natural thing to be doing.

Striker gave him a solemn nod. "Morning, Avery."

Garrick huffed.

"You coming to the meeting this morning?"

"Probably not." By the time they met, he'd usually be long gone.

"Want to check on the new calves or work the fence?"

"Fence. I'll sign the board."

Striker stood for a moment and watched him feed the kid in his arms, then left, leaving his questions unasked.

Garrick left them unanswered. He wouldn't lie, but he wouldn't snitch on Avery. Even though the goats were her project, he'd rather be here, doing this, than have her drive home in a compromised state.

When the goats were fed and nestled in the hay sleeping, he strolled out of the barn, the walking dead, too restless to head inside and try to sleep.

The task clipboard hung in its usual spot on the wall in the old barn. He signed himself onto fence duty and saddled up Rusty. The others usually used the utility four-wheeler, but he preferred horseback.

The partial moon was enough to ride by but not to work. He fetched his new high-powered headlamp from the gear bag he kept in his Jeep. With tools and supplies loaded in his saddle bags, Garrick rode out. The landscape was beautiful in the soft glow of predawn, and he inhaled the sweet fragrance on the mild winter breeze. Orange blossoms, from the grove to the north, scented the air for miles.

He worked for nearly an hour before the sun stretched over the horizon. Ahead, a bald eagle glided to the tree where its mate awaited.

This was the closest he got to happiness, a quiet morning wearing loneliness like a comfortable old coat. Guys like him weren't cut out for marriage and kids, and he'd made peace with it. But watching those two eagles perched on their usual limb, their white crowns aglow in the early beams of light filled his chest with a pang of...something.

CHAPTER TWO

S kylar McClure swung the sledgehammer with a satisfying crash. Drywall shattered. She hoisted the hammer and whacked again. With the back of her gloved hand, she pushed damp hair off her forehead, then began removing the stubborn chunks. The best part of renovating was taking out her aggression in the tear-down phase.

She glanced at the clock. "What?" There was only ten minutes until her online meeting with her coaching client? Why had she allowed her morning client call to run over? It put her behind on her renovating. This day had been planned to the minute. Boundaries. She needed better boundaries. But how could she end the call with her client in tears?

Debris covered the gutted living room. She scurried around, gathering, and filling a large trash can. No use. There wasn't enough time. Tonight, while Logan slept, she'd clean up and be ready for the carpenters arriving in the morning.

She cracked the lid on the crock pot, and the aroma of chili, one of her favorite winter meals, made her mouth water. They'd eat, and then she had another client call between dinner and bath time.

Life had been much easier when she was simply an aunt. But

this is what she had to do. As soon as she thought she had this whole mom thing down, Logan would hit a new milestone—or not—which was worse, and Skylar would have to figure it out again.

Skylar washed her dusty arms, pulled on a clean top for the video session, checked her reflection, and scoffed. Dust covered the slight wrinkles around her eyes and somehow got under her cap, giving her brown hair unwanted highlights. If her mama, a gentle and proper southern woman, God rest her soul, could see her ... she'd have an absolute fit. She raised her face skyward. "Sorry, Mama. This is what works for me right now."

She rinsed her face and slicked on some lipstick, hoping for a semblance of professionalism. This entire situation made her feel incompetent in all arenas. While not a great role model as a life coach, at least she had a firm grip on stress and juggling a busy schedule. That had to count for something.

If she didn't have to stop working on the remodel to take client calls, she'd progress faster. But if she didn't have client calls, she wouldn't have the income she needed to help fund the renovations. Because of the coaching and renovation business, she had to put Logan in preschool. This circle was so vicious it had fangs.

She drew three deep, slow breaths.

You're not a bad mother. You're a good enough mother.

Living in the houses she renovated saved money but brought challenges. She always had to have a safe and orderly area for Logan—that was nonnegotiable. Which meant rehabbing one of the bedrooms first and fast, even if it wasn't the most logical or cost-effective sequence.

Thankfully, Max, her boss and business partner, supported her priorities. She got to live in the houses they bought as soon as they were habitable. She'd even stayed with him and his wife for a few nights when they'd first bought this house. Loud and crowded with his four teenage boys, it was a real circus, and

Logan had been more withdrawn than usual. They'd moved out as soon as possible.

She set her tote by the front door and slipped into nicer shoes. After this session, she'd have to race to pick up Logan from pre-school, then whisk her to the appointment with the psychologist. They shouldn't be late. The speech therapist had called in a favor and gotten them worked in. Otherwise, they would've had to wait a month for an appointment. The parenting book stressed how she needed to get Logan's issues addressed before starting school.

While she waited on her laptop for her client to login, she opened the real estate app on her iPad. If she found a third property nearby, Logan could stay at the same preschool through the summer.

Funds were tied up in the two fixer-uppers they'd bought, and if she found a third, it'd be up to Max to finance it. Renovating and flipping houses turned a profit and their business was growing. But because they reinvested the money, her income still came from life-coaching.

A ringtone played on her phone. She was confused. Wasn't this supposed to be a video session?

Where was her phone anyway?

She followed the music, stepping over bits of drywall, paper, and wood, and found her phone on the table by the door.

It wasn't her client.

Cook County flashed on the screen. A chill ran down her spine, and she hesitated, tempted to press decline. She forced herself to answer.

"Hello?"

"Ms. McClure?" The voice was warm and familiar. "This is Deborah Marshall from Victim Services. We spoke a few months ago. How are you doing?"

"I'm fine. And yourself?" It had been trained into her to be polite, but nerves buzzed like she'd been plugged into an electrical outlet. "Is this about the appeal?" Clive Warwick had gone to jail two years earlier but had been working on getting the sentence overturned.

"Yes. I'm sorry to have to tell you this. They should have informed me, but someone dropped the ball. Anyway, I'm calling now. It's about the court date."

The room around her faded away as all of her focus zoomed in on the phone. "When is it?"

Deborah paused, then lowered her voice, which made her tone more foreboding. "A little while ago. And the charges were overturned. Clive Warwick is free. He's being processed out now, as we speak.

Skyler dropped onto a chair and tried to breathe. The phone slipped to the floor, clunking on the edge of her toolbox.

"Are you there? Are you alright?" Deborah's voice came from the dust below her.

With icy fingers, Skylar fetched the phone and dusted it off, wincing. The screen was cracked. No time to worry about that. Her heart hammered at the base of her throat. "How...?" It didn't matter how or why.

She had to leave.

Now.

"Are you okay?"

"I'm here. Thanks." She had to pack. Oh my gosh, she thought she'd have more warning. Skylar scanned the room, identifying essentials.

"I'm sor—"

"Thanks. I have to go." She ended the call. What should she do? Max. She had to call Max. Later. From the road, at a rest area. And Nadine, their assistant, was coming back from her trip tomorrow. They were supposed to have lunch the next day. She'd worry about that later.

Skylar slid her laptop and tablet into a tote, then ran into the bedroom and stuffed clothes into suitcases, cramming them in. There was no time to worry about folding them. Logan's toys and clothes filled the pink pony bag and a suitcase. Where's Pegasus? Logan always slept with the stuffed unicorn. She pulled back the sheet, searched under the bed, and rechecked all the rooms. Oh, no. Just when the day couldn't be any worse. Logan would have a fit if she didn't have Pegasus. The darn thing was nowhere.

She called off the search and lugged the suitcases out to the car. Relief! The stuffed unicorn sat beside Logan's car seat. She'd brought it along for the morning ride to daycare.

Back inside, she circled like a whirlwind, gathering items and filling her cooler with food for the road.

Once the SUV was loaded, she climbed into the driver's seat. Oh, hell! How could she forget her tools? She ran back inside, grabbed the toolbox, her power screwdriver, and drill case, hustled back to her SUV, and shoved it in the back with her suitcases. Then, on a whim, since she had space, she grabbed her roller and the two gallons of the costly paint she'd planned to use.

Max and his wife would handle what she'd left behind, including the chili.

At the red light, she quickly texted her client: *I'm really sorry. I'm under the weather. Let's reschedule. I'll call you tomorrow.*

It would take hours before Clive found her. But she wanted a good head start.

Skylar made the twelve-hour drive to her aunt's community near Chattanooga in eleven and a half. Not bad for driving carefully with a cranky four-year-old strapped into a car seat.

The clock displayed one-fifteen a.m.

Her eyes burned from staring at the highway. The dark, narrow streets of Aunt Janice's neighborhood were challenging to navigate, and the darn GPS took her to a dead end. She backed up and took a closer look at her map, then made a turn.

Relief washed through her. Down the road, with a light on outside, her aunt's home came into view.

A few years ago, she'd tracked down her father's older sister, and they'd been exchanging cards and emails and had spoken on the phone. This was her best hope.

She hiked Logan onto her hip, praying she wouldn't fully awaken, and approached the house.

Her aunt opened the door before Skylar knocked as though she'd been listening for the car. "Come on in. Y'all have got to be freezing." Janice's gaze darted around the dark street. She knew the reason for this visit.

Skylar followed her aunt into the warm house. Her aunt's sweet accent had always favored her mama's, and the aroma of dinner hung in the air, reminding her that many of the meals she'd eaten growing up were Aunt Janice's recipes. It felt like a homecoming. Like safety.

The clock chimed one thirty and brought her back to reality. This wasn't a family visit. She was in trouble.

"It's been too long." Aunt Janice offered her a small hug from the side opposite Logan. She hadn't seen Janice since her mother's funeral when she was ten. Her aunt's hair had turned salt and pepper gray, but her kind eyes and smile were the same. At one time, Aunt Janice had been an important part of her life, but ties to her father's family had been severed when her dad married Adrianna's mom, Vera.

Her dad's family had never liked Vera and she'd retaliated by cutting them off and lying about it—which was pure evil. For decades, her stepmother had led Skylar to believe Aunt Janice didn't want to see her.

When she'd learned Clive's conviction may be overturned, she'd reached out to Janice. If it hadn't been for Logan, she might've stayed in the Chicago area with Max and filed a restraining order. Done what she needed to do to arm herself. That man shouldn't be able to run her off. But she had to prioritize her niece, no—her daughter's—safety.

She put Logan down to sleep in the guest room with her favorite soft throw and stuffed unicorn, leaving the door cracked. Later, she'd slip in beside her on the full-size bed and try to sleep. Fat chance. She was more wound up than a long-tailed cat on a porch full of rocking chairs.

Aunt Janice set two cups of hot chocolate on the table and gave her shoulder a little squeeze. The kind gesture loosened the grip she had on her emotions, and tears pricked at the corners of her eyelids. Other than Max and his wife, she couldn't recall the last time someone had taken care of her.

"So, it's come to this?" Aunt Janice's forehead gathered into worry lines.

Skylar nodded numbly. A rich dark chocolate aroma wafted up from the cup. She took a fortifying sip and let the comforting sweet liquid clear her head.

"I followed the trial on the news." Aunt Janice shook her head. "And now you have Logan."

"Tessa arranged for me to be her guardian, just in case." She clamped her jaw shut and tamped back the fury...the excruciating grief. Tessa had been concerned enough to handle the paperwork for her child but not determined enough to leave, even after Skylar had directed her to resources that may've helped. "I couldn't say no."

Tessa had insisted—she'd begged.

"Does your stepsister help?"

"No." She scoffed. Vera had brought her daughter, Adrianna, with her when she married Skylar's dad. Adrianna was Skylar's stepsister, but Tessa had been half-sister to them both. Tessa shared a father with Skylar, but Tessa shared a mother with Adrianna. Why didn't Adrianna care about Tessa like she did?

"Not at all?"

"She's sent money a few times when I asked for help. I had to cut way back on work for a while." It had been a shocking and difficult adjustment for both her and Logan.

"I guess that's better than nothing." Aunt Janice pursed her lips.

It was barely better than nothing.

"I never met your half-sister," Aunt Janice continued, "but ... how tragic."

She nodded and drew strength from the mug of cocoa warming her icy fingertips.

"Tessa didn't want Vera to have her?" Aunt Janice tilted her head.

Skylar scoffed. "No. Vera wouldn't have wanted Logan anyway. Last I heard, she was somewhere in Spain. I think she's seen Logan once." Vera was Tessa's mother and a logical choice for raising Logan. But she hadn't put up any fight when Tessa named Skylar as Logan's guardian, or when Skylar adopted her. It might be cliché, but her stepmother was truly cold hearted.

"You certainly have your hands full. I wish y'all could stay here longer." Aunt Janice sounded genuinely regretful. "One month is it. This is a fifty-five and older community and there are restrictions on guests. People will probably start talking after a week. I'm afraid they're sticklers about the rules here."

"We don't want to cause any problems." At that moment, Skylar knew. They wouldn't stay more than a few nights, a week at the most. The regulations might say one month, but they should leave sooner. She couldn't drag her aunt into this mess. She was forty-two. Her father's older sister had to be close to eighty.

"I won't go back to Elmwood Park. Not until..." Skylar rubbed her cheek. It helped her think and soothed her. How long would she need to be gone? Forever? "I'm sure Clive will turn up. He thinks Logan is his."

"She isn't?"

"No. No! I've adopted her legally. Tessa had...well, she and Clive broke up and got back together a few times, and she... she didn't know who Logan's father was, but it wasn't Clive. Tessa didn't offer a father's name for the birth certificate." She took a sip of her hot cocoa. "Tessa and Clive broke up before Logan was born. But Tessa kept going back to him. She and Logan were staying with him when ...." It was so horrible, Skylar found it too difficult to continue.

The last time she'd seen her sister played on a loop through her mind. She'd warned Tessa not to go back, had practically pleaded, had given her the name of a good counselor, and even offered to pay. Could she have done more?

"And you think he's coming after you?"

She released a hard sigh. "I testified against him. And he seems to think that since he was with Tessa, Logan should be his."

A loud noise came from outside. Skylar startled.

Aunt Janice's brows drew together, and she stared at the door.

"That had to be a car backfiring ... or something," Skylar said.

They sat quietly listening.

Her pulse picked again, upending the comfort that had begun to settle over her. Could Clive find her here? He had brothers and friends who were loyal to him. Didn't law enforcement track you by your credit cards? It might not be too difficult for Clive to do it. Darn. She probably shouldn't be using her credit card. Was it a mistake to fill the gas tank when she'd pulled off the interstate? Or was she being paranoid?

"I appreciate you letting us come. We won't stay more than a few days. I don't have another plan on where to go. Not yet. But I'll figure it out. I'll get a loan from my business partner and buy a property to renovate, somewhere farther south and, I don't know... I started using my maiden name again when I adopted Logan. That might help." Providing her sister hadn't told Clive her other name. Oh, rats. It might not be difficult to look that up, either.

If she'd lived a normal life, she might have college friends to stay with, even people from high school. But after her father's death, her stepmother had moved them several times. Vera had reminded Skylar that she was the stepdaughter. Vera owed her nothing, and she was lucky not to be put in foster care.

Vera had put her in charge of cooking, cleaning, and caring for her younger sisters, leaving little opportunity for making friends. Because of it, Tessa had considered Skylar more of a mother than an older sister.

Aside from Max, Nadine was the closest thing she had to a friend, but she lived in Elmwood Park. Clive would be searching all of the suburbs where Skylar had worked and lived. He had connections and would find them there.

They sat in silence for a few minutes. Her aunt's black cat wandered into the room and stared at them with scolding yellow eyes as though asking what they were doing up so late. Then, the kitty began licking its paw.

Skylar finished her hot chocolate. Perhaps after a good night's sleep she'd be fresher and would be able to figure out their next step.

"There's something I need to show you." Aunt Janice pushed herself out of the chair and walked to the antique desk at the end of the room. After rifling through the contents, she pulled out a book and retrieved an old document. "This." Crisp paper crackled as Aunt Janice unfolded the yellowed sheets. With gnarled fingers, she handed it over. A faded old photograph attached to the papers, came loose, and fluttered to the table.

"What is it?" Skylar asked, examining the black and white polaroid of a rundown farmhouse.

"That old house, my dear, is part of our family's legacy. When we were children, your father and I visited our grandparents there at Christmas." Her aunt's gaze became unfocused, and a small smile curved the corners of her lips.

"This is the farm he talked about?" Skylar scrutinized the photo, looking for some sign of the memories her dad had shared.

"Yes. There were orange trees, and they grew strawberries. There were chickens, cows, and horses. Those were happy times.

It's not much now, but it's sitting on eighty acres. Your father was meant to inherit it. I've talked to my attorney several times and considered selling the property, but it generates an income. The land is leased to the neighboring ranch for grazing. I don't know the details. It's been leased for a long time. Your uncle handled that when he first got sick, and he set it up with a management company. A check gets deposited in my account every month. I'm old. My needs are met. I have investments and I don't need that income."

Aunt Janice folded her hands and sat taller. "It should be yours. If you like fixer-uppers, this will be a dream. I don't know what kind of shape it's in. My grandfather built it, and he was a good carpenter. But it's old. We had a renter, quite a while back, who wanted to install solar power. He dropped the project and left in a hurry for some family emergency. The house is likely a wreck. It might even be condemned." Aunt Janice glanced at the guest bedroom door. "It's probably not fit for Logan. Sell it. Find a fresh start."

"This is for me?" She stared at the photo with fresh eyes.

"I had it in my will to go to you, sweetie. But I want you to have it now. I have no plans to go to Florida. Michael was provided for in his father's will. This was supposed to go to your dad, anyway. It's yours."

Aunt Janice could have so easily left the house to her own son, Skylar's cousin. But she wasn't. Skylar swung her gaze from the photo to her aunt, who looked a lot like a fairy godmother.

"Once we transfer the deed," Aunt Janice continued, "you'll start collecting the rent."

"This is the answer to my prayers." Trellises with climbing roses, a front porch—Skylar couldn't help it—possibilities streamed into her mind. The house had potential, providing it had good bones.

"You may want to see it in person before you say that."

"Believe me, I've rehabbed some real dumps."

"It's Florida. There are bugs, alligators, snakes. It's not all white sand beaches. But there is a beautiful beach an hour away."

Skylar got out of her seat and circled Aunt Janice in a hug. "It's perfect for us."

Her aunt patted her back. "We'll make an appointment with the attorney and file a quitclaim deed and you'll own yourself a dump."

"A dump on eighty acres." Skylar could burst with the happiness bubbling inside her. She could hardly believe it. The sale of a few acres would certainly finance rehabbing the property and give her a fresh start. This was the place her father had talked about. It was almost like having a piece of her dad for her and Logan. Her mind raced with possibilities. It sat on eighty acres. How bad could it be?

CHAPTER THREE

Skylar's GPS cut out a few times when her cell reception fell off. She groaned. It was late, and Logan had been bored and fussy before falling asleep. She pulled off the two-lane state road and used the light on her phone to study an old-school paper map. The small town of Pine Crossing sat six miles behind her. Ahead stood a sign for Wren's Organic Produce—not on the map. She opened the map app on her phone and held it out the window. Please, please work, darn thing.

The map downloaded. There! Wrens Organic's Produce, a couple miles before Tall Pines Ranch, and after that, her farm. Yay! Relief washed through her. Finally, after two days of driving and sleeping at rest areas, they'd arrived at their new home.

She'd rehabbed enough almost teardowns to know it might be a major disaster. It didn't matter. This was hers. After transferring the property through the quitclaim, and tying up the other loose ends, Aunt Janice handed her the keys. She'd even insisted on stopping by the hardware store for a bug bomb. Seriously?

She pulled back onto the dark road and drove the last several miles. The fencing changed from three-rail white to something more difficult to see. But yes, there was a fence. Letters spelling McClure's Farm filled a rectangular sign hanging from an old metal arch marking the dirt drive. There was a gate. Not electric.

Skylar struggled with the old latch, and—ewww—something grimy got all over her hands. She pulled the gate open, wiped her hands on her pants, and breathed a sigh of relief. Then she had the task of shutting the darn thing behind her car. It seemed prudent. Any barriers she put between them and Clive, or his brothers, would help.

Aunt Janice had given her some cash, and she'd been careful not to use her credit cards. She had left no trail.

Clive won't find us.

Still, it made sense to be cautious.

It would be dawn in a few hours. Waiting until daylight to enter the house seemed better. She covered herself with a sweater, curled up on the front seat of her SUV, raised her face skyward, and whispered, "We're here, Dad. I'll do you proud." For the first time in years, she was home. Really and truly home. She closed her lids and fell into an exhausted sleep.

Skylar jerked awake, startled at the huge eyes and enormous tan body standing outside her car. And horns. The thing had horns.

"Cow," Logan said from her car seat. "Mommy. A cow." She pointed. Her face filled with wonder.

"Yes, it's a cow."

At least Logan started the day talking. That was a good sign, though her sentences were still short phrases. It was an improvement over the stretch of time after Tessa's death that Logan had stopped talking altogether. She'd only been two, but it had been alarming. The speech therapist said she was still lagging behind. Logan had the vocabulary. And some days she used full sentences, five or six words. She was very bright. But when she was stressed, she fell silent again.

Skylar surveyed the area. Large trees spread wide branches against the pink sky. Huge piles of brown palm fronds lay on the ground around shaggy palm trees that looked nothing like they did in travel brochures. It was astonishingly flat. Not a hill in sight. And there was so much green. Even now, in mid-winter.

In the first light of dawn, she could make out groups of cows freely grazing in her yard. "There are lots of cows. Aren't they pretty?"

Her forehead tightened. What were all these cows doing so close to the house? Was that right? Aunt Janice said the neighbors were leasing land, but didn't the livestock live in pastures? She swung her gaze around. A fence circled the property closest to the house, but a section to the west lay broken. Cows streamed through the opening like they'd been invited to a picnic of grass greener on the other side.

The darn cattle shouldn't be in her yard. It may not be safe to walk near them. Were some of them bulls? Did they randomly charge at people? She groaned. The number for the management company was somewhere in her paperwork. They could contact the ranch. How long would that take? Should she drive to the ranch and demand they remove their cattle? She didn't have the energy for that right now.

If she pulled close to the front door, they'd be able to get past the cows and into the house safely. She started the car and waved her hand outside the window. "Go. Shoo! Get away."

The large cow moved a few more feet, then wandered off to join the others closer to the fence. Thank God!

She parked near the door, hiked Logan onto her hip, and, carrying her battery-operated lantern, approached the steps leading up to the old white wooden house. For a moment, she simply stood on the wide, crumbling concrete step, taking it all in. There was no porch, which felt wrong. A covered porch, overlooking the countryside, would be wonderful. She'd build one as soon as possible.

Birdsong filled the morning, loud, as though there were extra birds here, and she'd not heard one car. Even the air smelled different, although it wasn't bad. She inhaled deeply. Sweet, yet familiar. Some kind of flowers? There weren't any blossoms in the immediate vicinity.

Paint peeled from the wood siding and the trim around the windows. Boards covered the windowpanes. Something scampered under the raised house.

Unease prickled over her arms.

You've seen worse. That's all cosmetic. Except for the furry creature that's under the house—a possum? Everything about this place was so different from the suburban homes she was used to up north. So strange.

She set Logan down. "Stay close to me."

"Okay." Logan clutched her unicorn in the crook of her elbow and sucked her thumb.

Skylar winced. They'd broken that habit, but this week had been full of change, and Logan needed stability.

The key turned in the front door lock. She cautiously stepped inside.

It wasn't as dark as expected. Her lantern cast a wide, bright glow, and early daylight poured through the back bedroom through an exposed window. Planks of wood sat at the end of the room near some unfinished shelving. She studied the area. It appeared surprisingly clean, as though it'd been swept.

Where were the insects her aunt had warned her about? Here and there, a dead bug lay feet up. But there didn't appear to be any major infestation. Had someone recently treated the house for pests?

She headed toward the room with light streaming through the uncovered windowpane. Her forehead gathered. A flashlight, a lantern—much nicer than hers—bottled water, and a small stack of books sat beside a sleeping bag.

Chill bumps raced down her arms, making the hairs on her forearm twitch. Was someone squatting here? She tried the flashlight. Wow! It was nice and bright. And new. The expiration date on a bottle of water was a few months out. With such clean, high-end camping equipment, the squatter probably wasn't a homeless person.

But who?

If someone was staying here, they'd have some explaining to do. And she needed a plan to protect her and Logan, to be ready if anyone showed up. It was a little late to think of getting a weapon, and she hated the idea of having a firearm in the house with Logan. She scanned the room. Bingo. There was a pry bar like the one she used when prying vinyl off of floors. She set it aside. It was pretty feeble, as protection went, but it made her feel better.

She shook out the sleeping bag. There were no pests, and it was in excellent condition and had another blanket stuck inside. Well, finders keepers. She'd brought bedding, but this would make a nice addition. Skylar spread it over the wooden floor and set out Logan's toys and a small device loaded with her favorite movies.

"Okay, sweetie. Sit right here while I get the rest of our stuff out of the car." Once her daughter was situated with books and toy ponies and listening to a video that Skylar could recite from memory, she organized their meal, which consisted of a bottled coffee for herself, and a juice box and a granola bar for Logan.

While Logan ate and played, she unloaded the car.

It took a dozen trips to haul in all their stuff.

The ceiling light didn't come on, which wasn't really a surprise. It was Thursday. She'd go to town and deal with the electricity. Or should she? If she had power, it would be obvious someone was here. And she'd have to sign up using her name and this address. Even though she'd gone back to her maiden name, living off the grid for a while longer seemed prudent.

On a whim, she tried the kitchen faucet. It ran clear. Running water? How? She walked outside, circled the house, and found what she was looking for—a working water pump, thanks to a solar panel. But the old, disconnected water heater had seen better days. There'd be no hot running water for a while. That would go to the top of her to-do list. For now, they'd make do with water heated using her camp stove. It'd served her well during a few of her sketchier renovations.

She pulled her shoulders back and summoned the determination that typically propelled her into a new project. This could work. The weather was nice and was predicted to be in the fifties and sixties. With running water, food, and shelter, they were good.

A truck drove past the house. She counted three men. A short distance behind them came a man on a motorcycle. The hairs on her neck prickled. Her SUV sat right out front. They were too exposed. In an abundance of caution, she drove her vehicle around to the back of the house and pulled between the thickets. Although pretty hidden, she dragged over branches and dried palm fronds. There. It was less visible.

They were safe.

For now.

Garrick jerked, knocked his head on the side table, and fell to the floor, coming fully awake. Sweat slicked his skin.

Another nightmare.

He disentangled himself from his sheets and found his footing. Heart hammering like a beast in his chest, he stood naked in his bedroom and rubbed the place on his head that'd hit the nightstand. That would leave a knot.

Using the bedding that had fallen on the floor, he blotted his face and pulled on his boxers. He willed the troubling images from his brain, replacing them with more pleasant memories of playing poker with his brothers last night, of the excellent steak dinner Jack had prepared. His brother had even made brownies.

The old refrigerator hummed in the dim house. Nearly zero seven hundred hours. He'd overslept. But five hours of sleep was cause for a celebration. Usually, he was lucky to get four. By the time he reached the barn, the morning meeting would be over. Win-win. He cracked a smile at that.

Since Jack had married Luke's sister-in-law, the tension between his two older brothers had eased, making the morning meetings more bearable. But, bottom line, after being away for so long, he was a grunt. They didn't want or need his input. His brothers and Striker could duke it out over being the boss. He didn't want to be around for all that posturing.

On the days he wasn't at the fire station, he chose to labor like a cowboy and go about his other interests. His skill set was vast but mostly wasted at the ranch.

While coffee dripped, he popped two ibuprofen and a Tylenol. He rubbed the scar where the bullet nicked his rib. He was lucky, but on some days, his injuries still talked to him. He had a prescription for stronger pain meds but rarely took them. That stuff messed him up, and he liked having a clear head.

He pushed his body into his routine of pull-ups, squat thrusts, hand release pushups, and flutter kicks, followed by two hundred sit-ups and topped it off with a three-minute plank. His abs burned. His arms were on fire and his back ached where arthritis had settled into that injury. Maybe he should've skipped the squat thrusts today, but at least now he had a reason to be sweaty.

Holding four jerky sticks and a go-cup of coffee, he headed to the barn, ready for a day working the ranch. He may even catch a few hours of reading at the abandoned farmhouse next door. He'd fixed up a space, a hideaway, where nobody could find him.

He tacked up Rusty, his red quarter horse, and rode into the west pasture, inhaling the sweet scents of morning mixed with the pervasive odor of cattle. Today, he'd check on the calves, a task typically involving two of them. He didn't mind getting an early start, working alone, and making a day of it.

Striker, their foreman, and Brick, one of their cowboys,

waved from across the pasture. He raised his hand, acknowledged them, and kept going. Before long, he located two calves, checked them out, and tapped on his device.

Shorty and Slim, the large gray guard donkeys, brayed as Garrick rode through the southeast pastures and approached the gate leading to the McClure's spread, eighty acres of leased grazing land adjacent to Tall Pines.

When he located and documented the three Brangus calves, movement at the far end of the field got his attention. Several head of cattle were clustered as though pushing at the fence.

Why?

He rode closer. Wire hung loose, and a fence post lay in the grass. Dammit. It hadn't been down the other day when he'd checked the fence.

Cattle pushed into the yard around the old house. Weeds grew tall in some areas, and trash hid in those patches. Someone needed to repair it today.

He pulled out his phone to text Striker, then stopped. Light shone through the cracks around the wood covering the window. His arms tightened, every sense on high alert.

They didn't own the old farmhouse, but he'd rid that roach hotel of bugs, cleaned the place up, and even repaired the damaged solar unit for the pump, getting the water working. It was his private sanctuary, and from the looks of things, someone was there.

Tension crept up his neck. The year before last, a gang of meth cookers had set up in a remote pasture of a nearby ranch. One man, a particularly nasty lowlife, had assaulted one of their employees and threatened his sister-in-law. That dirtbag was serving time now, but the others had gotten away. For months, he and his buddies had combed the countryside, searching for them.

Were they back? Using his space? The stuff he'd left inside? He growled. Those meth-heads might burn down the place and start a brushfire. Since Tall Pines leased it, he considered the

McClure land part of their ranch, and there's no way he'd stand for a criminal element on their property. Adrenaline set his nerves abuzz, but instead of shaking, he stilled, his mind growing more focused. The more adrenaline on the inside, the calmer he was on the outside. Although counterintuitive, it served him well.

Garrick tied Rusty to a fence post behind a stand of trees and crept toward the house. He circled the structure, stealthily moving from shrub to shrub, scanning the area for vehicles resembling those the meth dealers had used. A gray SUV had pulled tight between the thickets at the rear of the house. Clumps of branches nearly obscured the rear. Someone had done a poor job trying to hide it.

He stalked closer and snapped photos of the Illinois license tags. The vehicle may belong to contacts from out of town, or they could've used stolen plates. He tried the car door. Locked. There didn't seem to be much inside, just a car seat and an unopened juice box beside it. That didn't mean much. The car might be hot.

Even if it wasn't the meth dealers in the farmhouse, whoever had parked that SUV didn't want to be seen. Wood still covered the windows. That didn't bode well. And his stuff was in there. A nerd for the best gear, his new Fenix flashlight, Yeti cooler, and LED lantern cost almost what he made at the firehouse last week. There's also the sleeping bag his dad had given him for Christmas, with his military-issue poncho liner inside. That was irreplaceable.

But the other thing, the absolutely priceless thing, was the book of war poetry that'd belonged to his cousin, Brad, who died in action around the time Garrick took a round to the chest. He itched to get his stuff back. Those intruders might use it, trash it, or even sell it.

He pulled out his phone, ready to text his friend, but paused, debating what to do. Tate, a solid guy, would listen to him and respect his judgment. Flash was a wild card. Tate and Flash, along with a couple other men, worked for hire, or sometimes as volunteers, as local mercenaries, or superheroes, depending on who you talked to.

When he'd first arrived in Pine Crossing and met the two veterans, he'd joined in on some of their jobs. Now, between ranch work and his schedule at the fire station, he didn't participate as often. Sometimes, he missed it, but not as much as he thought he would.

He squeezed his forehead between his thumb and fingers while he debated. The thing to do was wait and recon. This was home, and he wanted control of what went down here. He excelled at working alone and had been recruited onto several task forces for special missions. He'd simply slip inside, gather more intel, and then, if needed, call in Tate and Flash. They'd return later, or he might take care of the target himself if there was only one or two. He never went anywhere without his blade and the compact Glock in his boot.

He pulled over the block that served as a step and silently removed the loose plywood from the back room, his usual entrance. He waited, alert to changes in the lighting, to sounds. The room appeared to be empty.

When he cracked the unlocked window, he paused and listened again.

Voices.

A man's voice, murmuring.

He stared inside but could only see a short distance down the hall. No sense in taking chances. He pulled his Glock from the leg holster and stuck it in his back pocket. In a fluid motion, he raised himself up and through the window, landing softly on the wooden floor. He'd been in and out of this old farmhouse enough to know every creaky board. It was his home away from home. And someone was trespassing.

A partial shadow fell on the wall outside the bathroom. A meth cooker?

Garrick quieted his breathing. The element of surprise was essential.

Whoever it was seemed to have disappeared. The hairs on the back of his neck prickled.

Walking on cat feet, he crossed the room and crept partway down the hall. From this vantage point, he could peer into adjacent rooms, far enough away to observe without getting involved.

He stopped. His lips parted in surprise. A kid?

There, in the glow of his new lantern, sat a little girl playing with a stuffed animal.

On *his* unrolled sleeping bag? What the hell?

What was she doing here? An image of another girl in another place came to mind and he quickly pushed it away. *Focus!*

Did this girl belong to one of the meth dealers? Had she been kidnapped?

He inched forward.

The child didn't look up.

Voices blared from the speaker of a device on the floor. There was something familiar about the words.

Then—from the corner of his eye—movement.

A metal bar. Coming his way.

He grabbed the weapon, spun to the side, ready to take the asshole down.

He halted.

A woman. Smallish.

"Get out!" she snarled, keeping a firm grip on her end of the rod.

"Calm down. I'm not here to hurt you or the kid." Garrick held tight to his end of the metal but lifted his free hand in a gesture meant to reassure. It also allowed him easier access to the 9mm in his pocket in case this bitch was completely bat-shit.

She spoke with an accent, familiar. Georgia?

Was it only her and the girl? He stilled, alert to any movement, listening for others.

Her gaze flicked to the room behind him. "You're trespassing. Leave. Don't come back. And tell whoever sent you she's not his."

"Lady, I think we have a misunderstanding. You're the one trespassing. I didn't come to hurt you." It's what he had to say, but it wasn't entirely true. If she was connected to that gang—if they'd kidnapped that kid—he'd need to handle it. He scanned the area again, wanting to confirm it was clear—but it was impossible without going room to room.

Even in the dim light, the woman appeared pale, her nostrils flared. Fear.

His paramedic training kicked in. "My name's Garrick. What's yours?"

Her tone was as hard as the metal in his grip. "My name's *get the hell out of my house.*"

"Hold up," he spoke calmly and kept his expression friendly. "Tall Pines Ranch leases this land. I've been taking care of this house. So how about we agree to have a little talk? Let's put down the metal bar, and I'll show you my ID." He was more than a little accommodating, and the paramedic ID would go a long way to inspire confidence. But she'd need to show him ID too. Who was she? Why was she here?

She stole a quick glance at the little girl on the sleeping bag. Fierce protectiveness burned in her expression. The child raised her face, and as the voices on her device continued, her big eyes shifted from the woman back to him. The girl squeezed her stuffed animal and sucked her thumb, her face trembling as though she was about to cry.

Ah, hell, he didn't want to scare the kid. This wasn't going as planned.

They stood in a stalemate for a long moment, each holding one end of the pry bar.

And then came music ... music he recognized. That *no worries* song. That's what was familiar. Disney's *Lion King* was playing in the other room.

Music filled the silence.

He stifled a chuckle at the absurdity of the situation. With his free hand, he removed his wallet from his pocket and let it hang open, flashing the two IDs he kept readily available. "See?"

"See what? It's too dark in here for me to read that."

He tossed it on the floor in front of her. "And I wear this." He touched the pager he always wore.

"What's that?" Still holding the end of the metal bar, she stooped down and pulled his wallet over, then stole furtive glances at the IDs as if he'd attack her if she took her eyes off him.

"A pager. I work for a volunteer fire department. Sometimes, we get called in when we're not on duty."

"A pager? Not a radio?"

He scoffed. "It's what they can afford."

While she studied his IDs, he waited patiently, letting her think she had some degree of power. She didn't. Even if she had a pry bar in each hand, she was no match for him. He kept his close-quarters combat skills sharp with mixed martial arts and Krav Maga training at the boxing club. It was difficult to tell her age. Late thirties? Her hair was thick and shiny, and her skin was healthy and smooth. The likelihood these two were with the meth dealers seemed pretty slim. Who were they?

"Here." She tossed his wallet back. "Skylar."

"Come again?"

"My name's Skylar. This is my house. It's belonged to my family for generations. We own the land those cows are grazing on. Or, more accurately, I own it." A hint of a smug smile curved her lips.

Huh? "Well, Skylar. I might need to check some ID, too, because I happen to know this property belongs to someone who lives in Tennessee." Their real estate agent had already approached an old woman about selling.

She huffed. "My Aunt Janice, who lives in *Chattanooga*, transferred ownership of the farm to me a few days ago. I have the paperwork as proof."

"I'll need to see it."

"Seriously?" Skylar set her end of the metal bar on the floor and shot him a *don't try anything* sidelong glance.

He worked to keep from laughing. Did she really think that carried any weight?

The child emerged from the room, the stuffed animal, a unicorn, pressed tight against her. "Mommy? I need..." She gave him a quick appraisal before glancing toward the bathroom. "It's dark."

"Okay, honey. I'll put the lantern in there. This man is leaving. He lives on the ranch that owns all those cows." Her tone said he'd better be telling the truth.

"I'll wait so you can show me your ID. And that paperwork." Garrick folded one arm across his chest and rested his other elbow on his hand, his thumb under his chin, a basic tactical stance offering the appearance of being relaxed. He could strike out or go for his Glock in an instant. He still wasn't positive the house was clear, but it looked more and more like these two were alone.

The woman led the kid into the bathroom using a lantern. *His* new lantern. His jaw hardened. They'd taken his gear.

He kept an eye on them until Skylar shut the bathroom door.

She had a pry bar, but that didn't mean she wasn't armed. She could have a weapon in the bathroom. He drew his 9mm and checked the house. When it proved clear, he stuffed his pistol back in his pocket and rested his hand on his right hip, ready.

This entire situation boggled his mind.

The little girl returned to the bedroom, and that *Lion King* song began playing again. It would be stuck in his head all day.

"The papers are in my tote." Skylar moved deeper into the bedroom with the girl and returned a moment later. Now that she didn't seem to be a threat, he indulged in a closer look. She wore baggy pants like a painter, and her flannel shirt hung open, revealing a tighter shirt beneath it. The honey badger was hot.

She extended an envelope.

He opened it and brought his attention to the paperwork. Unease washed through him. It appeared that she owned this property.

"I'm the landlord."

"I guess we're neighbors." He handed back the envelope.

"Apparently." She cocked her head, assuming her power. "And I'm requesting that you don't mention you saw us. To anyone."

That was an odd request. "Okay," he said slowly. "Do you want to—"

"Weren't you leaving?"

"I guess." He stood there awkwardly, his gaze shooting to the kid. His woobie, which had been inside his sleeping bag, sat balled up on top, serving as a hill for her toys. His woobie. His military-issued poncho liner that he'd hunkered down with in the field and later, in this cottage, on many a cold afternoon reading, was now covered with sparkly pink and yellow toy ponies. The sight made his insides clench. He fought back the urge to demand Skylar move the child and hand over his stuff. But they needed it more than he did. He'd get it later. "I'll let myself out the front door."

"Next time you want to visit." Skylar narrowed her gaze. "Use that entrance. And knock."

He moved through the house and out the front, casting a quick glance at the SUV in the bushes. What's her story? If she owned the house, why was she trying to hide? Skylar was running from someone. *She'd yelled, "Tell him she's not his."* Who had she thought he was?

And then it hit him. She'd said *next time.* Did she expect him to come back? Fresh energy charged through him. Was she interested in him? Nah. He'd gotten no signals, and why would he care? Skylar had a kid. He never got involved with women who had young children. Never got involved, period. Still, he stepped lightly as he walked back to Rusty.

Then his bubble burst. This situation messed up his family's efforts to buy the ranch. It'd already changed hands. But the owner hadn't wanted to sell. Real estate transactions were public records. He'd check on it.

He rubbed his forehead, confused. What good was the land to Skylar? Tall Pines had five more years on a lease. And despite the work he'd done to make it a habitable hideout for himself, the farmhouse was practically a teardown. How could she manage this place?

Chances were, they'd be gone soon.

Skylar lifted Logan to her hip and kissed her cheek, her heart still banging around her rib cage, a prisoner trying to escape. There were three things she knew for sure. For starters, she was rattled worse than she realized. Second, this was no place for a child unless she got busy making changes. And third. Yipes! That neighbor of hers was something else.

In the moment, she'd hardly noticed. But now that he was gone, now that he wasn't intimidating her with his ... his solid, masculine presence, his image was locked in her head. He lived at Tall Pines. Why had he been taking care of her farmhouse? Her gaze fell on the top-quality lantern, the sleeping bag, and the flashlight. The books. That stuff probably belonged to Garrick, but he hadn't said anything.

Dark-haired, light-eyed, and more handsome than a man had a right to be, Garrick could double as a rough and ready Hollywood star fresh out of an action movie. She wouldn't mind seeing him again.

Irrelevant. The very idea was absurd. Right now, it was all about survival. Rehabbing the house. Reinventing her life. That had to remain her focus. But she couldn't help it, a part of her pinged with attraction.

Her phone vibrated in her pocket.

A text from Nadine: *Miss you. How are you holding up?*

Skylar: *We're okay.*

Nadine: *Where are you?*

Skylar studied the question, her fingers hovering over the screen. Nadine didn't need to know where she was. They were becoming friends as well as coworkers, but everything they needed to do could be done virtually. Nadine might slip up and tell someone where they were.

Skylar: *out of town*

Nadine: *When r U coming back?*

Skylar cringed a little.

Skylar: *Not sure. Didn't Max tell you?*

Nadine: *He mentioned Clive. I hope you're taking some r &r. Make it a vacation. Meet someone.*

Had Nadine lost her mind?

Skylar: *Not happening.*

She laughed mirthlessly. She was on the run, and she'd told Nadine about her awful ex, Alan. She was supposed to have a vacation? Go out and meet someone? This was the worst time to think about that, even if she wanted to. Which she didn't.

Nadine: *There are good ones out there.*

Skylar: *We're ok as is, getting settled.*

Prior to her sister dying, she'd dated Alan. They'd discussed living together, but he'd resented the erratic hours she worked and took issue with the time she'd invested in Logan— tried to guilt her for doing what she had to do and became a demanding jerk.

Her renovating job was so physical, and the learning curve for parenting was so steep she could barely get through her days. Why make space for a man whose demands she'd have to accommodate and who she'd eventually disappoint?

She texted for a couple more minutes before putting the

phone away, her heart heavy, indulging in a moment of loneliness. Tessa was gone. Despite being eleven years older than Tessa, the two of them had been close. And now Max, Nadine, and her aunt were far away. Sentimentality wasn't her style since she moved from one home to another as she remodeled houses and they sold—but this was different, and she felt ungrounded. She wanted to keep Logan safe, but it had all happened so fast.

Now she owned this—eighty acres.

She gazed at the unfamiliar landscape outside and summoned resolve. This was the place where she'd put down roots and make a life for herself and her daughter.

CHAPTER FOUR

Each day, Skylar and Logan hiked a different section of her farmland. She imagined her father and aunt as children, running through the same fields she and Logan were walking, and a surprisingly deep sense of connection and family legacy filled her with purpose. Made her feel less alone. When she got the place fixed up, she'd invite Aunt Janice down at Christmastime. Wouldn't that be something?

While unfamiliar, this place wasn't so bad. Nadine had a point. She'd think of this as a vacation, like camping. It was time to regroup and come up with a plan.

The scent of flowers filled the air, and the weather was mild and sunny. Wildlife lived on the property: all kinds of long-legged birds, herons, and others with odd bald heads and long beaks—wood storks. Red-winged blackbirds perched atop fence posts, and bright red cardinals sang in the trees. And there were strange, large birds with colorful beaks. Caracaras.

Yesterday, a mama deer and her spotted fawn crossed the field in front of them. Off in the distance, piglets trailed behind a large wild boar, which, it turns out, was very dangerous. A flock of wild turkeys wandered the far pasture. She had half a mind to learn to hunt right about now because a turkey dinner, heck, anything fresh, would be wonderful.

They returned from their morning walk, her stomach growling and Logan cranky. "I'll have lunch ready in a minute, sweetie."

The meal of granola bars, meat sticks, a juice box for Logan, and bottled coffee for herself was less than appealing. Skylar tossed her dry protein bar in the trash. After roughing it for several days, it was clear this wouldn't work much longer. They needed good food cooked on a real stove and warm showers. She needed furniture—at least a mattress. Her daughter needed to get on a playground, to be with other kids,

It was Valentine's Day. When she was a kid, it meant cards and candy hearts. Thankfully, Logan was too young to understand. Skylar vowed to make it up to her next year, but perhaps she could go to town later to buy supplies and a chocolate-covered marshmallow heart for Logan. And she wanted to buy vegetables at the produce stand up the road. They could go there.

But she should give it one more day, just to be safe.

She followed Logan into her room, sat with her on the sleeping bag, and read her a book. The dim light strained her eyes. At this rate, she'd have a whopper of a headache. "Listen, kiddo. I'm going outside and taking the wood off the windows to make it nice and bright in here. Okay?"

Logan clutched a toy pony in each hand and walked them along the bedding. "Okay."

Skyler's heart sank. All the weeks and months of working hard, helping Logan socialize, and getting her to come out of her shell and talk would be lost if she didn't create a more normal environment and find a preschool. It was a risk.

After she'd testified against Clive at the trial, he wouldn't stop until he made good on his threats. He'd sent a message by way of his brother, and the words were seared into her memory. If only Clive wasn't so devious. In his polo shirts, wing tips, and power suits from his menswear store, he seemed like a regular guy, a catch, a real smooth talker—which made it all the scarier. Tessa had told her about his activities and how she'd feared for her life. Rightfully so. And Clive's connections, his friends, and his family would do things for him.

But a tiny town, hardly a spec on the map, well over a thousand miles from Chicago ... it was highly unlikely Clive would find them in Pine Crossing.

Would it be safe to start using her credit cards?

———

Garrick rode past the neighboring farmhouse, allegedly to make sure the fence repair was holding, but he had to find out. Was Skylar still there? Would his gear be there? What about Brad's poetry book? He could kick himself for not grabbing it the other day. Five nights in that dilapidated place would have most women running for a hotel. But Skylar hadn't seemed like most women.

Sure, he'd bug-bombed the place and made it somewhat habitable. But he was trained to sleep on the ground, filthy and covered in sand. His bar for comfort was pretty low. This was a woman with a little girl. She couldn't seriously be planning to stay.

He brought Rusty to a stop. Oh, hell. Across the yard, Skylar stood on his concrete block, prying the wood off a window. Some other windows were already uncovered, allowing the fresh air to flow through.

Wrangling the large sheet of wood, Skylar nearly lost her balance but pulled herself upright. He rode closer and fought back the urge to take over. Why make things easy? She'd be more likely to leave if it was a hassle.

She shouldn't try to do that alone. What if she injured herself? What would that kid do? He called over, "Can I give you a hand?"

"No. I've got this." She continued trying to lever the covering from the window. After a couple minutes of futile efforts, she scowled. "Didn't I tell you to come to the front door next time?" That accent. Georgia, for sure, or maybe North Carolina. The way she softened her I's to *ah.* But not twangy like Levi's, and not thick. She may have moved around or worked to eliminate it.

When he wasn't in North Carolina, he'd been based in Georgia for many years of his career in the military and had completed trainings there. He'd interacted with the locals. One in particular. He shoved Melody's memory aside. "How do you know I didn't try the front door first?"

Skylar cut him a quick side-eye. "You're still on a horse."

The wood fell to the ground in a loud *thunk.* Skylar stepped off the block he'd brought over from the ranch. Wearing gloves, jeans, and attitude, the woman seemed determined to do this on her own.

He watched her.

"Do you need something?" She sounded exasperated. "Or am I the only entertainment you can find this far from town?"

He chuckled. "It is pretty entertaining. I'll grant you that. But I'm here to check on the cattle and make sure the fence is holding up."

"It is. The cows are behavin'. You can go on now. As you can see, I have everything under control." She dragged the concrete block over to the next window, stepped up, and tried prying the wood, grunting as she struggled.

He'd avoided that window. Some idiot had used extra nails. The wood covering couldn't be removed without risking damage. He dismounted and approached. "Let me help."

She fisted her hands on her hips and stared him in the eye, the block beneath her raising her to his height. "What part of 'I've got this' don't you understand? This—" she swung her arm out, gesturing to the house "—is what I do. Renovations. Fixer-uppers."

Skylar resumed her attempts to jam the pry bar under the wood.

Garrick backed away and waited calmly. Minutes ticked by. He'd waited a lot longer in far less interesting situations. If the Army had taught him anything, it'd taught him patience.

Skylar had determination on her side, but he was stronger. Stronger than he appeared—had to be to survive his missions. He leaned an arm on Rusty and watched her work. The view wasn't half bad. Those work clothes and all that dust didn't hide how beautiful she was, their landlord. The owner of all the acreage they leased and wanted to buy. If he left her alone, she may get frustrated and leave, be more likely to sell. He should go.

But long ago, he'd taken a vow of service, and this woman needed help. What was her story? Why didn't she have the electricity on? Come spring, she wouldn't be able to survive for long, given the Florida heat and humidity.

Her accusations filtered into his memory. She'd asked who sent him. Who was she running from?

"Darn this thing!" Skylar growled. "You want to try? Have at it." She climbed off the step and shoved the tool at him.

He hesitated a moment, ambivalent, but his impulse to assist a woman in need triumphed over his self-interest. He pried the wood and, after a few careful tries, got the thing unstuck without taking off the window frame. Together, they lowered it to the ground.

"Thank you." Skylar blew a lock of hair away from her face and offered a grateful smile, guileless.

He had a flash of the person she might be under other circumstances. It pulled at him. Her mix of confidence, vulnerability, and pig-headed stubbornness was enormously attractive, and he had to remind himself that her staying on their grazing land may be a problem.

"Stack it over there." She angled her chin. "I may want to reuse it."

He arched his brows. "Yes, ma'am." Not only did she accept his help, but now she was giving orders?

After an hour, the remaining windows were uncovered, and the wood was stacked in the dilapidated pole barn. The place was a wreck. Didn't that intimidate her? The pole barn needed work, and the equipment barn out back was nothing but a ramshackle termite farm.

"Thanks for your help." Skylar wiped perspiration off her forehead with the sleeve of her blue work shirt. "I can offer you water. Or a can of warm soda."

"I'd appreciate a water." He had some in his saddle bag but wanted to catch a glimpse of what she'd done inside.

He followed her into the house.

Nothing.

The place was unchanged, other than a pantry-like area set up in neat rows on the kitchen counter. All canned goods and packaged foods. Not much better than what he'd been issued in the Army. And there were little jars of meat sticks. His lip curled. All those cattle outside, all that beef in the freezer back at the ranch, and they were eating little jars of mystery meat? "You still don't have electricity?"

"No." An odd expression flashed over her face. "We've been here less than a week."

"Some people would turn it on before they moved in."

"We're ... used to roughing it, moving around." She handed him a glass of tap water.

"You plan to leave soon?"

"No," she said firmly. "We're staying."

Huh. He rubbed his neck, scanned the room, and returned his gaze to Skylar. She seemed confident. "Is there a problem with the power company?"

Skylar exhaled hard. "I don't have what I need to get it turned on."

His radar told him the woman was lying. Why? "Is it a ... lack of funds?" If so, Tall Pines ought to put in an offer right away.

She could be desperate.

"Not exactly. Hey, do you have a ladder I can borrow?" She gestured to the hall.

He followed her to the bedroom, the one he'd fixed up for himself. Like the rest of the house, it was unfurnished. The girl lay atop his new sleeping bag, hugging the end of his woobie, and sucking her thumb. He stifled the urge to get his stuff out of there before it became covered with paint. Ah, hell. Between the toy ponies, something sticky, possibly jelly, and Cheerios, his bag was practically toast already.

Why were they still sleeping on the floor?

"The room's in pretty good shape." Skylar stood, arms akimbo, speaking like she'd done this a few times. "I've been making plans, searching online for subcontractors. But I'll fix this up for Logan first, so she has her room set."

He followed Skylar's gaze and noted two gallons of paint in the corner. "Are you planning to buy furniture, or are the movers bringing it?"

A deep groove formed above her nose. "It'll be furnished eventually."

Skylar had dodged his question. How did a woman with a kid have no furniture? Had they been homeless? She seemed too clean, too middle class, her fingernails too well groomed, to have been living on the streets.

"Anyway, I need a ladder for painting unless I drag that block in here. Do you think they have one next door at the ranch?"

In fact, there were several. Not only did he work at Tall Pines, but he also co-owned the ranch with his brothers and the foreman. He'd shown her his ID. Hadn't she realized he was a Stone the day they'd met? It didn't add up. But more to the point, why should he encourage her? It was a jerk move, but he searched for an excuse not to help.

In the moment that stretched between them, a brief flash of vulnerability moved over her face and tugged at something inside him. Despite sharing many qualities with a honey badger, Skylar was gorgeous.

He caved in. "There's a ladder."

She hiked her eyebrows and spoke very slowly, like she thought he was dense, "Do you think I can borrow one?"

He chuckled. She had attitude. "I can bring one by in a while."

"Good." She brightened. "The sooner the better. I'd like to paint later today or tomorrow." They strolled back into the living room. "I'm removing this wall and opening the room to enlarge the living area. Can you give me the names of good drywall guys or carpenters? I need someone with a license to pull a permit."

"I can. But don't you want electricity?"

She rubbed the side of her face. "I'll get it turned on."

They stood there, that *no worries* song playing softly in the background. The kid was seriously stuck on that story.

"I'll be back shortly." This may be shooting himself in the foot, but she was compelling. Too tough to be a damsel in distress, yet she needed him, nonetheless.

"If you have time when you come back, I could use a hand fixing the back door. I can do it, but the job would go faster if there were two of us."

"I can make that work. Tell you what, it's getting toward lunchtime, and I'm picking up lunch at the diner. Can I bring you something?"

"You don't need to go to the trouble." She glanced at the supplies on the counter. "We have...."

"It's no trouble."

"I've been craving a Greek salad. Or anything fresh. And Logan loves grilled cheese. So yes, we'd love it."

Either he was as dumb as dirt for helping her, or he was savvy, keeping tabs on her progress. *Keep your friends close and your enemies closer.* Which camp did Skylar belong to?

Amber, the counter server, moved the overflowing plate of pink frosted heart cookies beside the register, wrote down Garrick's order, and took his money.

A little early for the lunch rush, he waited on an empty stool at the counter and drummed his fingers on his thigh, the aroma of bacon and baked goods making his stomach growl. On the counter sat several additional platters of frosted cookies and a breakfast order. The omelet and buttered toast had him practically drooling.

It's okay to buy Skylar and her kid lunch and waste the sandwich sitting in his lunchbox. Okay, that he'd set aside the work he ought to do this afternoon. Skylar was hot and an enigma, and he was curious as hell.

He wasn't being disloyal to his family by helping her. He was being neighborly. And he'd give her his phone number because that's what good neighbors do. She had a kid. As a paramedic, he was well aware of the issues and injuries that can arise when you have a child. A beautiful woman with a lovely voice. He could listen to that accent all day. But this was an act of service, not self-service.

Why hadn't he mentioned her to anyone yet? He needed to, soon. She was digging in and intended to stay. This was pertinent information. He had to tell his brothers, and he didn't need a crystal ball to know it wouldn't go well. They'd been trying to buy that property. Could she sell them the land and keep the farmhouse? It wasn't optimal, although it might work.

But he probably shouldn't bring her lunch, a ladder, or help her with that door.

Amber returned with his order.

"What's with all the pink cookies?" he asked.

"Garrick." Amber screwed up her face. "Don't you own a calendar? It's Valentine's Day. We're giving them out with every order. I already put some in your bag."

Valentine's Day? That hadn't been on his radar in years.

He swung by the ranch, fetched the ladder, and returned to the farmhouse.

Once inside, he pulled his sandwich out of the bag and handed the rest to Skylar.

"Thanks. I'm so ready for this salad." A towel lay on the floor for a makeshift picnic in the living room. She called to the girl, "Who wants grilled cheese?"

"Grilled cheese?" Logan's face lit up as she came running into the room.

The kid was so excited over a simple sandwich?

Skylar unpacked the bag, and the way she laid the wrapped, heart-shaped cookies in a row on the towel, you'd have thought he'd brought her winning lottery tickets. "What are these?"

He hiked a shoulder. "It's Valentine's Day. They—"

"Wow." Logan lifted a cookie, enchanted with the pink frosting and red candy trim.

"It's Valentine's Day, baby. Aren't they pretty?" Skylar teared up and blinked a few times. "This is so nice of you."

Just a few cookies had her choked up? He hadn't done anything at all, but seeing her so touched and the kid so happy, he'd take the win.

Garrick climbed the wooden steps at Luke's house. Tall Pines held monthly meetings that included more people than the daily task assignment meetings. When he wasn't scheduled for the firehouse, he tried to make these, and today, for a change, he had news to share.

As soon as he stepped inside, the aroma of something sweet hit him, and he scanned the area for the source. They didn't typically serve food at these meetings.

Avery, his niece, carried in a container of cookies, set it in front of him, and slipped into the empty seat between him and Thea, the old woman who lived next door to him.

Avery cut him a stealthy glance, and he dipped his chin in acknowledgment. "Thanks," he said softly so's not to draw attention to their transaction. The golden color and bumpy appearance meant they were his favorite, peanut butter oatmeal. He should've told her to add chocolate chips. Still, his mouth watered.

Thea caught his eye and arched a brow.

He suppressed a grin. She didn't miss a thing. Despite approaching eighty, Thea was kind of amazing. Her healing teas and creams had transformed his dad.

"Where's mine?" Jack's gaze zeroed in on the container and he looked from Garrick to Avery.

"There are more in the kitchen," Avery huffed. "I'll get you some later."

"Hold on." Luke sat up. "You're giving our cookies away?"

"I want some." Wyatt, their youngest hand, who was like a son to Jack, swung his gaze to Jack and then Avery.

"I can make more. I'll go get them." Avery exhaled hard and shot Garrick an exasperated eye roll.

Hey, she could've waited and given him the cookies at the end of the meeting.

She returned with a loaded platter and took her seat.

His father came to life. "Send them this way." Bud reached for a cookie. "Let's call this meeting to order." Mostly recovered from his stroke, Bud had deeded the ranch to Garrick, his brothers, and Striker, but took great pleasure from running these meetings.

Avery spoke first. "We have seven goats now, including the babies. I'm planning to sell goat cheese and make goat milk soap. Thea's showing me how. I'll need more storage in the goat barn."

"That sounds good. I can help," Wyatt volunteered. Their youngest ranch hand hung on Avery's every word.

The corner of Jack's mouth quirked up, and he met Garrick's gaze. Luke's pretty, adopted daughter could read Wikipedia entries about the history of Teflon, and Wyatt would think she was brilliant and ask for more.

They discussed Avery's needs, and then Garrick spoke up, "There's something I need to—"

"Hold on. Striker's next on the agenda." His father held up a paper. A few years ago, Bud had a hip replacement followed by a stroke and had been fighting for his life. While Bud wasn't working like a cowboy anymore, he helped with the horses and took great pleasure in running the whole-ranch meetings.

"When did the meetings get so formal?" Garrick asked.

"When we diversified," Jack said.

Striker offered his general overview of the ranch's needs. Then, Luke presented the business and marketing report.

Garrick scooted forward on his seat, excited to have something of value to contribute. This seemed like a good time to mention buying the adjacent property. "Speaking of expenses—"

"We're next." Jack pointed to the sheet.

"I sent you a copy." Luke raised his palm, implying he should've checked his email.

After Jack gave updates on the horse breeding side of their operation, he and Dani presented their plans to start the equine therapy program using the miniature horses.

"Next month, we have our first group coming," Dani said. "Oh, and if y'all know anyone who wants a puppy, Macy had a litter of seven."

"Wasn't Wren supposed to get Macy spayed?" Avery sounded personally affronted. When their Border collie, Sadie, had a litter, they'd given a puppy to Wren.

"Yes," Dani continued, "and Wren's not happy about the situation either. By the time she took Macy to the appointment, she was pregnant. Wren thinks it's that stray she took in. She got it neutered, but apparently, the deed had already been done. The puppies are soooo sweet. Anyway, I wanted to let y'all know."

Garrick's mind wandered. He had to sit through a conversation about puppies? Unreal. He ground his teeth while he worked out what to say about Skylar. How much should he tell them? She'd occupied a fair amount of his head space recently.

Now, instead of catching a few hours hanging out at the farmhouse reading, like he'd been doing since he discovered it, he helped her. They'd removed the wood from the windows, and he'd repaired the back door and replaced the guts in her toilets and the kitchen faucet. She still didn't have power and relied on charging tools in the car or using batteries, which was damn strange.

"Earth to Garrick," Dani's voice broke through his thoughts.

"What?"

"Where were you? I asked if you thought any of the people from the Heron Park Veterans' Center would want to come out for the therapy program, maybe one of the groups that meets there? We're including some of the larger horses, too. Do you want to ask? Or can you give me the name of a contact?"

"I'll check." He shifted uncomfortably in his seat, feeling a little guilty. He'd only visited the Veterans' Center group a couple of times last year. Mostly, he used it as a cover story when he was going on jobs with Tate and Flash and when he'd slipped over to the farmhouse for quiet afternoons of solitude, reading. Those days in his private sanctuary were over unless they bought the farm and Skylar left. But if Tall Pines bought McClure Farm, the old house would likely be torn down. A pang of regret hit him. He really enjoyed hanging out there.

"Okay. That wraps it up," Bud said.

Garrick snapped out of his reverie. "I still have something for the agenda."

"Yes. New business." Bud sat taller, more official.

The room fell silent, and, almost comically, several heads turned his way.

He chuckled. "Don't be so shocked."

"Go ahead, bro." Jack lifted a hand, inviting him to speak.

"I met the owner of McClure's."

Luke asked, "The old woman in Tennessee?"

"No. Her niece. She recently acquired it, and she's staying there." He scanned the surprised faces surrounding the table.

"She can't stay there. That place is ready to be condemned," Striker said.

"True, but she's there. And she has a kid," he added. And thanks to hours of his heavy labor, the farmhouse wasn't in as bad a shape as it had been.

Luke tapped on his closed laptop as though it were paperwork. "Our lease is good for five more years."

"Why weren't we informed it was for sale?" Jack grimaced. "When Wes approached the owner, she wasn't interested. What changed? Did you talk to the new owner?"

"A bit," Garrick said.

"Is she planning to stay there?" Jack asked. Since expanding his horse breeding operation, Jack had been pushing to make their control of those acres official.

"Not sure." In his mind, he saw Skylar standing in the center of the room, describing her remodeling plans. "It wouldn't hurt to make an offer before she does too much work on it."

"You're thinking she'll sell? Jack asked.

"Possibly." Garrick's brows drew together. "She already seems pretty dug in and was asking about subcontractors. I think she's worked on houses before."

Jack leaned back and rubbed his chin thoughtfully. "She may need a little encouragement."

"We're not harassing her." Luke shot Jack a look.

"I never..." Jack winced. "A single mom in that dilapidated place. I'm just saying she won't make it a month. Especially as it warms up. Ask if she'll sell. Play up the angle of the heat, the snakes, the cockroaches, the old plumbing..."

"Just be straight with her," Luke said.

Garrick watched his brother and his half-brother volley, and it seemed like old times. Those two could really go at it.

"Next time I see her, I'll ask," he agreed. But would he? After helping her get the place habitable?

Bud's gaze sharpened. "Next time, huh?"

"Yeah, well...I've stopped by there a few times." He groaned inwardly. This conversation was heading in the wrong direction.

"How old is this new owner?" Luke raised a brow.

"I don't know." He scoffed. "I didn't check her driver's license." Actually, he had. When he'd viewed her paperwork and license, he'd been surprised to discover she was a few years older than him. "Close to your age, I guess."

"Is she single?" Jack's expression grew shrewd as he leaned forward.

"Possibly," Garrick called up his memory of Skylar. Nothing indicated either way other than the lack of a wedding ring. But Garrick had the sense she was alone. Very alone.

The corners of Jack's mouth lifted. "Turn on the charm. See what you can find out."

"Right."

"I'm counting on you, bro." Jack swung his gaze to Luke. "I think we should work up an offer. Carpe diem."

"On it." Luke nodded.

The meeting ended, and Garrick slipped out before they grilled him anymore. He'd gone into the meeting excited but walked out feeling opportunistic. It was too soon to make an offer. Unless Skylar wanted to sell, but he didn't get that vibe from her.

He headed back to his cottage to get ready for work at the firehouse, grateful for the distance from his brothers.

CHAPTER FIVE

S kylar wasn't ordinarily paranoid, but the whole Clive situation had her looking over her shoulder. She stood beside the window, the place where cell reception was best, and nervously chewed her finger while she listened to the phone ring.

Pick up, Adrianna. Most of the time, her calls went to her stepsister's voicemail. But she needed to know what Adrianna had heard. Deborah, from Victim Services, had nothing.

Adrianna answered, "I only have a minute, but I took the call because I saw it was you."

"You left a message. Clive contacted you?"

"He did. Hold on." Adrianna spoke to someone in the background. "I'm back. Yes. Clive called. He's really angry and asked where to find you and Lizzie."

The hairs on her arms prickled at the mention of Clive and the confirmation he was looking for her. She'd told Adrianna that she was calling Lizzie by her middle name, but in this case, it was a blessing that her sister hadn't been paying attention. "What'd you tell him?"

"The truth. I don't know where you are. Where are you anyway? Weren't you decorating houses outside of Chicago?"

"Not decorating. Renovating. And Max, my business partner, took over my projects. I'm ... it's best you don't have my address."

Adrianna sighed loudly. "Okay, well, I have a video conference, so I need to go."

"But ..."

"I really need to go. Text me. Bye."

Skylar stared at the phone for a beat, her chest tightening with disappointment. There was no, "How are you? How's Logan? Do you need anything?" Adrianna was in her mid-thirties now and hadn't become warmer with age.

It shouldn't be surprising. Adrianna was simply being true to form, but wasn't she the least bit concerned that Clive was out? Where was Adrianna's loyalty to Tessa? Didn't she care at all? Was she a narcissist like her mother?

She'd chosen to treat Adrianna as a sister. Had loved her. Skylar had been the one to make soup and crackers for Adrianna when she was sick, had helped her with homework, babysat for countless hours, basically parented her while Vera went clubbing with boyfriends. When would she get it through her head that she'd never get love from them? They were busy living their own lives. Life with her stepsister and stepmother had always been a give-and-take relationship. She gave ... they took. And she hadn't minded when Adrianna was young and needed her.

For a while, she'd hoped they might be friends. Sisters. That was a stupid fantasy.

Tears pricked the corners of her eyes but she blinked hard, refusing to cry. *You don't need them. You can do this.* Starting over down here might be lonely and challenging but she didn't need her stepsister's approval or love to move forward with her own life.

Holding her cracked phone, she wandered away from the window. Noonday sunshine poured into the room, lighting up the dust motes and making it warm. She wiped the sweat from her forehead and pulled her shoulders back finding the determination that carried her through renovating the pitiful homes she'd remodeled. If she could gut a house and turn it into something beautiful, she could certainly build a new life and make the farmhouse their new home.

Her stomach growled, but none of that highly processed, room-temperature food appealed to her. If she ate one more protein bar or peanut butter sandwich, she'd scream. After the meal Garrick had brought, she longed for real food.

They needed air conditioning, refrigeration, and laundry facilities. She wanted to make it more comfortable, and she needed to charge her devices and power tools. The SUV would be out of fuel if she kept running it to charge everything.

It was time to go into town, get the power turned on, and pick up supplies.

Skylar pulled the branches away from her SUV and strapped Logan into her car seat. She scanned the area. Cattle stood in the sunshine, and birds glided over the landscape. She warily pulled onto the road and drove to the nearby farm.

She held Logan's hand as they walked into Wren's Organic Produce stand. This was bare bones and fresh from the field. An aisle cut between plywood counters covered with bins of lettuces, tomatoes, and citrus fruits. Jars of honey and what appeared to be dried herbs sat arranged in neat rows to the left. "There are so many oranges here."

"It's still citrus season." The woman at the end of the produce stand stood. She wore a sundress with a shrug covering her shoulders, had long brown hair, and was probably close to the age Tessa would have been. Beside her, a large yellow Labrador retriever, wearing a service animal harness, came to attention, his astute gaze sizing them up. "It's all local," the woman continued. "And we have strawberries. They're really sweet."

Skylar paused as she lifted the pint of berries. Although the woman faced them, her gaze was unfocused. She appeared to be visually impaired and seemed completely at ease despite working alone. That had to be a sign this area was safe.

"Puppies!" Logan tugged her hand and pointed. "Can I pet?"

Her chest lifted at Logan's excitement. There, beneath the counter holding bins of romaine, was a long crate containing several puppies. They were adorable, and the dark one reminded her of Panda, the dog she'd had to put down a few years earlier, before Logan. "Yes. They're cute."

"You can pet one." The woman stepped closer. "I'm Dani, and this handsome dog is Lucky. He's a special dog. You can't pet him. I'm blind, and he's in a harness, which means he's working. But I can let you hold a puppy if your mom watches you." Dani's unfocused gaze seemed to stare right through Logan.

"I don't know if you should." Skylar fought back the urge to head over to the crate and hold a puppy herself. She wanted a dog, probably more than Logan did, but not now.

"Please, Mommy?" Logan gave her a look that melted her heart.

"Okay. Only petting. We can't take one home." The next thing she knew, they were "trying" all the puppies.

Logan squealed as the black one licked her chin. "Please. Please, can we get him?"

"Not today." Skylar gathered her strength and paid for their selections.

"Are y'all new in town or visiting?" Dani asked.

"We recently moved into the farmhouse east of Tall Pines." She gasped. It was too late. The words were out. Did she just tell this stranger where she was living?

"Well, hey there, neighbor. I'm Dani, and I live at Tall Pines. My husband's a rancher." Dani told her about the honey and creams and a bit about the businesses in town—a coffee shop offering wonderful baked goods, a diner with great home-style food, and a bar with decent music and dancing.

Bags of veggies, fresh romaine, oranges, and strawberries weighed down her arms as Skylar hauled them back to the car and drove into town. This was good, being out with Logan. And Pine Crossing offered more than appeared when she'd driven through in the middle of the night. On the way to Heron Park, they stopped at Mac's Diner for a late lunch.

As they were finishing, the woman who'd been working at the counter strolled over. "Hi there. I'm Amber. Your server left. I'm covering her tables." Her kind eyes danced with delight as she took in Logan and her unicorn. "Such a cutie. What's your name?"

Logan turned away and hugged Peg.

Skylar scanned the room. There were only a couple of older men dressed in beat-up jeans and work boots, a young family, and a few women occupying booths. It seemed safe enough to talk to Amber.

"Go ahead. You can tell the lady."

Logan stared at the table.

"I'm Skylar, and this is Logan. We're new in town." She wasn't ready to tell the woman where she lived.

"Welcome to Pine Crossing. I hope you like it here. Say, do you like crafts? There's a craft store up the street, and they have classes. They might even have something for the little one on Saturday mornings."

Logan stared up at her.

"Thank you," Skylar said. "I'll keep that in mind. "Logan likes coloring and clay. Don't you?"

Logan nodded slightly.

"That's okay," Amber shifted her gaze between Logan and her. "It's perfectly okay to be shy. When I was your age, I stuttered and hated talking. Now listen to me—you can't shut me up. Would you care for dessert? We have excellent pies and ice cream."

"You can get dessert," Skylar said.

Logan grinned. "Ice cream."

Amber reappeared with a bowl of ice cream topped with whipped cream, sprinkles, and a cherry.

"Wow." Logan gazed at the sundae in open-mouthed wonder.

Well, that got a reaction out of her. This was an excellent choice. And when they got their water heater and electricity, living in Pine Crossing would work fine.

Clive would never think of searching for her here, and he'd be trying to find a Lizzie. Clive wouldn't be searching for Logan McClure. They'd be okay.

———————

Skylar shoved aside tingles of trepidation, produced her identification, and paid the deposit at the electric company. If all went as planned, this weekend, they'd have lights, and soon she'd have a hot shower. "I can't tell you how nice it will be to have the electricity on. And air conditioning. Who knew you'd want to have AC in the winter?"

"It's usually muggy on the days leading up to a cold front." The clerk shrugged as she finished entering the information into the computer. "Let's see. We can have someone out next Tuesday."

"Tuesday? Don't you just flip a switch or something? I'm surprised I had to come in and do this in person."

From the tone the clerk used, she'd heard this before. "Sometimes we can do this online. But you're a brand-new account, and this address hasn't had electricity in over ten years. We have to do an inspection first. I can get someone out there on Tuesday afternoon. If everything's in good order, Wednesday is the earliest we can get you power."

"Really?" She didn't even try to hide her disappointment.

"Thank you for your business." The clerk was on automatic pilot now. "At the bottom of that paper is a customer satisfaction survey. You can fill it out online."

"If I had electricity and internet, it would be easier to do that."

"True." The clerk began typing on her keypad. She was finished with their conversation. "Have a nice day."

Deflated, she forced a cheerful voice as she walked Logan outside. "Ready to go to another store?" At least by the time the power was on, she'd have the new water heater installed. She'd stop at the home store on the way out of town. And while she was at it, she ought to find a local real estate agent to discuss selling a few acres. Her credit cards were filling fast.

Something seemed off when she approached the car. She stared at it, a sinking sensation washing through her. The back rear tire was completely flat.

Her breath stuck in her lungs as she searched for the source of the leak and came up empty. Did someone do this intentionally? Was it Clive or one of his friends? Last she knew, Clive drove a maroon convertible, but if he sent a friend or colleague, they could be driving anything.

She scanned the area as she called the roadside service.

"We'll have someone there in ninety minutes to two hours," the representative said.

"You can't get someone here sooner?" She scrutinized the bushes, alcoves, and anywhere someone might hide. The streets were nearly empty. She was being paranoid. The call ended, and she shoved the phone back into her purse.

"Let's wait in the car." She strapped Logan in her car seat and lowered the windows but felt uncomfortable and exposed. If someone had intentionally tampered with her tires, sitting there, in the open, was a bad idea.

"Come on, honey." She unbuckled Logan, and they started toward the building. But as they approached the entrance, several employees exited. The woman she'd spoken to a short time ago stepped out and locked the door, then got in her car and left. Skylar checked her phone. Five o'clock.

"Mommy. Peg wants to go home." Logan pouted. She'd missed her nap.

"I'm fixing the tire, then we'll go to another store before we go home." She could do this. She renovated homes. "You'll sit here in the grass, and I'll take care of it." How difficult could it be?

Very difficult, it turns out, when your spare is flat too.

How had this happened? Frustrated, she rubbed her cheek, barely holding it together. She was the one who took charge. She was the one who helped people. But now she needed help. Ugh. And she knew nobody.

Strike that.

She knew one person.

About forty-five minutes after getting the call, Garrick rolled up to the power company parking lot just as a road service tow truck pulled in. There was one huge difference. In the back of his Jeep sat a brand-new tire that would fit Skylar's SUV. She was lucky he'd been in Pine Crossing talking to Tate when she called. And since Tate was buddies with the guy at the tire place, he was in and out in a heartbeat and made it to her in record time.

While Skylar sent the roadside service away, he got her tire changed.

"I really appreciate you bringing me the tire. But I would've changed it. Or even asked the tow-truck guy. I pay for that service." Skylar stood behind him.

"No worries. You have to keep an eye on munchkin here." He lifted his chin toward Logan, who giggled. "You like being called munchkin?"

"Munchkin is in *Wizard of Oz*." Logan's eyes grew wide with delight.

"That's right, munchkin." His wink earned him a smile.

A few minutes later, he wiped his hands on his bandana while Skylar strapped her girl in the back. Dressed differently today, nicer, she seemed unaware of her beauty, and he fought back a ping of attraction that muddied the waters. This was the woman he needed to sweet talk into selling his family her land. A woman who acted like she had some kind of secret. What was he supposed to say? "Hi, neighbor. I know you're just moving in, but we want to buy your farm." That seemed wrong.

"Turn on the charm," Jack had said. But he wasn't a smooth operator like Jack. He'd never had any trouble finding women. But banter wasn't his strong suit, and he wasn't about to try to con the woman out of her home even if it would be in the best interest of the ranch.

"I need to pay you back." Skylar looked up at him. "I'm not set up with a bank yet. Can I buy you a gift card or something at the home store, or...."

"I can wait until you have it. I know where you live." That sounded stupid. Or creepy. He waited for a beat, unsure what to say or do. Should they shake hands? No. Too weird. He shoved his thumbs in his pockets. "Glad to be of service."

"Well, thanks again."

He held her gaze, energy shooting through him.

Color crept into her cheeks.

Did she feel something, too? Nah. Probably the heat.

"Tomorrow night, we're supposed to get a cold front. That's why it's so muggy." That's the best he could come up with? Standing this close to her must've made his IQ drop about thirty points.

"That's what I hear." She met his gaze.

Flecks of paint covered her arm and fingernails.

"Looks like you already painted." He'd meant to offer to help her.

"Yes. Logan's room." She picked at a bit of paint on her finger. "It made a huge difference. I need to wait to do the rest of the house because of the remodeling, and it's difficult cleaning up without a hot shower."

"Right." He held her gaze again.

She cleared her throat. "I guess I'll be off. I have to buy a water heater. I owe you one. More than one by now."

Skylar climbed into her vehicle and backed out.

It took a moment before he realized he'd been acting like a dummy, watching her drive down the road, a funny feeling filling him. He ground a rock beneath his boot, uncomfortably agitated. How did this woman get him so unsettled? Self-sufficient, he only needed a few solid guys to hang out with. And now this ... complication.

Skylar stirred him up and made him irritable. Maybe it's the kid. Logan touched that place he preferred to keep shut. Although younger than that girl in the desert, she had the same innocent expression.

It would be better if they left. Sometime in the next few days, he'd talk to her about selling. And now he'd built up a little more credit. Skylar would be more receptive. Helping her had been a brilliant move. Strategic. He was a good neighbor and a savvy businessman.

He climbed back in his Jeep. He'd done a good deed and would reward himself with a brew at Turner's Tap. And if he met a hot woman to blot out the image of Skylar seared into his brain, all the better.

CHAPTER SIX

Outside of the glow of Skylar's cell phone, inky darkness filled the house. She'd been looking forward to moonlight shining through the windowpanes, but the last couple of nights, it'd been cloudy, and now—this. Wind whipped around the old house, and branches fell. Rain hammered the rooftop. A strong, serious rain—the kind that washes everything clean.

Lightning blinked on and off like Mother Nature's fireworks. Thunder boomed, and a particularly loud crack shook the house. Fortunately, Logan liked thunderstorms. Her daughter might be afraid of people, but the weather, no problems there.

She opened the weather app on her phone. According to the weather service and almost every person she'd talked to, a cold front was behind this squall line. The forecasters debated calling it a no-name storm, approaching a hurricane in intensity but smaller, and in the winter, coming from the north. Too bad she'd already removed the wood from the windows.

Several communities were already without power. At least she didn't have to worry about a refrigerator full of food going bad.

Rain pummeled the farmhouse as the rumbling moved into

the distance. She opened a flood zone map on her phone. They were in the clear. They'd be okay. This house had weathered many storms.

She snuggled with Logan under the blankets on the sleeping bags. She'd laid the new one over her well-worn bags from home. Now that she was back to using her credit cards, she'd gone online and found a store selling beds, but they wouldn't be delivered for several weeks. She groaned and shifted position, achy from sleeping on the hard floor. This wouldn't work. Hadn't she suffered enough? She opened a website and ordered air mattresses. Knowing they were coming made the thought of lying back down more tolerable.

She breathed in the fresh paint scent and tried to settle herself enough to sleep, but her lids popped right back open. Ruminating and watchful, she tried all the techniques she preached to her clients—breath counting meditation, visualization, making a gratitude list. When she kept busy during the day, she was too tired and focused on work to think. But at night, in the quiet, the voices of her fears grew louder.

Thankfully, she had Max to oversee her two projects up north. It cost her, but the projects wouldn't be a total loss. When she got her electricity and WiFi, she could resume her client calls. That would help. Finances mattered, but they weren't at the top of her worry list.

She turned the lantern on low, hoping the light would be calming. This wasn't anxiety. This was fear. Clive had threatened her.

Logan wasn't his. The math didn't add up. Tessa had been with her friend in Oregon when she'd gotten pregnant. Maybe Clive wasn't really interested in Logan. Maybe Logan was a pawn. He might simply be after revenge. Skylar had encouraged Tessa to leave Clive, and he was the type to nurse a grudge. He'd lost his business when he'd been sentenced to fifteen years— time he deserved to do. They'd called it manslaughter. Even if

Clive hadn't meant to kill Tessa, he'd meant to hurt her. He'd done it before. Why on earth had Tessa kept going back?

Something whacked the window.

Skylar jerked.

She got to her feet, grabbed the metal bar, and stood flattened against the wall, heart pounding in her ears, inching over to the window to investigate.

Leaves stuck to the windowpane. She peered out.

It was only a branch. Nobody was trying to get in. Still, she waited for a long moment, listening.

Convinced they were safe, Skylar laid back down.

Logan turned in her sleep, clutching her Pegasus. Sometimes, when Logan slept, Skylar saw Tessa in her. Like tonight, the way her mouth fell open a bit. Her heart pinched, and a wave of grief rolled through her. It was still difficult to believe her baby sister was gone.

She kissed the top of Logan's head, and her nose wrinkled. The child needed a real bath. They both did. She'd been heating water on the camp stove and washing them up. Tomorrow, the power company would send someone out to inspect, and the next day, they'd have electricity. Soon, they'd have a hot shower and shampoo. They could get through a couple more days.

She checked the time. Midnight. She'd been lying there, ruminating, for two hours.

Her phone vibrated. No name. An unfamiliar phone number.

A text appeared: *I will find you.*

She gasped and stared at the words, then touched the screen, ready to delete. No. She should take a screenshot and email it to Deborah at Victims Services. It had to be Clive.

How did he get her number?

At least Clive didn't know where they were.

When daylight finally crept into the room, Skylar slipped into a sweater and opened the bedroom window to chase the damp odor from the house—and the troubling images from her brain. Fresh, cold air rushed in, nothing like Illinois, but she welcomed the crisp, wintery breeze. The view, not so much.

Branches littered the yard.

Skylar pinched the bridge of her nose in frustration. Didn't she have enough to do without having to gather limbs and debris? She pulled the covers over Logan and padded into the living room. Bottled coffee, even at room temperature, was exactly what she needed.

A drop of water hit her hand.

She took another step, almost slipped, and caught herself. What in the world? Her socks were soaked. She stared at the floor.

A puddle?

Out of habit, she reached for the light switch, but of course it didn't work. She found the powerful flashlight that'd been there when she arrived and aimed the beam upward. Drips steadily plopped from a spreading dark area on the ceiling. Her stomach turned. Oh, for crying out loud. Water spots like that usually meant a roof leak. This was just too much.

She set a plastic cereal bowl under the primary drip and stared at the ceiling. This was the first hard rain since they'd arrived, but there'd been no sign of water damage when she'd examined the house.

Crumpling to the floor, she buried her face in her hands and groaned, heaviness settling over her. *Universe. Why do you hate me?* She'd always tried to be good, to do the right thing, to help.

What would she tell her clients?

Quit sitting like a lump on the floor and get moving. Pull yourself together. Self-pity is not an option.

She'd worked on some real dumps. She could do this. Filled with fresh resolve, she forced herself to her feet and fetched towels to dry the puddle.

Someone knocked on the door.

She peeked out the window, then cracked the door open. "Garrick?" It was early. She was a mess, the house a bigger disaster than ever, but her heart lifted at the sight of him.

"Are you two okay?" he asked. There was something in his voice this morning that made her wary.

"Yes. We are but...." She rubbed her cheek. "Why do you ask?"

"That was a bad storm. I worked at the fire station last night. We had a few calls. I just drove by to check on you."

"We're fine. Thank you."

"You might want to step outside for a second." He looked to the right.

She stepped outside. A chill seeped through her wet socks as she stood on the cold concrete steps. Her stomach dropped. "Is that tree...?"

"It appears it was hit by lightning, and the wind probably did the rest. That limb might've gone through your roof. You can see it better from the road." Garrick's tone softened. "But you and Logan are okay?"

"Yes. We're okay, but there's a leak. That explains it." The tree had split. A charred streak ran vertically along the trunk, and half the tree lay on her roof. She exhaled sharply and shook her head. The tree would need to be removed and there was no telling how extensive the damage was. "I guess I'll add that to the list."

Garrick's gaze wandered over her house, the nearby pasture, and the yard. It seemed like he wanted to say something. He rubbed his chin. "Let me know if you need anything. I can get you the name of a tree guy. Maybe a roofer, too."

"Thanks. Text me their numbers."

"You sure you want to stay here?"

"Like I told you before, this is what I do. Rehab houses. It's no big deal. I've got this." She lifted her chin, mustering a confident tone. "And I should have power by tomorrow. They're coming out to inspect today."

"Over a thousand customers lost power last night. You may get a text saying your appointment is rescheduled until the power is restored. When there's a storm, everything gets reprioritized."

"Oh." She should've thought of that.

He stood there a beat, his eyes meeting hers with some kind of question.

"Is there something else?" she asked, growing uncomfortable.

"No. Just checking in. Have a good one." He strolled back out to his Jeep.

She closed the door and blinked back tears. *Get a grip.* Be strong, for Logan's sake.

But perhaps they ought to find a hotel for a few nights. Was there a hotel in Pine Crossing? She hadn't seen one. What she'd give for a long hot shower and a soft bed.

She glanced at the ceiling, the water dripping steadily. They were okay. Funds would come in next month. She'd line up a roofer, get the floors redone, whatever needed to happen. It was logical. She'd plan. This house would be wonderful. They were safe. That's what mattered most.

Garrick opened the door to his Jeep, fighting back the urge to do something. The woman was in a house without electricity and she had a tree through her roof. Fear, despair, exhaustion, he'd seen it all, in combat and working as a paramedic. Now, despite her bravado, those painful emotions were etched on Skylar's face.

This was his neighbor, not some random person. And he'd looked her up. She was good people.

The other night, he'd asked his techie brother, Luke, to do a deep dive. Skylar McClure had a clean record. Divorced, she'd changed her name a couple of years ago. The funny thing was, Luke found no evidence of Skylar giving birth to Logan.

Skylar was some kind of life coach and had a website. More to the point, she was a legit house flipper, part of a small renovation business out of the North Chicago area. Likely, she had the knowledge base to rehab the house, which made it urgent to get an offer soon. It was a stupid move to refer a roofer. She didn't need to fix the house to sell. They'd buy it as is. If she improved the structure, who knows what she'd want to do with her property. They could lose the grazing land.

Why would she want to stay? Wasn't her business back in Illinois? When it came right down to it, Skylar might be as anxious to sell as they were to buy.

He stared at the tree impaled on the farmhouse roof. The situation wasn't life-threatening, but she and the kid were sleeping on the hard floor with no electricity, eating processed crap, and the temperature might hit freezing tonight. Why did she choose such an uncomfortable situation?

Meanwhile, he had too much room. Skylar could use his guest bath and the two extra bedrooms until her house was in better shape. Maybe she'd want to work out a trade. He was terrible in the kitchen. If she'd cook, he'd give her free rent.

Did he really want her and the child underfoot? It's not that he brought hookups home, and they'd be in the way, but he had a policy of keeping things with women superficial.

But Skylar was in a bad place, and he'd sworn long ago to be of service, especially to help people in dire situations. It wasn't just words to him. Even if it seemed corny, that oath, spoken from his soul, really meant something. The fact he no longer served in the military didn't change his promise. It was made to something larger. It was made to God. Then he'd gone and taken another oath when he'd become a paramedic. He had honor.

Skylar needed him. Inviting her and the child into his too-large home was the neighborly thing to do—and it would position him perfectly to convince her to sell.

He climbed out of his vehicle and approached her door.

It opened before he knocked.

"What?" Skylar folded her arms across her belly.

He shoved his hands in his pockets, searching for the right way to put this. "Not to insult your ability to handle things, but why don't you bring Logan and stay at my house next door until you have ... power, a roof, whatever."

She lifted her chin. "No, thanks. We're fine."

"I have room, a hot shower, comfortable beds in my spare bedrooms. We can work out some kind of deal."

"What kind of deal?" She narrowed her eyes skeptically.

"No. Nothing like that. I mean, you can stay and have free rent and all. And in exchange—"

She scoffed.

He raised a palm in halt motion, "—maybe you cook some dinners, bake some cookies or something."

She fisted a hand on her hip. "Do I look like Betty Crocker?"

"Betty... like the cake mix?"

"Never mind." She shook her head and stared at the floor, then swung her gaze back toward the bedroom where she stayed with Logan. After a long moment, she said, "Okay. But only because I saw your ID, and you're a paramedic. A good guy. And ... no funny business."

"Promise. No funny business. This is totally legit. A neighborly offer. And once or twice a week, I work a twenty-four-hour shift, so you'd have the place to yourselves."

Skylar rubbed her cheek and stared at the kid for a beat. "Okay. It shouldn't be for too long. It depends on how soon I can get workers out here."

"Need help gathering your stuff?"

"Sure. Thanks."

He stepped inside the farmhouse and let her direct him on what to do while she got the girl organized.

She drove behind him in her SUV, then followed him inside, carrying the child on her hip.

"That one has twin beds," he gestured, "the other is bigger."

"Logan will take the one with the twins."

He shut his laptop and moved his stuff out, then helped them set up the two guest rooms. This is how he found himself unloading her SUV, carrying in boxes and suitcases—even his sleeping bag and woobie.

"Oh, can you put that camo blanket in her room?" Skylar asked. "It's her favorite."

Garrick groaned inwardly and held his sleeping bag tucked under his arm. She'd done a piss-poor job rolling it up. "Got a preference for the sleeping bag?" He asked mostly to find out what she'd say. Would she admit it wasn't hers?

"It's got grape jelly on it." Skylar wrinkled her nose. "Do you have a laundry?"

"I'll take care of it." There's no way she'd get it back. The first thing his father had bought him in years, it was a damn good sleeping bag.

He set the sleeping bag aside and fingered the soft fabric of his military-issue poncho liner. Under Logan's watchful gaze, he spread his blanket over the kid's bed. His woobie had sentimental value, but he'd get it back later. They'd had enough disruption for now.

"Whose bed?" Logan gestured to the extra twin in the room.

"That's nobody's. This one is yours, for now."

She put her unicorn on the spare bed. "Peg's."

Then she dragged her bag of toys over and climbed on her bed. Logan held out a small pink horse. "You want it?"

Had he stumbled into the twilight zone? "Uh...no. Thanks. I just got off work, and I need rack time, I mean bed. I'm going to try to sleep."

Logan stared up, openly curious.

"Never mind." He backed out of the room. A room now filled with pink and yellow ponies and little girlie clothes and toys.

He handed Skylar a stack of clean sheets. "I don't keep that bed made up."

"Okay. Thanks. Can I..." She gestured toward the bathroom.

"Make yourself at home." A tender feeling hit him out of nowhere, and he fought back the urge to touch her. The woman looked like she needed a hug.

"Thanks..." Skylar's brows drew together. "I'm a little surprised you live in such a nice house. I guess I figured all the cowboys live in something like a bunkhouse. I must watch too much TV."

He chuckled. "Sometimes we hire day worker cowboys. And we do have a bunkhouse. Three cowboys live there, the two hands and the foreman."

"How do you rate this nice little house?" she asked.

She owned the McClure land. They leased it from her but had a larger spread. Wasn't she aware of the business end of their situation? He studied her. "You really don't know? I showed you my IDs."

"No...."

"I'm Garrick Stone."

She stared at him, the expression on her face changing as awareness dawned. "Stone? As in the Stones who own Tall Pines?"

"That's right. I own a share of the ranch." He waited for that to sink in.

"Oh. I didn't.... It was kind of dark the other day. I didn't catch your last name." Her brow furrowed. "And you're a paramedic?"

"I am. And I work the ranch on the other days."

A couple beats of silence passed.

"Do you think we can get showers now? I haven't had a hot shower in over a week. You can probably tell." She touched her hair.

That's not what he'd expected her to say. "Sure."

While she got settled, he slipped the stack of books he'd had at the farmhouse into his room, resting his hand on his cousin's poetry book. Safe. Images of Brad played in his mind. He opened to the back where he'd started his own poem.

Sand in my nostrils,
Grit in my shoes,
On beleaguered field he paid his dues,
and so valiantly fought
through cover of night...

It was unfinished, meant to be a tribute to Brad, but everything he came up with felt inadequate. Heart squeezing, he stepped outside and sat on the porch. What was he thinking, bringing the woman and her child into his house? It must be his sleep-deprived brain. He'd worked two twenty-four-hour shifts with several intense transports. Was he up to this commotion?

His phone buzzed.

Levi: *Saw Janie on my last run—told me the girl's doing better.*

Garrick: *Did you ask about the mom?*

Levi: *She's being moved out of intensive care.*

With Levi's words, the tension inside of him unraveled, which was surprising. He didn't ordinarily care so much, but the little girl deserved a chance to live and to have her mom.

He'd intentionally blunted his emotions. It was easier that way. But even in his shutdown state, he understood the situation was about more than the two females at Heron Park Mercy. It was related to the rusty hinges on the vaults inside of him. About that little girl who'd been in the wrong place. He should've known she was there.

He might be emotionally stunted, but he wasn't stupid.

An eagle swooped down and came to sit on the tallest branch of the lanky pine near his cottage. He'd only ever seen it out in the pasture. The majestic bird peered down at him before taking flight again. For a moment, he envied the way it soared through the blue sky, unfettered.

Life hadn't been easy before last week, but it'd been simpler. Now, his attention went in all kinds of directions. Skylar and the kid inside, the girl in the hospital, and the tasks before him. His brothers were counting on him to soften Skyler up and make a bid on her land. That could wait until they were both rested and fed.

His stomach growled. He grabbed a stick of jerky on the way to his room and texted Skylar not to bother him. After a long nap, he'd figure out how to convince the woman her house wasn't worth fixing.

Steam filled the bathroom. Glorious steam, and the scent of Logan's baby shampoo mixed with Skyler's coconut bath products. She breathed it in, reveling in the simple luxury of a hot shower. Skylar slipped into comfy clothes. How wonderful it was to feel really clean for a change. Even Logan seemed perkier.

After getting her daughter set up with her *Wizard of Oz* movie, the new favorite, she unpacked and took inventory of Garrick's cabinets. She scoffed. This was pitiful. Nuts, beef jerky, a few frozen meals, and wrapped packages of beef in the freezer. Did he even eat here? An excellent cook, she'd bought a variety of fresh vegetables, and the man was in bad need of home cooking.

She picked up her phone and found a text.

Garrick: *Sleeping. Make yourself at home.*

Fine, that's the second time he'd told her that, so she may as well embrace it. She defrosted the beef in the microwave and set to work chopping onions and carrots, assembling a stock pot of vegetable beef soup.

A loud noise came from the master bedroom.

She whipped her gaze in the direction of his door. What was Garrick doing? Moving furniture? Hadn't he gone in there to sleep?

Now, there was silence.

She made biscuits and popped them into the oven. With the soup simmering and the biscuits baking, she fished around in her tote and pulled out the glossy real estate advertisements she'd picked up in town. Wes Blankenship appeared friendly in his photo, and his card said he specialized in rural properties.

She called his number.

"You want to sell ten acres?" Wes seemed interested.

"In five-acre parcels, or I could sell twelve in three acre plots, if possible. Won't I get more money if I sell smaller pieces?"

"I'll check on zoning. I can get you buyers for five-acre tracts. You say you're leasing the land at the moment?"

"Yes, but I'll try to get out of it. At least part of it. It's being leased by Tall Pines."

"Hold up," Wes said. "Are you in the McClure place?"

"Yes. How did you—"

"I've spoken to the owner, Janice."

"Janice's my aunt. She recently transferred the property to me."

"That explains it."

"Explains what?"

Wes sounded wary. "Do the folks at Tall Pines know your plans?"

"No. Why? I thought I'd have you check the lease and possibly contact them on my behalf." Skylar stared out the front window. A man wearing a cowboy hat rode into the area on horseback and stopped outside the barn.

Wes was silent for a long moment. "They might be interested in purchasing the land."

"But I can get more money if I sell smaller parcels, right?"

"That's usually true."

"I'm thinking of the eastern boundary, on the other side of all those trees. Let's get it started. We need a survey and..."

"I still think you ought to reach out to the ranchers leasing the pastures. They're your neighbors."

"It's my property. They don't get a vote."

Wes seemed hesitant. "Are you planning to live there? The farmhouse is probably in bad shape."

"Yes. I'm actually in the renovation business. So, no problem."

"Look, Skylar, I'd like to help you, but to be perfectly ethical, I'm already representing Tall Pines. And around here, ranch folks typically offer land to their neighbors first."

"Except, I need to get the most money possible."

"You've read the lease, haven't you? You may find it difficult to get a buyer willing to assume the lease for that parcel for five years before they can build."

"I realize that. But there may be someone out there." They ended the call.

Dammit! Wes wouldn't help her amend the lease.

Tension moved into her jaw, and she took a moment to settle. She opened and shut the drawers a little too hard as she moved around the kitchen cleaning up, the slamming sound oddly satisfying.

She didn't need this condescending agent mansplaining real estate to her. She'd bought and sold at least a dozen homes, although, to be honest, Max had handled more of the business end. Which had been fine. She preferred the hands-on.

Why couldn't things go easily for her, just once?

She'd have to find a different real estate agent or approach Garrick. He didn't seem the least bit interested in her property. In fact, he'd been helping her. Wes might not have a good read on the situation.

While the soup finished cooking, she called an inspector, a roofer, a carpenter and checked in with Max. In addition to being her business partner, Max and his wife were dear friends and sort of like parents, the good kind, who loved and supported her.

"Hey, kiddo." The sound of Max's gravelly voice came over the speaker like a warm hug. He was fifteen years her senior, and she loved that he called her a kid.

"I need a sounding board." She updated him on the farm-house and ended with the lease dilemma.

"I have faith you'll figure it out. And I have no doubt you can turn that farmhouse around. At least you made it there, okay. How's the peanut taking all this?"

"Logan's good."

He filled her in on the jobs back up north. "Say, I hate to be the bearer of bad news, but I should mention that dirtbag showed up."

Skylar had to sit down. "You talked to him?"

"He came to one of my job sites, asked a few questions, and tried to throw his weight around. Asked me where you were."

She stared out the back door toward a large garden. "What'd you tell him?"

"Do I know where you are?"

"No," she said slowly.

"That's right. And I never will, even if you tell me. But don't tell me. Not yet. Just check in. Good to hear your voice. I'm having Nadine upload everything to one of those shared documents things. You can follow along and keep an eye on the project. If everything goes right, we'll have a tidy sum in a couple months."

A couple months? That seemed like a long time from now.

"Which is good—" He coughed. Max must be smoking those awful cigars again "—because Monty needs friggin' braces. And now Mikey wants to go to that out-of-state school. It's gonna cost a chunk of change."

This wasn't a good time to ask Max for another loan or an advance on her portion of the profits to tide her over. And she owed Garrick several hundred dollars for a new tire. It hadn't been Clive. There'd been a hole in the side wall. But now she had to deal with a roof leak, too.

Her heart sank. If only the funds she'd reinvested in the business were available. It had seemed like a good idea to purchase that second property. Max had warned her, but she'd been on a roll and the projects had seemed doable at the time.

She looked around the room. It was clean and comfortable.

Beyond the garden, shrubs gave way to a wide fenced-in pasture spreading over the flat land like a throw rug. You could spot someone coming from a good distance. They'd be safe here. The universe didn't hate her completely.

In the background, *The Wizard of Oz* started up again on Logan's player. She could watch the house land on the wicked witch all day.

Skylar dragged in three slow breaths, in for six counts, out for eight. It was time to video chat with one of her remaining coaching clients, and she needed to look like she had it together.

CHAPTER SEVEN

G arrick dropped to the living room floor for a squat thrust, then stopped. Would he wake his guests? He moved into his bedroom and completed his workout.

On the days he didn't go into the firehouse, he checked the task board, claimed a chore, and got an early start, often finishing as the others were getting started. Not today. He needed to talk to his brothers. Instead of tacking up Rusty, Garrick strode into the early meeting and took an empty chair among the men discussing schedule changes. The storm had blown down limbs and damaged a storage shed.

Striker stopped mid-sentence.

Jack widened his eyes.

Brick and Wyatt simply sipped their coffee and waited.

"To what do we owe the honor?" asked Luke.

"Fair enough." The fact that it came from Luke softened the dig. He'd skipped a lot of these meetings.

Jack scoffed. Subtle wasn't in Jack's wheelhouse. "This got something to do with that SUV with Illinois plates?"

"Is that the *landlord*?" Luke asked as if he didn't know. After helping him scour the internet the other night, Luke probably had a large file on Skylar. His brother Jack was a bulldog, but what you saw was what you got. Luke was another story. The man could get a job as an intelligence analyst. He came off as chill but had an extensive tech skillset.

"Yes. That's what I need to talk about." The cottage sat across from the bunkhouse. It wasn't like he'd planned to keep them a secret. "It's the woman who owns McClure's. She's there with her kid."

"She's at your house?" Jack asked incredulously. "I'll admit to telling you to charm her, but—"

"It's not like that." Garrick huffed. "Anyway, I heard her talking to Wes on her phone. She called when she thought I was sleeping."

"She's talking to a real estate agent?" A deep crease formed on Jack's forehead. "What'd she say?"

"Hold up. Wes is in on this?" Luke's brows lowered into a dark ledge. Wes Blankenship had negotiated their purchase of Tall Pines. "He's working for us."

"I've talked to him several times about purchasing that property." Jack grimaced.

"She could transfer the lease to another buyer," Striker said.

Garrick shook his head. "She said something about wanting to sell smaller parcels, three to five acres."

"Hell, no. She can't do that," Jack said angrily.

Garrick offered a small shrug. "Skylar told Wes she wants to let go of the property on the far east side."

"Where we're grazing the Brangus?" Jack had claimed the western pastures for his new horse operation, and they needed the ones farther east for grazing cattle.

"How's it coming getting her to sell all of it? Have you talked to her yet?" Luke asked. "She can't be thinking of living in that dump. Not with a kid."

He huffed. "I'm working on it, waiting for the right time." Skylar and Logan had just gotten settled. Swooping in with an offer to buy her land after her flat tire and the roof issue would be wrong.

"So, her car was parked there—overnight?" Jack arched a brow.

"Yes." Garrick glanced at Striker, who pulled his hands back in a *leave me out of this* gesture. Their father had been friends with Striker's father and had gifted their foreman ten shares of the business. He had a vote, but he steered clear of conflicts between the brothers.

Luke and Jack exchanged a meaningful look.

"You think it's wise to get involved with her?" Jack asked.

Indignation climbed up Garrick's spine and tensed his neck. He forced himself to remain steady. Jack was one to talk. Did he have the memory of a flea? His dating Dani had caused a lot of friction in the family.

Luke frowned. "Why can't you go to Turner's or Heron Park...."

"No. I said it's nothing like that." Garrick slammed a hand on the table a little harder than intended. In fact, he'd gone to Turner's the other day. And there'd been a group of women visiting from Ohio, among them a hot redhead—just his type. But he'd had zero interest.

All he'd been able to do was think about Skylar and how grateful she'd been when he'd shown up with that new tire. He was seriously off his game. "I'm doing things my way. Trust me." He jammed a hand through his hair. "I've handled more complicated situations. Her roof is damaged, a tree came down on it, and the power isn't getting turned on until—who knows with that storm. The timing hasn't been right."

"So, you ... what? Invited her to stay with you?" Luke asked.

"Seems like if she had to drive out from a hotel in Heron Park, rehabbing the farmhouse would be less attractive. She'd be more open to selling." Now, it was Jack's turn to frown.

In the light of a new day, he saw how inviting Skylar to stay in his cottage might look like a rash move. After working two back-to-back twenty-four-hour shifts, with multiple transports and only a few cat naps, it could've been a bad call. But it wasn't. It was the right thing to do. The only choice, really, for someone with honor. So, Jack needed to get off his back. He chose diplomacy. "Her staying there could be strategic. Now I know her plans."

"True," Luke conceded.

"Maybe," Jack said.

Yesterday, he'd left Skylar and Logan to get settled while he caught a few Zs. An hour in, a nightmare had caused him to knock the glass of water off his bedside table, spilling it all over the damn floor. That's when he'd heard Skylar talking to the real estate agent.

He'd come out a short time later, loaded for bear, ready to confront Skylar. She'd been standing barefoot in his kitchen wearing yoga pants and an oversized beater of a sweatshirt that fell off her shoulder, exposing a stretch of soft, naked skin. She'd showered, and her thick, glossy hair hung around her shoulders. The house was filled with the pleasing scents of shampoos, floral stuff, and food. And he'd been hungry.

She'd been covering a pan of homemade biscuits and vegetable beef soup simmered in a pot on the stove. The entire scene had disarmed him, something that she seemed to easily do. The soup was the best he'd ever had. Was he supposed to eat up, tell her they wanted to buy her out and send her and the kid packing? That seemed pretty harsh.

"So, she hasn't agreed yet?" Jack demanded more than asked, his tone accusing.

"I'm positioning her to be more receptive, moving in when she's softened up. She was wound pretty tight when she first got here."

"Sounds like a plan." Luke closed his laptop.

"We're calling Hiram." Jack's nostrils flared. "She can't parcel off acreage and sell."

"It's a little soon to get the attorney involved." Garrick's pulse picked up. A legal battle with the beautiful woman under his roof didn't set well. "I'll talk to her and be back with the report."

"When?" Jack asked.

"She's getting it inspected, got some people coming out to give her estimates today and tomorrow. Might be in such bad shape she'll abandon the project."

Jack leaned forward, his elbows on the table. "That's a lot of ifs. Hiram can still check the lease. If we're leasing the land the house sits on," he turned over his palm, "she might have to go. Simple as that."

"I doubt the land under the house is included in the grazing rights." Luke winced.

"Except the house was abandoned. Russ implied nobody would ever live there. Russ said the lease was drawn up in a hurry because the owner was sick. That's how he got such a good deal." Jack said, referring to the previous owner of Tall Pines, a man Garrick had never met. "So, Hiram ought to check."

Garrick's insides twisted. "No. It's not that simple. Something is going on. She's running."

"What kind of runnin'?" Jack asked.

The room stilled. Wyatt's gaze sharpened. "From who?"

"I don't think it's those meth dealers."

"Is she in trouble?" Jack asked. "We've got the new horses. People are scheduled to come out for the equine program next month. We can't have issues here again."

"I don't have details. It's a hunch, things she's said." He wasn't about to tell them she'd almost caught him off guard and cocked him upside the head with a metal rod. He'd stopped her, but she'd been expecting someone, and she thought they'd sent him.

"You'll find out?"

"Right. I'll get the story. In the meantime, she's at my house, and I'll work on her."

"Make it fast. And I'll call Hiram," Jack said. "One way or another, she won't be our problem."

Problem? Skylar didn't feel like a problem to him. Garrick grimaced, a spark of anger igniting in his chest. He needed to get busy before Skylar invested any more money in what would likely be a tear-down.

Skylar and Logan stepped into the pleasant midday sunshine. She breathed deeply, inhaling the fresh, floral-scented breeze, and her spirits lifted, infused with optimism. This is why people came to Florida in the winter.

The branches littering the ground around Garrick's house were gone. A short way down the drive, men loaded debris into the bed of a pickup truck. She scanned the immediate landscape with a fresh appraisal. Majestic trees spread wide canopies over the drive running down the center of the area. A cottage sat nearby, and a sprawling house sat adjacent to the barn. Toward the road, a larger ranch house sat near the entrance. And there were barns and all kinds of pens and corrals. This was a working ranch. As she studied her surroundings, a vision for her own property started to form.

"Ponies!" Logan pulled out of Skylar's grasp and ran toward the corral.

"Wait! Logan. Wait for me."

Directly across the driveway, the blind woman from the produce stand walked among several ponies with a hose. "Hi. Er... this is Skylar," she called out as she approached the fenced-in area. "We met at the produce stand. And I have my daughter here, Logan."

"Hey there. Welcome to our menagerie. Jack mentioned y'all were here." Dani shut off the water.

Skylar studied the smallish horses. "Are these ponies?"

"No. They're miniature horses. Like regular horses, but shorter. Does Logan want to pet one?" Dani asked.

Logan clung to the bottom rail of the fence and shook her head. "No. Too big."

"Maybe not," Skylar said.

"I'll bring Gracie over. She's real gentle."

Logan's face got all pinched, and she whined. "No."

"It's okay. You don't have to touch it," Skylar said in a soothing voice. This was a lot for Logan. "I think she's afraid."

"They might be more afraid of you." Dani drew closer and lowered her voice. "Some of their owners were mean to them before they came here. But Gracie is sweet. I'll bring her over and you can watch me brush her."

Logan stood several feet away, enrapt, watching Dani care for the horse.

"You ought to get Avery to show Logan the goats," Dani said. "They're smaller, and we have a few babies."

"I will, thanks." After a few minutes, Skylar grasped Logan's hand. "We need to be going, but if it's okay, we'll come back tomorrow."

"Sure thing. No extra charge." Dani chuckled.

They climbed into her SUV and drove the few miles from Tall Pines to the entrance of the McClure Farm. Her farm. It was a mess, but it had potential—and it was hers.

As she parked, a call came in from the property inspector.

"We're running a couple of hours behind," he said. "Several of our employees are without power, and there're trees down."

Discouraged, she unbuckled Logan and headed inside to wait. When she opened the door, a dank odor filled her nostrils. Clumps of the ceiling lay in soggy piles on the floor.

Disappointment settled over her shoulders. This was a bigger job than she'd anticipated and if she didn't get it cleaned up immediately, she'd be looking at a mold issue on top of everything else.

She put cheer in her voice and got Logan settled in the

freshly painted bedroom with paper, crayons, and her *Wizard of Oz* movie. "You play. This shouldn't take too long."

The soggy mess required a shovel and she'd worked up a good sweat by the time the property inspector arrived. The power company van pulled in right behind him. Skylar checked the time and groaned. More workers were due any minute, and they were about to overlap.

The roofer drove down her dirt driveway, and moments later, both the subcontractor handling the carpentry and the electrician showed. The house became a three-ring circus of workers talking about the storm and vying for her attention.

The roofer seemed annoyed. "Lady, didn't we have a—"

"Ma'am, you need to see this wire..."

The contractor raised his hand in a *what gives* gesture. "I've got another appointment in an hour."

"Just a second, please." If she wanted to rehab this house, she needed to get along with these men, especially the one pulling the permit.

The electrician frowned. "Trees damaged the power lines. The one through the roof ripped out some of the wiring in the attic. It'll be a couple weeks, minimum, before you have power."

She asked the contractor, "Can you talk to him and set it up?"

"Lady," the house inspector said, "you have a huge issue with termites. The subfloor in that bedroom's like honeycomb. You'll need to get the place tented and replace the subfloor. It's dangerous as is."

Her heart sank as she stared at the chewed-up flooring beneath her. From this side, it didn't appear too bad.

One by one, the various subcontractors gave their reports. All bad news.

Aunt Janice's words played through her mind. "It might be condemned. Sell it and use the money for a fresh start." But this house was the closest thing she had to roots... to her dad. She'd lost her mom at ten years old and two years later lost her father. With him, she lost any sense of family, of belonging. And now she had this. A piece of her family history. She needed to hold on to it, to renovate—and she enjoyed it. But logistics were an issue. She had nowhere else to stay, and it might take weeks, a couple of months to get the repairs done. Could she impose on Garrick for that long?

He'd come to the Veteran's Center on a mission to discuss the equine program at Tall Pines but had been herded into the group getting ready to start. Resigned to waiting until after the meeting to make his inquiry, he sat in a chair opposite the group leader. Garrick scanned the faces of the men sitting in a circle. A couple he recognized from the few times he'd attended last year.

Before getting injured, completing his education, and becoming a clinical psychologist, Dr. Cameron Austin had been a Platoon Sergeant in the U.S. Army. Angry scars cut through half of his face, and he had a prosthetic left eye, but the gaze in his right eye focused intently on the veteran talking. Doc's patience and quiet acceptance of the man's experience invited openness.

The veteran choked up, drew a shuddering breath, and finished his story.

Garrick shifted in his seat. He ought to feel something. Compassion might be a start. At the moment, the best he could come up with might be numb.

The aroma of freshly brewed coffee and donuts from the shop down the street filled the room. His mouth should be watering; he loved those chocolate-covered donuts, but today, they couldn't penetrate his armor.

As he listened, his stomach clenched. Acid churned at the base of his throat. He could relate. He'd experienced something similar. It wasn't one of the memories that came back to haunt him, but he preferred not to think about that incident.

Dr. Austin leaned forward. "Thanks, Sean. That took courage. Courage then, and courage now ... to tell it. It hurts coming out. But when we dull ourselves to the pain, we shut down our capacity for happiness too." The doc moved his gaze around the circle, making sure they all caught that last part.

Sean squeezed one hand over the other, shaking a little, his knuckles white from the strain, and he stared at the floor, gathering his composure. Trying not to look weak.

It was okay to cry. That's what the doc said.

They seldom did.

Garrick gathered and released a long breath, responding to the tension in the room, to the feelings ramming the walls inside his vaults.

Tom, one of the three other veterans in the circle, dipped his chin in acknowledgment. It was difficult being here, dealing with the shit. Nobody wanted to do it—until they couldn't *not* do it. Until facing it became the lesser of two evils.

Doc Austin understood. He was open about his past, the outpost where he'd been stationed, the situation that took his eye and scarred his face. He'd been to hell and back and didn't mince words. But he didn't push the guys beyond what they could handle. Doc had your six. The group had your six. God had your back too.

But ultimately, you were the one who had to face your inner demons. It was a solo mission. The guys in the group would be waiting for you when you came up for air.

Tough as the men in the circle were, it still took a helluva lot of grit. Healing wasn't for the faint of heart. He'd been called brave all his life. Since he was a kid and helped save his friend's little brother, and then a few years later, that incident with the wounded dog. He'd rushed in to help, despite his fear.

"Garrick's my brave boy," his mother had bragged to the neighbor. Seems like the only time she took a break from fighting with their father was when Garrick did something outstanding. And then, for a few minutes, she noticed he existed.

He might be brave, but laying his crap out for others to see, or rehashing the worst days of his life in front of an audience, took a kind of resolve he had yet to find.

They moved on to the topic for the day—chill. Powering down, getting sleep.

"How's your sleep going?" the doc asked.

Garrick stared at the clock near the door. Stay. He could stay. He was choosing this, and he wasn't the only one with issues.

The guy missing a finger spoke up. Good.

If the guy talked long enough, Garrick would have an excuse not to.

Doc Austin asked if anyone else had something to say.

Crickets.

"So, everyone's getting a great night's sleep?" Doc looked around the group expectantly.

The guy beside him made a sound between a snort and a chuckle.

"That's what I thought. Okay, we'll cover the basics." The Doc reviewed sleep hygiene, mindfulness practices, medications, and therapies that helped with PTSD. There were additional resources, a flyer about an upcoming class.

Garrick rubbed his forehead. "Who has time for all that?"

"Who has time not to?" Doc recited the laundry list of issues tied to long-term sleep deprivation.

Why had he mentioned his nightmares during those sessions when he first came to Pine Crossing? It might be paranoid, but it felt like the doc aimed at him with all his comments.

He scoffed. They all knew going without sleep had been part of the job. Now they were supposed to reverse it on a dime and sleep like a friggin' baby? Get real. Plus, in his new job, calls came in at night. When the tone dropped at the station, they were up and out the door in a heartbeat. It didn't pay to sleep deeply. And if you were at home when you got the alert, you had to be clear enough to drive in—which was the main reason he wasn't much of a drinker. He'd never forgive himself if he was too drunk to help someone in need.

When the group broke up, Doc approached him. "How's the job going?"

"Fine."

"That's great." The doc nodded skeptically. "There are people out there who might find some of those calls triggering."

"No issues." He glanced at the door. The doc was cutting too close to the bone.

It wasn't that he didn't trust the doc in particular. It's that he didn't really trust anyone since he'd come home, since that day when his comrades had fallen. How could he replace them? It felt like a betrayal.

Doc Austin handed over a glossy business card.

Garrick turned it over in his hand. "New card."

"New look. Better paper. Paid for them myself." He huffed a soft laugh. They both knew the VA budget didn't cover frills.

"Same number?"

The doc met his gaze. "Call or text if you need to talk."

"Thanks." He shoved the card into his pocket, mostly to be polite. He didn't need it. Didn't want it. He'd had those few private sessions when he first came to town. "But I probably won't call. It's all good."

"The QR code on the card links to some decent meditations. Give them a listen. Might help you sleep."

Right. He was gonna sit around meditating like some yogi. Get real. All of this soft, touchy-feely stuff made him itch.

He should've gone to the gym.

Frustrated, he stormed out to his Jeep.

Halfway to Pine Crossing, he realized he'd forgotten the reason he'd gone to the Vet Center. He was supposed to talk to Doc about the equine program at Tall Pines.

Garrick strode into Hudson's Farm and Ranch Supply. Lauren

Hudson, Tate's younger sister, was stocking the shelves near the register. "Hey, Garrick. It's been a minute."

He lifted a shoulder. "They've been keeping me busy at the station."

"The guys are in the back." She angled her head toward the door along the rear wall between the fishing tackle and hunting supplies.

He knocked two quick taps, signaling it was one of the team, then punched the code on the keypad and pushed through the door. This large room at the back of the shop doubled as storage and meeting room for Tate and a few of their other veteran brothers. They were good guys, taking specialized jobs, and were headed by Tate, who'd grown up friends with the local deputy and was plugged into all kinds of local connections. They had an understanding. Deputy Kurt shared information in situations where he had limited power and Tate could get the job done more efficiently. Sometimes legal, sometimes operating in a gray area, often a dark gray, they were fast, accurate, and at times, well paid.

When he'd first joined them, there'd been a rush and the satisfaction of a job well done with a brotherhood of men who shared similar skills. Doing something that mattered. However, his participation declined when he accepted the paramedic position. And he still ranched. He had two jobs now. They had to understand.

Tate left the new guy at the back of the room. "Good to see you, G-man. You up for some excitement?"

Garrick hated the nickname but couldn't shake it. That's what he got for disclosing his one-time dream about going to work for the FBI. "You have a job?"

"Affirmative G, getting a woman's car back. Her scumbag exboyfriend cleaned out her bank account and stole her vehicle."

"And she went to the sheriff?" It slipped out. They wouldn't have taken the job if she'd gotten results the usual way.

Tate winced, mildly put upon. "Yeah. And the guy's in debt,

and if she wants her car back ... they're dragging their feet. Anyway, Flash got his 20, and we're heading out at seventeen hundred." He leaned on the shelves where they kept an inventory the public didn't see. "You in?"

Flash examined his Glock 19 and stowed several extra mags.

Garrick swung his gaze from Tate to Flash, then to Ron, who sat with the new guy in the back, near the police scanner where they listened to calls.

His brows drew together. When he'd first come to town, he'd joined them on jobs that'd included finding a runaway teen, breaking up a gang of small-time car thieves, providing security for a high-profile rock star, and a few sketchier jobs. And they'd spent hours combing the countryside searching for an elusive group of meth cookers.

Judging by the kind of gear they were organizing, they expected trouble. Some jobs were messier than others.

He'd worked the ranch that morning, ran errands, and been to that group at the Vet Center. Skylar was back at his place with Logan. And he'd promised his brothers he would deal with the property issue. He couldn't do messy today.

Tate raised a brow.

"Nah, I've got stuff to do. I'm checking in. Needed to pick up feed." But if they were short a man for the job, he ought to stay. "Unless you need...."

"No worries. We've got it covered." Tate's gaze darted to the new guy. "Hawk's a solid guy."

He nodded slowly, glancing at Hawk, his replacement. "Gotcha."

"Tomorrow's tournament night. My house. Are you coming?" Tate lifted a palm.

"Right. My days have been all mixed up from working extra shifts. I'll be there."

Garrick paid for the feed and left, a surreal sense of not fitting in anywhere increasing as he climbed into his truck. He missed that feeling of absolute belonging and trust. Of knowing his place, his job. Of connection.

Becoming a paramedic was supposed to help him get it all together. Consolidate his skills. But now, between ranch work, the firehouse, and Skylar staying at his place, his life was in more fragments than ever. Where did this piece with the guys at Hudson's fit? He'd think about that later. For now, he owed it to his brothers to talk with Skylar.

———

The aroma of roast chicken hit him when he entered his house. Not the rotisserie kind from the grocery, but richer, more savory. Garrick's mouth watered.

"There you are," Skylar greeted him as she laid out silverware and napkins.

He never ate there, at the table. He preferred to sit on the couch and watch TV while he scarfed down his carry-out.

Mashed potatoes, green beans, and pans of both cornbread and biscuits sat on the stovetop. Steam rose from something sweet. Was that cherry cobbler?

"Woman, you never told me you were a wizard in the kitchen." His stomach growled, and he decided to push the talk out until after dinner.

"I can cook." She hiked her brows. "When I'm in the mood."

A smile stole over her lips, and at that moment, he wanted to hug her. Instead, he snagged a hot cherry from the edge of the pan.

She tapped his hand. "Get your dirty mitts out of there. Wash up. We can eat in ten minutes."

When he'd offered her the deal, he'd expected her to simply cook. Basically, keep the fridge stocked with the kind of food he could heat up. He hadn't expected her to set a table and serve a family-style meal. He hadn't planned on eating together. "You didn't have to ...."

"Don't worry." It was like she'd read his mind. "Once I get rolling with the remodel, I'll have some long days. I'll prepare food we can heat when we have time. Do you have a crock pot?"

"No." He rubbed his head.

"You might want to buy one." She got Logan situated on a stack of books, raising her to table level. "And we might want a booster seat."

He pulled his head back, surprised. How long was she planning to stay?

A short time later, he slathered butter on hot cornbread, sopped up gravy with a biscuit, and shoveled in huge mouthfuls of succulent chicken and dressing. He moaned. The woman could cook.

"Does it feel windy in here?" Skylar tilted her head.

He glanced her way. Logan nibbled a chicken drumstick, and Skylar had a forkful of green beans.

"I think you're creating a vacuum." She laughed.

"Huh?"

"You know, with your speed eating."

He grinned sheepishly. "Force of habit from years in the Army. And it's good."

"Glad you like it."

She served warm cobbler with vanilla ice cream for dessert. He had seconds.

After getting Logan bathed and into bed, Skylar came out holding a mug and sat with him in the living room.

He clicked off the remote. The MMA fight was starting, but it appeared she wanted to talk.

"Want coffee?" she asked. "Or will it keep you up?"

"I don't need coffee to keep me up."

Skylar looked at him quizzically, the cut-away neck of that same beater sweat-shirt from yesterday falling partway down her upper arm. She had a nice neck, smooth, and she probably wasn't wearing anything underneath. He brought his attention back to the topic. "I've had trouble sleeping since getting back."

"Back from where?"

"I served overseas. Army. I said during dinner. Fast eater?" He waited a beat for her to remember.

"Oh. Right. Where?"

"Mostly Afghanistan. A few other places."

"I figured since you're a rancher and a paramedic...." She gestured to the landscape outside the window. "So, you were in the military? For how long?"

He knew a lot about her, at least what they'd found online. She had a right to know a little about him. "I left the ranch in Montana when I was twenty-two. Enlisted with my cousin. Got out a few years ago." She didn't need all the details.

"You were in a long time." Skylar seemed to study him as if searching for evidence of something.

He nodded.

"Did you...fight?"

He huffed. "Yeah. Did my fair share of tours."

"And you were what? Like a foot soldier with a gun or..."

"Yeah. Kind of." The edge of his mouth hiked up a little. She had no idea. "For a while. I did a lot of extra trainings. They give you time off when you're not deployed, and I used it to take classes and improve my skills. Eventually, I changed my MOS, that's your specialty, to combat medic."

"What made you change to that?"

He shrugged. Ran his thumb over the remote, itching to put the fight on and tune her out.

"And because you were a combat medic, you work as a paramedic?" she asked.

"You could look at it that way."

Her eyes narrowed. "What other way would I look at it?"

He ground his molars back and forth. What did he want to tell her? Becoming a combat medic had a lot to do with taking a round to the chest, with his cousin and buddies dying in action. But that wasn't the reason he'd become a paramedic.

"Seemed like a good fit." He lifted a shoulder noncommittally, feigning indifference. It was a deep and sensitive topic. She didn't need to know. "What did you find out about the house today?"

Skylar groaned and rubbed her cheek while shaking her head. "That bad?"

"Worse." She began listing the issues they found.

Inside, he cheered. Thank God. She probably couldn't wait to unload it and leave. His task was already done for him. "So, it's too big a job? You gonna sell it?"

"No." She drew back like he'd slapped her. "I already told you I rehab houses. Plus, it's been in my family for generations. I'm just saying it's more work than I expected."

"Are you sure you want to take that on?" He leaned forward in earnest, elbows on his knees. "The land is being leased. You can't even use it for another five years."

Her forehead wrinkled. "Right. I was thinking about that."

"The land lease offers you an income stream, but have you considered how much money..."

Her gaze sharpened.

He bit back the words. Why couldn't he ask her to sell? It seemed simple enough, but she was offended when he implied she might want to. This was a touchy subject. He needed to approach it strategically.

Skylar's lips moved like she wanted to say something.

They sat there for a long moment. She was so beautiful and smelled so damn good. He fought back the craziest urge to kiss her. That would go well. Kiss her, then ask her if they could buy her land. He stifled a laugh.

"What's that smile for?" she asked.

"I wasn't smiling."

She snorted. "Yes, you were."

He hiked a shoulder.

She shook her head like she didn't believe him. "Anyway. Do you think we can stay here a while longer? Until the roof's replaced?"

He leaned back on the couch and squeezed his forehead. What kind of hole had he dug himself into? But watching her sitting on that chair, those soulful eyes—and he had the extra space. He might regret this later. "Sure. You've cooked a couple of excellent meals."

"Thank you!" She brightened and nearly leaped out of her chair. "Tell you what. Give me a list of your favorite meals, and I'll make sure you get them."

"I can handle that." He grinned despite himself. No more reheated diner food or bumming dinner invitations from his brothers as long as she was around.

"But Garrick?"

"What?" Of course, there was a catch.

"I grocery shopped today, and I'm a little short on funds."

"Right. I'll call Martha at the grocery in town. She'll bill me for whatever you need. You're cooking, I'll buy." He and Tate had helped the couple who owned the local independent grocery apprehend some chronic shoplifters. It was easy after installing a few hidden cameras and following the guys when they left the store. Now, the grocery store owners were like their best buds.

Skylar stretched. "I'm tuckered out. It's been a rough ... couple of weeks." She walked into the hall and checked on Logan, left the door cracked, then headed into her room. He waited but didn't hear her door click shut. Skylar was willing to put herself in a vulnerable position to keep a watch on her daughter.

The honey badger probably kept the pry bar under her bed, just in case.

No. That wasn't it.

Warmth flooded his chest. She trusted him.

He rubbed his face and moaned. Her trust made him feel like a real shit. He'd give it a few more days before asking her about selling. More information from the attorney might offer clarity anyway. There was no reason to act prematurely.

Before heading to the poker game at Tate's house, Garrick swung by Heron Park Mercy. He'd rarely been in there out of uniform, not working. The beeping in the background, the slight disinfectant scent, and the shiny floors all seemed a little off when he was dressed in civvies. He'd entered from the parking garage one other time when their ranch hand had been assaulted, but other than that, they were lucky. He didn't usually need to use the public entrance.

He rode the elevator and strode directly to the room in pediatric intensive care where they'd put the kid the last time he'd visited.

She was gone.

He found the nurses' station. "What happened to the girl in 306?"

"Are you family?" asked the woman at the computer.

She wasn't the one he knew. He scanned the area and deflated. He didn't recognize anyone working this shift.

"No." He stuck his hands in his pockets. What was he doing here?

A puzzled expression crossed her face. "I can't—"

"I worked the call. I'm not in uniform today." It was unusual, but he needed to find out how the girl was doing.

The nurse pursed her lips, her distrust understandable. She had a job to do.

"The girl was in pretty bad shape." He got out his ID and flashed it.

"You're the one who worked on her?"

"Yeah."

"I'm amazed you got those IVs in." The nurse's expression warmed as she recognized one of her own.

"Thanks." He could insert an IV in the dark, in a helicopter. That girl had been challenging, but he'd never doubted his ability to get the job done.

The nurse tapped on the computer keyboard. "They moved her to 471."

That was a good sign. He smiled inwardly. A regular pediatric unit meant she was doing better. He stepped lighter as he navigated the hallways, but stopped when he approached the girl's doorway. There were voices in there.

"We'll visit your mom, and then we're going to my house for a week," a woman was saying. "Your mother will join us tomorrow or the next day. We'll swim in the pool and go to the beach. Sound good?"

"Can we build a sandcastle?" That was the little girl.

"Sure, we can. Now, let's gather your things."

"If you'll sign here." That sounded like a discharge nurse. "Then you and your aunt can be on your way."

Satisfaction washed through him. The child was being released into her aunt's custody, and her mom would be okay. He stood back as the three of them exited the room. The little girl glanced up at him, curious. Small scabs dotted her face, and a trace of bruising remained, but her skin glowed, and a ribbon held her clean hair in a ponytail. She wore a shirt the color of sunshine and held a white teddy bear. Cleaned up. No blood. Looking good.

He dipped his chin in acknowledgment.

"Can I help you?" the nurse asked.

"No thanks." Something inside him tightened as he stood aside and allowed them to pass. She was okay. He'd done that— saved her. Did it even the score? He couldn't save them all, but she was alive because of him. Him and something bigger.

He didn't claim all the credit.

The three made their way down the hall and waited for the elevator. He should feel elated. And part of him did. So why the twisty sensation in his chest?

The mouth-watering aroma of pepperoni pizza filled his truck as Garrick drove to Tate's for their monthly tournament night. The sprawling stucco ranch style house was perfect for the larger poker crowd that gathered in the living room at two, sometimes three tables.

He carried the pizza boxes inside and saw two of his worlds converging—the guys from the firehouse were there with his veteran friends from Hudson's. Sure, they all knew each other; this was a small town, but it was still a little strange. Sometimes, he made the regular poker game at Tate's. Other times, he played with the guys at Zeke's place behind the firehouse. Tournament nights combined the two groups and had a few other men mixed in. The couches were shoved close to the sliding glass door, and two tables filled the center of the room.

Most of the players had already arrived. Kurt, a local deputy, stood talking to Zeke, who had his trademark bottle of kombucha tea on the table.

"Hey, Garrick. I'm collecting the buy-ins. Fifty dineros, my man." The fire chief sat, passing out the chips and reminding people to toss a few bucks into a jar for snacks and drinks.

"Back in a second." He nodded to Zeke on his way into the kitchen, where he set the three pizza boxes on the counter closest to the family room.

Tate caught his eye in acknowledgment as he listened to Hawk speaking, too low for Garrick to hear. Flash stood to the right, his face hard.

Garrick went on high alert.

Flash drained his beer, then headed out the glass door opening to the deck and made a call.

Unease snaked up Garrick's spine. What was wrong?

Laughter drifted in from the other room. More men arrived, and the sound of Cody's Tennessee drawl joined the others. Voices rose and fell. Zeke said something, and there was more chuckling. Molly, the female firefighter on their staff always joined in for the firehouse poker games, but she never showed up for these events. It's a shame, really—she was a decent player and good people. Aside from the fact she and Levi were working, she'd once commented that there was too much testosterone in the room on tournament nights.

Garrick opened a pizza box and pulled out a slice, his attention focused on the guys in the kitchen.

Hawk joined Flash on the deck.

"Something up?" he asked.

Tate huffed, moved closer, and helped himself to pizza. "Nah. It's all good." The hard set to his jaw said otherwise. Tate trusted him, but he didn't need to know the details. Sometimes, plausible deniability was preferred. His buddy was protecting him.

Out on the deck, Hawk and Flash seemed to be having a disagreement. Something had gone sideways.

"Hey, G." Ron moved through the kitchen, barely greeting him, and made a beeline for the guys outdoors. The two men said something to Ron, glanced toward the living room window, and lowered their voices, but their facial expressions and posture told him the issue wasn't over. The men outside seemed to come to an agreement. Ron strode off the deck and headed toward the side of the house.

A moment later, Hawk checked his phone and left in the same direction Ron had gone.

"Guess we're short two players." Tate lifted his brows. "Let's get this party started." He carried his beer and plate of pizza into the other room. "Pizza's on the counter. Help yourselves."

Garrick followed Tate and swung his gaze from the men in the room to Flash, on the deck, texting. Yes. Not knowing was best. But the uncomfortable feeling of not being an integral part of their group didn't sit well.

A moment later, Flash entered the room and cast a quick glance at Tate, nodding almost imperceptibly.

The game started.

"What happened to Hawk and Ron?" Cody asked, eyeing the two empty seats.

Tate waved his hand dismissively. "They had a schedule conflict." He added his chips to the pot. "How'd that deep sea fishing trip go, Zeke? That rod I sell you do the trick?" His question signaled the topic of the missing players was closed.

"Caught me a real nice grouper ... had to toss him back." Zeke shook his head. The season didn't open for another couple of months. Talk turned to fishing and which deep-sea charters were the best.

After stopping at the hospital, Garrick had fought the urge to go home. Hanging out with Skylar was going better than expected and he wouldn't have minded calling it an early night and spending the evening with her.

It was good he'd chosen to play poker.

Whatever was going down with Hawk and the guys had his senses sharpened. Tonight, he was picking up on everyone's tells, the way Tate rubbed his thumb and forefinger together whenever he was bluffing, how Cody handled his chips. After the first few hands, Garrick took the lead.

Throwing caution to the wind, he upped the ante. He only held two pair, but the other players were holding worse. On a winning streak, he was raking in the chips. Players froze out and Garrick assumed a seat at the winners' table with Cody, Tate, Flash and Kurt. As he continued to win, his mood elevated considerably. The payout would be a few hundred bucks. It's not that he needed the money, but it was still a rush to come out ahead.

Within the space of a couple seconds the room filled with the noise of Kurt and Zeke's radios, and the beeping, and chirps of the pagers and phones Garrick and Cody wore.

And Tate got a text. His expression remained neutral, but the color drained from his face. He slid his gaze to Flash.

Then everything happened very quickly.

Zeke backed away from the table, his expression a storm.

Kurt jumped to his feet and cursed under his breath. "I've gotta go."

Garrick stood, ready for action, the tension in the air palpable

Zeke eyed the piles of chips at Garrick's seat. He addressed the group, "Sorry guys, we've got a call." He swung his gaze from Cody to Garrick. "Both y'all need to come."

Then Zeke and Kurt were out the door.

Shit. On his night off. When he was winning. With only a brief pang of regret, Garrick left his chips on the table and hurried to leave with Cody. Duty called.

Behind him, the other players broke into loud chatter.

In a tone of authority, Tate said, "That's it for tonight, guys. We'll roll this pot into next month's game. Everyone here is already bought in."

Conversations, speculations faded into the background. Garrick hustled outside. He grabbed his med kit from the back seat of his truck and climbed into the passenger seat of Cody's vehicle.

His stomach twisted. He had a bad feeling.

Garrick rode with Cody in Rescue Two, Rescue One having already been dispatched to the scene. They were calling it a potential mass casualty incident, an MCI. There were three known victims, one suspect under arrest, and the area was a designated crime scene. Shots fired. They'd need their vests. That's all they knew.

At the scene, blue and red lights flashed, and yellow crime-scene tape already defined a perimeter. Zeke and Walt, their other firefighter EMT, had pulled in ahead of them. Deputies appeared to be Mirandizing a man by a squad car. Levi was loading someone into his rig.

Kurt and another deputy stood near Molly, who was giving CPR to someone on the ground near the house. Garrick fought back the impulse to run over.

Zeke pointed to the landscaping at the far end of the house, where a woman hovered over someone. "You two, over there."

Zeke and Walt approached Molly while Garrick and Cody headed toward the shrubs.

Garrick's stomach clenched.

Hawk. Moaning. Thank God he was conscious.

A woman applied direct pressure to Hawk's leg while a deputy stood behind her, grimacing.

"I heard gunfire and called it in," the woman said. Blood covered her hands, and determination etched her face. "When I looked out the window, I had to do something. I've had first aid training."

She'd put herself at risk, but her actions had given Hawk a chance.

"I'll take it from here." Garrick moved into the space and applied a pressure bandage to the wound, getting Hawk stable enough for transport. He started two large-bore IV ports, and Cody got a drip going.

Hawk groaned, grimaced, and swore a blue streak. "It burns like hell."

"Hang in there, man. You're gonna be okay." Garrick must've said it half a dozen times.

Within moments, he and Cody had Hawk loaded into their bus and were on the way to the ER. A few more minutes and Hawk would've been in serious trouble.

They rolled Hawk through the ambulance entrance at the ER and got him transferred to the trauma team. Sometimes, people who took a round to the leg lost a limb. Hawk's bullet entry location was farther out, 9 mm through and through, and didn't seem to have nicked a major artery. But, at the very least, Hawk had a difficult few months ahead of him, and there could be nerve involvement.

While Cody cleaned the rig, Garrick filled out the report.

He'd finished tapping on the tablet when Cody showed up in

the doorway, his lips set in a grim line. "Molly was working on Ron. He didn't make it."

His stomach dropped. He figured it'd been Ron but had clung to hope anyway. He liked Ron. They'd hung out at Tate's. Worked a few jobs together. Gone skeet shooting. He nodded slowly.

Cody shoved his hands in his pockets, continuing. "Died at the scene."

The words twisted in Garrick's chest. He huffed, a painful sound.

"At least they got one of the shooters," Cody added.

The drive back to Pine Crossing was quiet.

A few hours ago, Ron had pushed past him to get outside and talk to Flash. A sinking dread washed through Garrick. If he'd worked that job with them.... He liked to think he was smarter, would've seen it coming, could've taken evasive measures. But the bottom line was you never knew. It could've been him.

A sobering thought. A shitty situation.

When they pulled into the Pine Crossing firehouse, Zeke was already there. "There're sandwiches and drinks on the conference room table. Come in and eat."

"Not hungry," Garrick called over as he pulled his gear from the rig.

"I'm not asking." Zeke folded his arms in front of him.

Cody and Garrick exchanged a look before heading to the conference room.

He took a seat and rubbed his face. The odor of the food made his stomach clench. He recognized the bags as the ones from the diner. "Since when does Mac's deliver?"

"Since the fire chief made a special request." Zeke handed over a cup. "Drink up."

"What is this?" Garrick's lip curled as he stared at the contents.

"Hot tea with extra honey and cream. Like my grandma served up when we were sick or had a problem."

"Do we have a problem?" Garrick raised the cup to his lips and tasted it. Not bad. He drank it straight down. Zeke gave him a refill.

Zeke's gaze bore into him as though trying to say something. "Do we have a problem? Your buddy was killed tonight. You guys hung out...." He paused meaningfully, then opened the bag, pulled out sandwiches wrapped in foil, and slid them across the table. "Eat."

Levi and Molly joined them and helped themselves to food.

Garrick took a bite of the sandwich and washed it down with more tea. Within seconds, he'd polished it off and felt a few degrees better.

"What a night, huh?" Cody said.

Levi filled them in. "The woman sustained a head injury in a struggle with the guy they arrested. She was pretty beat up, probably a concussion, and she'll need more than a few stitches. Some guy had come around with a couple other men, causing trouble. Two got away. It had something to do with a stolen car." He shrugged.

Garrick's food turned hard in his gut. The story made no sense to Levi, but in Garrick's mind, it clicked into place. He didn't know all of the details, but this had to be related to that job, the one he'd thought seemed messy. Yes. It could've been him.

"I want you to take a few days off," Zeke continued. "Rest. Walt's got your next shift."

"I don't need—"

"That's an order."

They polished off the food and drink and spent the next hour comparing notes and debriefing. A call came in, and Levi headed out the door with Molly.

He stood to leave.

Zeke approached him. "Call me if you need to talk. Or call Cam."

"As in Doctor Cameron Austin?" Garrick raised a brow.

"You told me you saw him when you first came to town."

"Fair enough."

"Give him another call," Zeke said softly but in a steely tone that left no room for argument. "I'm mentioning it as a friend. After what you've been through. And you knew Ron...."

He balked. "I'm fine."

"Yeah. I was fine, too. Until I wasn't." Zeke aimed his bottle of nasty kombucha tea toward him as he spoke. "Nip it in the bud, bro."

"I'll take it under consideration." Garrick groaned inwardly. That's what he got for confiding in Zeke.

CHAPTER EIGHT

The clock read zero three hundred. Garrick had already finished his morning PT and was dressed for ranch work. His sleep issues had worsened since Ron's death, and he figured he might as well make good use of the time. He drained his first cup of coffee and found a thermal go-mug to carry to the barn. It was never too early to work, as far as he was concerned. When he'd been deployed, many of his assignments had been under the cover of night. Working in the quiet and dark had become a pattern that suited him.

A familiar prickle crawled up his spine, and he stopped pouring, experiencing the strong sense that someone was watching him.

His pulse picked up a little as he slowly moved his gaze to the rear.

The munchkin.

Logan stood behind him, her chin wobbling, clutching her unicorn.

"Logan? What's wrong?" What was she doing in the kitchen at this hour?

Her tiny forehead gathered into wrinkles. "I had a bad dream."

Join the club.

He studied her for a moment. Dancing pink ponies covered her PJs, but she looked like she was about to cry. She stuck her thumb in her mouth, then pulled it out and buried her face in her stuffed animal.

What was he supposed to do? He squatted down to her level. "What do you need?"

She shrugged.

"Want a glass of water?"

"Okay."

He spotted her plastic cup next to the sink, got her water from the fridge, and held it out.

She stared at it. "Ice?"

Seriously? He popped a couple cubes into the glass and handed it down to her.

Her face shone with approval.

"Hold Peg?" The unicorn was wedged under her arm.

He accepted the stuffed animal and set it on the counter.

Her tiny hands held the glass, and she drank, never taking her innocent eyes away from him. They were blue. And her hair was straight and lighter than Skylar's. In fact, this kid bore only the slightest resemblance to her mother. Did she take after her dad? What had happened to her father? He and Luke had found a record of a divorce when they'd looked up Skylar, but it was fifteen years ago. Perhaps Logan was the product of a random hook-up.

Ordinarily, he'd hustle out for an early start. Instead, he sat on the couch and waited for Logan to finish. It was taking forever. The kid must be sipping it one drop at a time.

Finally, she handed over the glass.

"You'd better go back to bed. I have to work outside with the horses." He'd muck the stalls, then mow the south pasture so they could bale it tomorrow.

Logan brightened. "Will you ride a horse?"

"Maybe later."

"Can I see?"

"You need to go back to bed. It's too early to get up."

"Tuck me in?"

He glanced from Logan's room to Skylar's room. Her mother should do the tucking in. He didn't want to go in there alone with the kid and have Skylar hear him. But she was asleep. "I don't think I should."

Logan's features scrunched into a worried expression. "I don't want to go by myself."

Was he wrong, or was this kid more talkative than usual? "How about you get your blanket, and I tuck you in here? We can put a show on the TV and let it play while you sleep."

"Mommy says no TV at bedtime."

"Right." He rubbed his scalp. "This is different since you're lying down in the living room."

That faulty piece of logic seemed acceptable.

"I need my blanket." She looked at him expectantly.

"Go get it."

Her lips trembled.

He disappeared into her room and returned carrying her soft throw.

"No. The big one."

Huffing as he about-faced, he retrieved his poncho liner, her new favorite blanket.

She climbed onto the couch. He got her organized, covered her with his woobie, and turned on one of those nature shows his dad was always watching with the woman who lived next door. Two hours of botanical gardens. If that didn't put the kid to sleep, nothing would.

"I'm going out, and you stay here. If you need anything, wake up your mom. Do not open the door." He put his hand on the doorknob.

"Wait!"

He turned. "What?"

"My Peg." She'd sat up, face pinched, about to cry.

"It's here. On the counter." He fetched the stuffed animal, set it beside her, and turned to leave.

"But she wants a kiss goodnight."

"What?" Was he hearing correctly?

Logan extended the stuffed animal.

He stared at the slightly worn, plush white unicorn with a pink horn and shimmering wings. There's no way he was kissing that thing. "I think she's just tired and wants to lay down."

Logan wasn't buying his suggestion and pushed the toy toward him. "Kiss."

Oh, for the love of hell. Was he really doing this? No. He was not putting his lips on her stuffed animal. He thought for a moment, then made a fist, kissed his thumb, and blew on it. "There. It landed right on her."

"It did?"

"Magic." He nodded solemnly.

She grinned, a mouth full of tiny teeth, kissed her hand, and blew on it. "Magic." She whispered. "Did you feel it?" She pulled the covers over her face, then peeked out and giggled.

"Go to sleep now. You hear?" His throat clogged with emotion and the words came out gruffer than he meant them to.

Go-cup in hand, he let himself out. Once in the barn, he leaned on the stall and laughed heartily, straight up from his belly.

Home life was full of females, a unicorn, and—magic kisses? Where had he come up with that? Warmth filled him again, and he moved horses into the ring so he could clean their stalls. Laughing over Logan wasn't a bad way to start the day, but he'd better not get used to it. If he was successful, they'd buy Skylar's land, and she'd leave.

CHAPTER NINE

S kylar parked close to the farmhouse and lowered the window, allowing a pleasant March breeze to flow in. "You wait here a second. I need to talk to those workers, and then we'll visit the puppies." Visiting the puppies had become shorthand for shopping at the produce stand and talking to Dani while Logan played with the pups. They'd leave with vegetables fresh from the fields.

"Can we go swimming?" Logan asked.

"Maybe. After the puppies."

Despite meeting with subcontractors and running to the home store, she still managed to take Logan to the solar-heated swimming pool up by Dani's house. Logan took to the water like a fish. In fact, while she might be worn around the edges, her daughter was positively blooming. Logan enjoyed visiting the horses and feeding them pellets. Dani had helped her brush the smallest mini. Logan smiled more often, and the sound of her sweet laughter when Garrick teased her made Skylar's chest lift with joy.

The termite treatment was finished, the sub-flooring would be done today, and the wall guys were scheduled for next week. Then the flooring would be delivered, which meant she'd need to rent saws and borrow some other tools. Everything had been scheduled with minimal deposits and the promise of more.

When she stepped from her car, her cell phone buzzed. It was her realtor, an older local man, Pablo Vasquez. Putting Pablo in charge of approaching the management company seemed cleaner. More businesslike. She didn't want to do anything to jeopardize her arrangement with Garrick since staying with him was going so well.

She leaned on the door. "Do you have good news for me?"

"I found you a buyer."

Her heart leaped. "That's great! I can get out of the lease?" Pablo knew someone who'd expedite the closing, and she'd have what she needed to move forward with the remodel. "That's the best news. Are they buying four three-acre parcels?"

"Hold on," Pablo said. "Not so fast. I sent you an email on Monday and another yesterday. Didn't you get them?"

"No." She opened her email. "It's not there."

He sighed heavily. "Check your spam, chiquita."

Skylar opened her spam folder. There it was. And there was one from Adrianna, too. That was weird. She'd read it later—and check her filters so she wouldn't miss any other important messages. She opened the email from Pablo. What? "You couldn't get me out of the lease? But you found a buyer who wants the land even if it's being leased."

"The buyer is the ranch."

"But what about selling it in the parcels?"

"In theory, you can sell parcels to different buyers. But nobody can touch the land until the lease is up. That makes it less attractive. The ranch presented a fair offer. I think you should consider accepting it. I'll email you a copy. You can hold out for a better offer. But ... it would take a special buyer to be willing to wait five years."

She sat back down in the driver's seat. The ranch would own land on two sides of her. She stared over the fields to the east, green pastureland that would remain as is, which should be okay.

This is a good thing. There wouldn't be construction noises all the time. But it made her uncomfortable being boxed in by the ranch. Still, she needed the cash. "Okay. Find out how fast we can close."

After speaking to the workers, she drove to the produce stand and found Dani talking to a familiar face, one of the hands from Tall Pines.

"Howdy," the hand greeted them. A little on the young side, he sounded more like Texas than South Florida. Hadn't she seen him working with that young woman in the goat barn?

"Hey, yourself," Skylar replied. "We came to visit the puppies and buy more tomatoes."

"Have you met Wyatt?" Dani asked, "Is little Logan with you?"

"Wyatt." Skylar nodded to him and nudged Logan. "Say hello to Wyatt and Dani."

"Hi," Logan whispered. "Can I see the puppies?" Logan moved toward the crate of tumbling puppies to the right.

Happiness lifted Skylar at Logan's complete, clear sentence. Her daughter was becoming more comfortable around the people at the ranch.

They spent the next ten minutes having puppy time. Maybe they'd get one when she finished the house—if there were any left.

A truck pulled in, and a man wearing black jeans and a black leather vest with an American flag on it, emerged. Chains rattled as he approached the stand. "Hey, Dani. Have you been taking good care of my puppy?"

"Bear! I sure have. She's had her shots and is ready to go."

"Excuse me." Bear moved into the space with Skylar and Logan. "This is my new best girl." He opened the crate and removed the puppy with a white spot on her ear.

"Give her lots of love," Dani said.

"You know I will," Bear called over his shoulder. He looked adorable carrying the small pup out to his truck.

Logan's lip trembled.

"It's okay," Skylar said. "They need to go to their new homes."

"But that was my favorite." Logan whimpered, ready to pitch a fit.

"Logan. I need help. Can you do a special job?" Dani trailed her hand along the counter as she neared. "Do you see that puppy with the black feet? He needs some extra cuddles, so he doesn't miss his sister."

Logan's gaze shot to the black-pawed squirmer, and she reached her fingers through the crate.

Skylar removed it and placed the black and white puppy in Logan's lap, watching over her. "It looks like he's wearing boots."

The puppy licked Logan's hand and she giggled.

A familiar Jeep pulled in, and a moment later, Garrick approached the farm stand. His gaze landed on hers and held for a moment, making her insides flutter. "Hey Garrick." She greeted him, feeling stupidly tongue tied, and forced herself to focus on the dog. It had been way too long since a man made her heart pick up like this and there was no way she'd let him know she was interested. He was their host and one of the ranch owners. Should she say something about accepting their offer? This didn't seem like the place for that discussion.

"What's all the commotion?" Garrick asked.

"Bear left with a puppy," Dani said. "And Skylar and Logan have come to visit. Logan has the important job of comforting the puppies left behind."

Dani's words hit the mark, and Logan grinned as she gave the puppy a kiss on top of his head. "It's okay, Boots."

"Logan loves dogs," Skylar said, ridiculously happy he was there. "Me too, if I'm being honest."

"Their mama came from my sister's dog, Sadie, at the ranch," Dani explained. "I haven't been able to convince Garrick to take one."

"I'd take one in a heartbeat if we were settled." Skylar stroked the little bruiser.

"What brings you in, Garrick?" Dani asked.

"I was at the diner in town, and Jack thought you might like me to drop this wrap off for lunch." Garrick placed a sack on the counter.

"Garrick, you are my hero." Dani ran her fingertips along the wooden countertop until she came to the bag.

"No worries. I'd best be getting back." He nodded to Skylar and strolled out.

"Garrick really is a nice man." Dani rang up Skylar's tomatoes. "Hey. If you have free time, you ought to bring Logan to the barn this weekend. We have a group of kids coming out to brush the minis. I can email you the information we created for volunteers."

"I'm not sure." Skylar's groaning to-do list ran through her mind.

Dani persisted. "We could use the help, and Logan might enjoy it."

Skylar had plenty on her schedule, but Dani had been so welcoming. "Sure. We'll help." She carried her bags to the car, and they headed home, or rather, to Garrick's house, which was home now. This situation was comfortable, perhaps too comfortable. She needed to be careful. But she found herself singing along to her playlist and grinning, enjoying the unfamiliar, bubbly sensation of happiness.

CHAPTER TEN

After getting off work at zero eight hundred, Garrick headed to the Cedar Bay Boxing Club for a hard workout and an hour of sparring and Krav Maga. His sensei had recently returned from vacation, and he'd missed their regular sessions.

His trainer showed him no mercy, and he cursed himself for not finding a different sparring partner the past couple of weeks. If he wasn't exhausted before, he was finished off now and couldn't wait to get a hot shower, but he needed to stop at the feed store on the way home and pick up a new post-hole digger.

Tate waved him over to where he and Flash were loading supplies into the bed of his truck. "G-man. Just in time. You up for a job?"

"Uh..." Something inside him tightened, and the scene where he'd found Hawk played through his mind. "Maybe. What's with all the lumber?"

"We're doing some work for a woman in Heron Park. Got a few hours?"

He hadn't hung with the guys since Ron's funeral. Still, he was wiped after a twenty-four-hour shift and the grueling workout. He'd been looking forward to an easy afternoon napping and reading.

But they were short two men. They trusted him to help, and they'd have his six if he ever needed them. Lacking a pressing excuse, he climbed into Tate's truck.

"We're building her a chicken coop," Tate explained.

"Which is actually...?"

"Chicken coop. For real. That's why all the lumber."

His stomach growled. "Do we have time to stop at the diner?"

"No. We'll be late." Tate focused on the road.

Flash tossed him a pack of beef jerky sticks.

He peeled back the wrapper and bit off a chunk. He liked jerky, but it wasn't the sustenance he needed.

"A chicken coop?" Tate didn't strike him as the kind of guy who went around building barns for people. "Does she have the birds yet?"

"No. I'm driving her to get them tomorrow, so the job needs to be done today."

He arched a brow. "Is this someone you've been seeing?"

"No. It's a favor. Friend of my dad. Her husband was a special agent. Worked undercover," Tate said as he steered them west.

"Put away a lot of lowlifes," Flash added from the back seat.

"Where is he now?" Garrick asked.

"Same address as Ron, my man," Tate said solemnly. "The Veterans' Cemetery. Served ten years before going into law enforcement. Could've retired next year. Killed in the line of duty." They were silent for a long moment. Ron's funeral service was still fresh in their minds.

Tate glanced over. "He was a good guy. I promised my father I'd help his widow."

Tate's dad had spent decades running their store before Tate and his sister took it over. Now, the man was an expat in Costa Rica. Garrick had sensed the elder Hudson had more going on than simply being a feed store owner, but Tate was tight-lipped about it.

He wadded up the empty jerky wrappers and stuffed them in the side of the door. "And that means building her a coop and getting her birds?"

Tate gave him a *don't ask* look that meant there was a lot more to the story.

Garrick didn't care. He was just here to help his friends and leave as soon as possible.

They parked in front of a newer house, large for the area, with manicured landscaping, pigmy date palms, beds of roses, and other flowers. The three men spent the next four hours busting their backs and busting each other's chops, seeing who could come up with the best insults. Flash was the one to beat, but Garrick got in a few good ones.

The client, a gorgeous woman named Carla, wrote them a hefty check. She wasn't as old as he'd imagined.

"You don't need to—" Tate held up his palm, trying to decline payment.

"Don't be silly. I insist." Light sparkled as it caught the diamond bracelet on Carla's wrist. She waved the check until Tate accepted it. "And I appreciate you upgrading the security system last week. I feel much better now."

"Call if you need anything." Tate caught the woman's gaze, and they exchanged a look.

Unless his radar was off, Tate definitely had something going on with that woman. And she was at least ten years older than him.

They rode back to the shop. Garrick made his purchase and headed home.

It was nearly seventeen hundred hours. Garrick usually didn't pay such close attention to the time, but there'd be a home-cooked meal for him if he got there on time. It was seriously motivating. It was hot. It was good, and Sky would be there eating with Logan.

Garrick parked next to Skylar's SUV, and at that moment, it hit him. He liked having them there. Two weeks in, on the nights he was home, they'd fallen into a pattern. They'd eat dinner, and then he did the dishes while she got Logan bathed. Then she'd read Logan a story, and sometimes he listened in. She was a good mom. When Logan was settled in bed, he and Skylar sat in the living room and talked. Sometimes, they watched a movie. His old self would've given him a hard time, but he liked it. The routine was comfortable.

He hadn't done anything like this in years, not since Melody in Atlanta.

Now there was Skylar, Sky as he liked to call her, and he hadn't even kissed her—yet. That was about to change. In the time she'd been staying with him, he'd given her space, and it had gone better than he'd expected.

It was time to take things to the next level. There'd definitely been something in that look at the produce stand the other day, and there'd been moments of closeness when they were hanging out after dinner. But this arrangement was unlike anything he'd ever done before.

He stalked inside on a mission. "Hey, Sky."

Silence. He moved from room to room, searching.

The aroma of cheesy lasagna wafted over from the stovetop. The table was set. Nobody was there.

When it was evident they weren't home, he scanned the house for a sign of where she'd gone. "Skylar?"

Where was she?

Garrick strode outside and walked around back.

Sky and the neighbor woman, Thea, were in deep conversation, standing in the middle of the large garden as long rays of early evening sun spilled over them. He liked Thea. The local healer knew a thing or two about life, about plants. A Red Cross nurse, back in the day, she was training his sister-in-law, Dani, on medicinal herbs. And she was his dad's new best friend. In fact, Thea was likely the reason his father was up and working again.

Thea wore a serious expression as she listened to Sky and watched Logan digging in the dirt with a garden trowel. After a short time, they seemed to come to an understanding.

Sky took Logan's hand, helped her to her feet, and brushed her off. Thea returned and handed her something. That's when Sky looked his way, her face flashing bright and beautiful when she spotted him.

Logan broke into a run. "Gricky."

What was she calling him? He winced. It was worse than G-man. But despite Logan butchering his name, her delighted expression made him smile. "Hey, munchkin. Whatcha doin'?"

"We're making a garden." Logan bounced on her toes.

"Garrick, when did you get home?" Sky asked, her sweet-as-sugar accent reeling him in. How had these two females captured his affections so quickly?

"Just now. What's in the bag?"

The three of them walked inside together.

"Herbs. Something safe for Logan. Go wash your hands, sweetie." Sky pointed Logan toward the bathroom, where a little white step stool with horses on the sides and pink glitter trim was positioned in front of the sink. When he'd found it online, he'd had to buy it. The stool was practically made for Logan.

"Why does Logan need Thea's herbs?" Tension moved into his forehead. "Is something wrong?"

"Logan's perfect. But she has some issues. Tied to, well, events that caused her stress. You may have noticed her shyness and how she doesn't talk much."

"But it seems like it's gotten better."

"She has." Sky pulled butter out of the fridge, stopped, and looked directly at him, her tone filling with warmth, "And she likes you."

"Does this stress have something to do with that pry bar? How you yelled 'she's not yours' that first day I met you?"

Skylar rubbed her cheek. "Yes." She abruptly turned, ending the conversation, and removed a covered bowl from the fridge. Then she pulled something wrapped in foil from the oven, her movements stiff.

The atmosphere had shifted. It didn't take a trained analyst to tell he'd upset her. He moved into the kitchen and leaned back on the counter, gripping it with his hands. "You gonna tell me about it?"

"Would you uncover the salad and set it on the table?"

She was stalling.

He did as requested but returned and stood right beside her. "What's going on? You've been here a couple weeks, and I've been waiting for you to say something. I have a right to know if you're in some kind of trouble."

"It's probably better if you don't." She turned away.

He came around in front of her. "Tell me. Maybe I can help."

"I doubt it." Sky's forehead got all wrinkled, and for a moment, it seemed like she might cry.

He closed the distance and drew her into a hug. "It's gonna be okay."

She rested her face on his shoulder, sighing one of those long sighs, sinking into him. "I hope so."

He lowered his face, cupped her cheeks in his hands, and moved his thumb over her skin. So soft. "You can tell me. I want to keep you safe," he whispered.

She looked up, and the next moment they were kissing. It felt like such a natural thing to do—and it ended too soon. For a quick moment, they held each other's gaze as though surprised.

Then, with unspoken agreement, he covered her mouth with his, and she parted her lips. He took the kiss deeper, tasting her, tilting her face for better access, arousal lighting a bonfire inside him.

He pressed her against the counter, claiming her mouth,

thoroughly enjoying her body against his, their kisses growing increasingly passionate. There was only Sky, the sweet scent of her skin, her soft curves.

She broke away and whispered, "Logan."

His heart thudded at the base of his throat, and it was almost painful to let go. After watching her for over two weeks, suppressing his desire, he'd done what he'd only thought about— and kissed her. It wasn't enough. He wanted her, now. And if Logan wasn't there, he'd happily finish what they'd started. But the bathroom faucet shut off, and the stool moved.

Logan padded into the kitchen. "I'm hungry."

"It's dinner time." Sky slipped right into mom mode.

"This isn't over," he whispered roughly.

The flush climbed back into her cheeks.

"I meant the conversation." He chuckled. "But that too." Now he knew. She wanted him like he wanted her.

They ate. The food was good. It always was. But he hardly tasted it for thinking about later, after Logan was in bed.

A fire had been lit inside of her, and Skylar hated to put it out. But she banked it and somehow got through dinner, even though, when her eyes collided with Garrick's, her breath caught.

Garrick was looking at her with intention. She didn't want to encourage him, but her body betrayed her. Sleeping with him had to wait. Right now, it would complicate an already delicate situation. There were her issues with Clive, her issues with the lease, and the sale of the land. She and Logan needed to stay here, and she couldn't blow that up because she was attracted to Garrick.

She rubbed her cheek, pressing on the joint that got sore when she clenched her teeth at night. Why did life have to be so complicated? It wasn't fair. Couldn't she just be a single mom, moving to Florida and living freely on her farmland? Why did they have to be staying with the man whose family was leasing her land? It'd been years since she'd really been interested in someone. She was in her early forties. She wasn't dead. But everything had changed when her sister was killed.

Wound up from a big day, Logan wanted two stories read to her, and her back rubbed. It was after nine when she faded, and Skylar came out to have her own time, which these days meant sitting with Garrick watching TV and talking about nothing.

After the conversation and that kiss before dinner, it would be different tonight. She glanced at her bedroom door, tempted to turn in early. No. That was the easy way out. Eventually, they'd need to talk about Clive, about the lease, and whatever this was between them. It was supposed to be nothing. House-guests. Impersonal, like a vacation rental. It was nothing like that. Hanging out with Garrick at the end of the day had turned out to be the best thing going on in her life, besides Logan.

She slipped into the kitchen and reached for the coffee, then paused and opened the dried chamomile Thea had given her. Logan drank a little cup of the tea with honey after dinner and should sleep better tonight. Her daughter drank it, but Skylar didn't have to. Thea said it would soothe her nerves, but she hated tea. Wasn't she suffering enough? She sealed the tea bag and chose coffee instead. She didn't do herbal tea. She liked her coffee bitter and black, and it didn't keep her up.

Cars crashed, and voices yelling blared from the TV. Good. An action movie made an excellent distraction from the talk they needed to have. She got comfortable at her end of the couch, sipped her coffee, and tried to catch up on the show, an older one with Dwayne Johnson.

Garrick turned off the TV and leaned forward, resting his elbows on his knees.

Ugh. Her luck had run out. "What?" She fought the urge to take her coffee into her room and sit at her computer, perusing flooring materials and light fixtures and.... Adrianna's email! How had she forgotten? She pulled her phone from her pocket.

"Can that wait? There's important stuff we need to discuss." Garrick glanced toward her, his face tense, and appeared to be gathering his thoughts.

She studied him. His eyes were more brown than green, and they were kind, but sharp. Alert, reminding her of that eagle she'd spotted in the tree.

"Sky," Garrick began.

"Yes?" She loved that he used that nickname, the one her dad had used.

"Tell me what's going on. When I found you at the farm-house, why were you so...." He twirled a hand in the air, as though searching for a word, and not wanting to call her crazy.

"I know. I was a mess." She felt a lot better now, in his home. It was safe here.

"Who did you think I was that first day?"

She gathered and released a long breath and tried to organize the situation in her head. She may as well tell him the truth. "This guy was in prison back in Chicago. And ... I ... I helped put him there. He got his sentence overturned, and he's out now."

"Does this guy have a name?"

"Clive Warwick." She bit her thumbnail, then caught herself.

"What happened? You seem pretty shaken up."

She looked Garrick straight in the eye and felt her muscles tense. "He killed my sister."

"Damn, Sky."

"He pushed her down. She hit her head. He said it was an accident. But he'd done it before. I can almost say I saw it coming. I mean, not that day, but I had a bad feeling about him, and he ... he was rough with Tessa, and threatened her, gaslighting her. He was a nasty, controlling son of a bitch." Memories filtered in. The night when her sister had called her, scared, and Skylar had driven by and picked Tessa up at the end of Clive's driveway. Another night, Tessa had come over, and Skylar took photographs of the bruises. She'd begged her sister to go to the police. Tessa had left him that time but went back a few months later.

"And you testified against him."

She nodded.

"The situation wasn't worthy of WITSEC?"

"I guess not. The trial was pretty straightforward. They probably didn't think I needed it. But he has loyal brothers and friends, and he managed to get a couple of messages to me. I turned them over to my Victim Services liaison, but there's no way to prove he was actually behind them."

"That's tough," Garrick said earnestly. He seemed unflappable, serious but caring, and strong enough to handle what she was telling him.

She rubbed her cheek. "I gave her pamphlets, showed her resources for domestic violence. I was training to be a life coach, so I was learning about different services. But you can't make someone get help. Even if you love them and part of them knows they need it. I told her if it happened again, I was calling the police myself. She got really angry and said I'd make it worse. That she'd cut me out of her life if I interfered. But I should've called."

Garrick waited.

She choked up a little. "I tried to warn her."

"And this guy has a grudge against you?"

"Big time. I testified. I had photographs of my sister, texts, and emails she'd written to me ... even a recording she'd made of him threatening her. Even though it wasn't all admissible, it painted a pretty damning picture. And when he went to prison, he lost his business. And his reputation. He owned a custom menswear shop. Really high-end clientele, but when the scandal surfaced, they dropped him. The shop closed. I think there was some kind of financial mismanagement ... I don't remember that part. I was too upset."

Anxiety constricted her throat, and she could barely drag in a breath. "He threatened to kill me," she whispered, as though saying it softly made it less true. "But I can't prove it. Deborah from Victim Services believed me, and she's been my contact. She's the one who told me when he was released."

She folded her arms over her belly. Focusing on the remodel had been a good distraction, and dredging all this up made her stomach ache.

"And you think he's coming for you?"

She shrugged. "Probably. He's been searching for me. I've heard from a few people, and then there's this." She opened her phone and scrolled to the horrible message that came in the night it rained so hard. It occurred to her she might have mentioned this to Garrick sooner. She handed over her phone.

Garrick's gaze sharpened. "It doesn't sound like he knows where you are."

"No. I don't think he does. And Logan was Lizzie before. Elizabeth Logan. We called her Lizzie. Now she's Logan McClure. It seems like that would make it more difficult."

"What does Logan have to do with this?"

"Oh." She winced a little. "He thought Logan might be his daughter."

"I'm not tracking."

"Sorry. It's complicated. Logan's my half-sister's daughter. My niece. I adopted her. It's what Tessa wanted."

Garrick's mouth parted, stunned. "She's not yours?"

"No. She's mine. Legally. She was only two. I'm her mom now."

He exhaled hard. "Right. How do you know this guy's not the father?"

"I believe my sister. She broke up with Clive for a few months and stayed with a friend in Oregon. That's when she got pregnant, and she didn't know who the father was. I think it was a one-night thing. I had Logan's DNA done. All it takes is a paternity test and he'll see she's not his. It's pretty simple and will prove Clive isn't the father. The place for her dad is blank on the birth certificate."

Garrick rubbed his hands over his face, his brows drawing tightly together, and he was quiet for a long moment. Then, he seemed to fill with energy like someone had plugged him in. "I need everything you know about Clive."

"Why?"

"I know some people who may be able to help. And someone who's got computer skills. It's better to be proactive in this situation. You don't want any surprises."

"Other than the basics—names, address, and work stuff, I don't have a whole lot of information."

"Tell me what you know."

For the next couple of hours, she searched her brain for any details she knew about Clive, all that her sister had shared. She pulled up her social media and examined the threads for clues. Then she searched through the texts still on her phone. And the phone message was still there. Tessa called when she and Clive were in the middle of a bad fight. He didn't realize it was being recorded.

Garrick sent the text thread and emails to his phone and asked her questions.

Drained, she leaned back and closed her lids. Opening those doors stirred up all kinds of old memories, pain, and grief. Tessa would never again sit beside her on the couch eating Ben and Jerry's as they talked and wiled away the weekend binge-watching *Heartland* or *Yellowstone* or one of the many home shows they watched on HGTV.

Garrick moved, and in the midst of her grief, she felt the warmth of him beside her.

"Are you okay?" he asked, covering her hand with his.

She cracked her eyelids and met his gaze. He gave her that little grin that made her all mushy inside. The man was seriously good-looking, like fantasy material handsome, and he was giving her a hot look. It hit her squarely in her belly and woke up all of her lady parts. But there was something else that reached into her chest and touched her. He looked so kind, so protective, so.... *Oh, no.* She really liked him. She could fall for him.

Garrick held her cheek and covered her lips with his. She welcomed his kiss, parting her lips, and their kisses became demanding, open-mouthed, his tongue tasting hers, their mouths locked together. Then he backed off and nipped a trail along her neck. His warm hands lit little fires wherever they touched. She surrendered and got lost in the moment. It felt so good to be kissed. His skin smelled clean and wonderful, and his whiskers sent shivers over her skin as they scratched her. It had been too long since she'd had this.

Soon, she laid back, her arms circling his neck, his incredible, hard body pressed against hers. She dragged her foot along the back of his thigh. Chills moved over her skin as his lips traced a path across her shoulder.

Wait! The voice of reason broke through. She needed to have the lease talk with him and take up the mantle of landlord. She couldn't do the deed with this man. That would make a complicated situation even worse.

With heroic effort, she grasped his face in her hands. "No. This can't happen. The timing isn't right. I need to talk to you. I need to have some space to think."

He sat up, exhaling hard. "What's the problem?"

"For one thing, I'm your landlord. I wanted to ask about Tall Pines buying the east side of my land."

"What are you talking about?"

"I accepted the offer earlier today."

He jammed a hand over his scalp, appearing confused. "You said the east side? Not all of it?"

"No. Of course, not all of it. Only twelve acres at the far side. They border the road."

"You aren't interested in selling the entire spread?"

She drew further away from him. "That was never on the table. In fact, I'd kind of like to see if y'all would break the lease.

When it was originally created, nobody was living there. Now, I'm there with Logan, and we want to do something with it. At the very least, landscape the yard, make a garden around the house, and add a porch and a garage. And honestly, I could sell the back section by the dirt road to a developer and get a good price. I could live off of that for a while."

Garrick's jaw tightened as though all his muscles had turned to granite. "The lease is for five more years."

"I know. But circumstances have changed."

"You want to put a—" He winced like he'd eaten something very bitter, "—subdivision in there?"

She'd lived in several places. Born in Athens, Georgia, she'd spent most of her childhood in Charlotte, then Memphis, come north with her stepmom, settled outside of Milwaukee, and later moved to Chicago. It had all depended on her stepmother's boyfriends. Years of living around cities had altered the way she appraised rural and urban areas. This place, where ranch met farm, was positively empty. Practically barren. "What difference would a dozen or so houses make?"

"A huge difference," Garrick said, aghast. "It would be like dominoes. Once you start tearing up the pastureland for housing, there's no end to it." He scooted a little farther away. A shield had come up, cool and hard.

This conversation made her head hurt, and she was too tired to think. "I'm heading into my room. It's almost midnight, and I've got an eight-o'clock client call in the morning." She grabbed her cold cup of coffee and stormed to her room, shutting the door this time, needing a barrier until he went to bed.

They wanted to buy all of her land? There's no way that would happen. What was she supposed to do? Where would she go? That was her house. Her family legacy. A connection to her dad. Based on Garrick's reaction, the outlook for breaking the lease was dim. She'd talk to Pablo later. He might have more luck with the family. Her chest sank. At least they'd bought the east end. She'd have cash in a few weeks.

She scrubbed her hands through her hair in frustration, hating how the evening had gone downhill so fast. Hating that she and Garrick had argued. There was a lease, and they were counting on using her land. It was cut and dry, business, legal. And she was taking her anger and frustration out on him. It was pretty here. And quiet. She could understand why he wouldn't want more neighbors.

Too wound up to sleep, she forced herself to read, getting lost in a novel until her eyelids drooped.

As soon as she turned off the light, in that hazy place of almost sleep, her lids popped open, and she bolted upright. Adrianna's email. She'd forgotten to read it.

She grabbed her phone and located the message in her junk folder.

Skylar,

Clive was in touch. He wants to know where you are so he can return a box of Tessa's belongings he had in storage. I don't know your address, but I gave him your phone number. Hope that was okay. Send me your address.

Adri

What! Hadn't she told Adrianna she didn't want Clive to find her? Thank heaven Adrianna didn't have her address.

Her heart pounded at the base of her throat. *It's okay. He has your phone number but no address. He can't find you.*

Wait. Did Adrianna give Clive her new name? What was in the box of Tessa's belongings that he'd had in storage? Her sister had always kept journals. There'd be personal information in there. Would there be anything about Aunt Janice? Her mind raced with possibilities.

Why hadn't Clive simply shipped the box to Adrianna?

Was there even a box? Or was this a ruse?

She fell back on the bed, staring through the dark, rubbing her thumb over the cracked screen of the phone glowing in her hand. Anxiety buzzed through her like sparks of electricity. She was strong. This, too, would pass.

She took ten deep, slow breaths and shoved aside thoughts of Clive. She could do this. Fix up the house and live there until the lease was up. Then, she'd do whatever she wanted with the land. She'd continue coaching and leasing the grazing land and perhaps locate another fixer-upper in the area.

This life could work. They had to be safe. After all, they were thirteen hundred miles away from Clive.

Garrick drank a glass of cold water, took a cold shower, and lay on his big, empty bed. Top-of-the-line, this new mattress was supposed to help him sleep, but his mind raced. He hadn't expected Sky to be in the mood after all she'd said, but attraction had mixed with a fierce urge to protect her, and something had come over him. She'd been on his mind for days. He was a man. He was into her, and it'd been a long time.

Talk about a boneheaded move. She'd been upset. He hadn't been thinking with his brain.

He lay in bed, his thoughts swirling in a fierce tangle. His brothers had bid on a land purchase without even discussing it? The deal was he'd talk to Sky first. And some creep had killed Sky's sister and might be after her and even Logan? The situation was so messed up it almost made the incident with Ron and Hawk fade into the background.

Ron was gone. Hard to believe. Last month, they'd gone shooting. They hadn't been close, but the heaviness of grief settled over him anyway, calling up memories of other fallen comrades. He fought those images back and focused on the fact that Hawk was okay and would be transferred to a rehab unit soon. The little girl from the accident was with her aunt. Sometimes, there were happy endings.

He ran through all kinds of people and chores weighing on his mind, but no matter where he directed his attention, it kept coming back to Sky and Logan. He had to do something.

It was nearly zero two hundred. Garrick texted Luke.

Garrick: *need help, check into Clive Warwick, recently released from prison.*

There was no point waiting for a return text. Luke was happily married and probably sleeping like a baby. Next, he texted Tate, who would likely be up or open to an early morning text.

Garrick: *Need help with a situation—Clive Warwick*

Tate: *come by tomorrow.*

Thirteen hundred miles was a long way, but if this guy blamed Sky, if the creep thought Logan was his, there was no telling what lengths he'd go to. He'd already sent a threatening text. Garrick wanted to protect Sky, to show her he cared—but what the hell? She had to go talking about selling to a developer? Wanting out of the lease? She didn't plan to leave. That part didn't bother him. He wanted her around. But his brothers had put a bid on the property without even telling him? He rubbed his hands over his face.

At this rate, he'd be up all night.

And then he remembered Doc's card. He fetched it from his dresser, scanned the QR code, and opened the website. There was a whole section on guided meditations for sleep. He squeezed his forehead, feeling like a wimp. This is how low he'd fallen. But he was desperate for rest. Hoping to fall asleep while it was playing, he chose the longest one and allowed it to play through the speaker on his phone. It'll never work....

Well rested after four and a half hours of dreamless sleep, Garrick skipped his PT and strode out of the house. There was no way he was missing the morning meeting today. They had some explaining to do.

He stalked into the room as the others were getting coffee and sitting down. Brick and Wyatt were at the end of the table talking to Striker. Jack was pouring coffee, and Luke sat at the long side of the table with his laptop open.

"Hey Gare, got your text." Luke glanced over meaningfully, signaling that he'd already done some digging. "Let's talk."

"The invisible man shows up." Jack held out a cup of coffee.

Garrick accepted the bitter brew, offering Jack a squint in return, biting back his fury. "You put in a bid for Skylar's property without telling me? When I'm supposed to be working on her? You didn't think I needed to be kept in the loop?"

Jack scowled as he took his seat at the head of the table. As ranch manager, he ran the daily meetings unless he was in Ocala checking on horses. "If you'd ever—"

Garrick scoffed. The muscles in his arms tensed and he fought back the urge to fist his hands.

Luke raised his palms in the sign of stop and spoke over Jack. "You're right. I should have talked to you. We should've looped you in. I'm sorry. It's our bad."

Striker glanced over, visibly concerned.

Garrick took in Luke's apology, settled a few degrees, and gave Striker a look that said he didn't need to worry. Jack might be a hothead, but it wasn't Garrick's style to get physical with his brothers. While they'd easily had an advantage when they were young, with all his training, there'd be no contest now. He wouldn't let it come to that. But he was enraged, and they had some explaining to do.

Jack had the good sense to back down. "The real estate decision happened kind of fast. Wes knew we were interested and wanted to act quickly before some developer planning long-range put in an offer. You were on board with buying her property, weren't you?"

"Right." Garrick nodded slowly. He'd been all in for buying her land, but he wasn't sure what he wanted anymore. "But I need to be able to trust you to keep me informed, or I look like an idiot."

"Agreed. We'll do better." Luke said, then turned to Jack.

"Agreed." Jack looked at Luke and continued. "Like Luke said, our bad. So, no problem, right? Although we're paying more than we ought to. How'd it go, getting her to sell the rest?"

"She's not interested." He hated being in this position, blowing an opportunity to impress his brothers, to bring value, but there was a limit to what he'd do. "I can still work on her. The problem is she wants us to release her from the lease so she can sell more acreage to the north, by that dirt road. Smaller parcels. For a subdivision."

Jack leaned forward and slapped the table. "Hell, no."

Garrick lifted his hands in a conciliatory gesture. "We've got time to convince her not to. As long as we have the lease."

"Get a start on convincing her," Jack said.

Striker cocked his head. "How's it going with her there, anyway?" Their shrewd foreman didn't miss a thing, and, living across from the cottage, he'd probably been keeping tabs on them.

"Fine. They're not a problem. I'm not there much, and neither is she," Garrick said matter of factly. "But there is an issue. Her sister's ex is searching for her."

"The guy she was running from?" Wyatt asked.

Of course, Wyatt would be connecting the dots. He'd been in a serious altercation with some meth dealers and had developed a watchful eye, not a bad thing, but a hell of a way to get it.

Luke lifted a brow in question.

Garrick dipped his chin in response, signaling that they'd keep the Clive intel between the two of them until they knew more. "I'm still gathering information. When I have something relevant, I'll let you know." Why stir up a hornet's nest if the man wasn't heading this way?

Dayworker cowboys coming to help with calving was next on the informal agenda. Calving had already started, but the crux of it was in the next few weeks. They expected thirty calves. It was interesting, and for a change, he got involved in the plan. "I'll talk with Zeke and schedule around it." Since Zeke had given him extra time off following Ron's death, he'd been more avail-able to work around the ranch and liked it. All the skills trained into him, cowboying in his youth, were coming back.

Jack parted his lips in surprise. "Good. Thanks."

He nodded. "No worries." An unsettling realization moved through him. He'd been AWOL at many of these meetings, yet he owned an equal share of the operation. He'd simply been depositing his own small chunk of the profits without giving it a second thought. For too many months, he'd been skating by on minimum efforts.

There were days when he'd first left the Army that he'd head into town and hang with Tate and Flash, taking jobs with them despite having a job right here. And last winter, he'd fixed up the farmhouse and slipped in there for hours to read when he could've been checking with Luke and Jack to find out what else needed doing. He'd always appreciated the strength of a team. And the one in front of him was pretty tight. How had he missed that?

When the meeting broke up, Garrick and Luke rode the golf cart back to Luke's house and headed directly into the office. His brother opened two computer screens. "Hold on a sec. I need to respond to this."

While Luke tapped on the keyboard, Garrick surveyed the area. Luke had red teamed at hacker's conventions a few times, and he'd since been hired by a few well-known companies to challenge their security. Luke had a VPN and buddies in several countries with computer skills that were put to use by various national security organizations.

"Okay." Luke swiveled in his direction. "Talk to me."

Garrick leaned forward. "How is this guy out of jail if he killed Sky's sister? They just say, 'Oops, you're innocent, now go?' After putting him away? Sky is sure he's guilty. Did you read the information I forwarded you?"

"They're not saying he's not guilty. The prosecution was at fault and didn't cover all their bases. This guy's bad news. Must have some connections. He's been in and out of trouble a few times and was supposed to have immunity in one of those earlier cases, but they used some statements they weren't supposed to use. It's a damn shame."

"More than a shame." Garrick squeezed the bridge of his nose. "He's a danger to Sky and Logan. We've got to do something. I'm talking to Tate later today."

"You're meeting up with Tate to talk about protecting *Sky?*" The corner of Luke's mouth curved up. "I take it they're excellent house guests?"

He snorted.

"That's how it is, huh? Play house long enough, and sometimes it gets real. I ought to know." Luke grinned full-out. "And she adopted her niece. I thought I took on a handful. But Avery was damn near grown, and she didn't have a violent background."

"I'm not saying I'm in it for the long haul. Nothing like that. She's good people. I'm only helping out a friend."

"That so?"

Garrick winced. They weren't having a relationship conversation. Obviously, Luke had been living in close quarters with women for too long.

"Living single all your life suits you?"

He scoffed. Why did Luke even care? And who was he to make assumptions?

At that moment, the chasm between them was evident. Despite being brothers, they really didn't know each other. When Garrick had enlisted, Luke was already off performing in the rodeo circuit. There were long periods when Garrick had no contact with his family, preferring to cram in additional training or go to Atlanta during his leave.

"I had that thing with Melody in Atlanta and thought it was the real deal. Got burned pretty bad."

"Sorry, man."

He huffed. "I told her upfront that I'd be deployed more than I was home." For a long while, he'd liked being over there, where the action was, a hard charger. It might sound arrogant, but he'd thought he was born for it. Born brave. Wanted to defend the defenseless, save the world, save whoever needed saving. Whenever he signed up for extra training, he couldn't wait to get back and put his skills to use.

Until things went to hell. He was injured, and a couple comrades were killed, and Brad. When his cousin died, it was a game changer. He'd begun looking at his situation with less *hooah*.

Luke stopped typing and continued the conversation. "She didn't like you leaving?"

He scoffed. "The thing is, I told Melody, and she said she'd support my choices. I bought her a nice rock, and we were engaged. I trusted her, man. She was gonna be my wife. I trusted her with my Hemi 'Cuda convertible while I was gone."

"You could afford that car?" Luke gaped.

"Helped a buddy restore his. When he died, come to find out, he'd willed it to me."

"Damn. You lost your friend and gained a car. But this isn't going to end well, is it?"

"No. When I left again, Melody wasn't cool with it at all. When I came back for a stretch in the hospital, she gave me an ultimatum. Said I loved my job and my car more than her."

"And?"

"She might've been right. I couldn't let down the guys on my team." He shook his head. "She kept the ring and trashed the car. Said it was an accident. Only an accident where you run into a sledgehammer from several directions over and over." He exhaled hard. "I sold it for a fraction of what it'd been worth."

"Ouch!" Luke expelled a soft, mirthless chuckle. "I get it. When I got injured, and I couldn't perform, my ex took all the money she could get her hands on while I was laying there with my leg in a cast, watching my dreams go up in smoke."

Garrick huffed. "Damn. We're unlucky in love, bro."

They both laughed.

"But sometimes things change." Luke glanced toward Ellie and Avery, talking in the other room. "I got lucky."

"Your luck's better than mine."

"You're not even taking full advantage of the proximity? Skylar's hot."

Tension clamped his jaw tight. He might not be in it for the long term, but he didn't want Luke disrespecting Sky. "True."

"So, how do you want to help this woman you don't care about?" A wry smile curved Luke's lip. He wasn't buying the whole "only friends" thing.

Garrick slapped a hand over his fist. "Stop this, mother—"

"Sure, you want to mess him up. But I'm talking virtually. You want to really sock it to him? Get him where it hurts the most." Luke shifted his gaze to the computer. "He may be wealthy, but the guy didn't get rich from his fancy men's clothing store. It appears he also owned a number of pawn shops. Most of them closed when he went to prison."

"Yeah?" What was the relevance? Some of the guy's businesses closed. What good did that intel do him? He wanted to hurt Clive.

"Two of the shops are still open." Luke swung the large computer screen toward him. A live feed camera showed somebody walking into a pawn shop. "That's one of Clive's brothers. He runs this store for Clive."

He scratched his chin. "How do you have a video of this?"

"I'm using the wi-fi camera across the street, and I zoomed in." Luke lifted his shoulder. "Here's where it gets good." He tapped a few keys, and documents along with names and numbers that made no sense appeared on several screens. "He's running a credit card scam out of there. Collecting information. Calling current and former clients and ...well, it's a phishing operation. Ripping off lots of people. Been going on the whole time Clive was locked up. As far as I can tell, nobody's traced it back to him."

"No shit?"

Luke pressed his lips together and nodded, obviously enjoying this.

"And we use this, how?"

"I'm still working that out. Let's think about it. There's got to be a way. In the meantime, I'm trying to access the cameras inside his shop. He's got safeguards, but I can get around them. The good news is we have a fix on the guy. I saw him there yesterday. So that means he's not here—yet. I've got a motion-activated video stream set to record, and I can view it double time. It will alert me when there's human activity. I'll find out what he's up to, and we can make a plan."

"Damn, Luke. I'm glad I'm on your good side. How do you have all this so quickly?"

"I saw your text when I got up to use the bathroom, and I couldn't go back to sleep." Luke chuckled. "It's been a while since I've had cause to get creative like this. Kind of miss it."

"You won't get in trouble?" He wanted Luke's help but had planned to handle Clive the old-fashioned way.

"Nah."

Garrick nodded slowly. "Let's go for it." He knew his way around the tech he needed as a medic. But Luke spoke an entirely different language, a coding cowboy crusader. In addition to online security, troubleshooting, and a buffet of the usual offerings, Luke's start-up offered discreet services to savvy clients who knew enough to ask for them. Some of his clients were near the top of the food chain. Garrick copped to more than a little awe and pride that he was related to Luke. And it was fun hanging out with him.

Luke fetched them cappuccinos from his new machine, and they spent the next couple of hours brainstorming worst-case scenarios for Clive.

CHAPTER ELEVEN

The first long rays of light filtered through the window beside the desk in Garrick's guest bedroom. Skylar logged into her coaching session and walked her client through a stress buster hack, the STAR POWER approach. Today, they were focusing on reframing thoughts, the power of catching stinking thinking, and replacing it with PPT, or power-ful, productive thinking.

It was a well-accepted fact that people often came to coaches with the exact issues the coaches needed to work on themselves, and she'd fallen into stinking thinking several times lately. It wasn't productive to dwell on *what-ifs* and worry about Clive. But her talk with Garrick last night had brought everything to the surface. When her appointment was over, she'd check into taking self-defense classes in town. She'd seen a flyer. Perhaps that would offer some peace of mind.

"Don't you think so?" The woman on the screen looked at her expectantly.

"Would you care to repeat that? The connection got wonky for a second." The connection in her brain, that is. She focused back on her client and wrapped up the session with an action plan and another appointment on the calendar.

If she was doling out advice and techniques, perhaps she ought to be making a plan and follow it herself. She had Nadine as well as Max and his wife a thousand miles away. She needed a support system closer. Thea and Dani could be part of her support system, and she was supposed to meet them in the garden in ten minutes.

She hurried into Logan's room, stepping over the books and toys. Logan wasn't in her bed. A momentary flash of concern spiked before she checked the living room. There was Logan, on the couch again, wrapped in that camouflage blanket.

Garrick had spoken about being in the Army, and he'd quietly stored the items from the farmhouse on his utility room shelves. The camouflage blanket, like the other supplies, probably belonged to him, yet he hadn't taken it from Logan. She smiled. He was a good guy. Really decent. Perhaps it wouldn't hurt to take things to the next level with him. They'd be roommates with benefits, friends, and a little something more, only while she was here. She didn't need a man making demands on her time, laying out all kinds of expectations. She'd tried that, and it hadn't gone well. Work and Logan kept her busy enough.

"Mommy." Logan looked up from her *Moana* video. "I want to go to the beach and see the waves like Moana."

Skylar practically gaped. Logan was talking in complete sentences? She'd positively blossomed since coming here. Was it the puppies? The horses? The fresh air? From Logan's point of view, life was slower and quieter—better.

Once she got over her shock, she groaned inwardly. Her promises about how wonderful it'd be when they moved, the beach, the fish, and the palm trees, were coming back to haunt her. "We're going over to the garden for now. I promise we'll go to the beach soon." It was nearly an hour away, but she owed Logan a day of fun after hauling her to visits with subcontractors and asking her to be patient.

Dark, sandy soil covered Dani and Thea's hands as they set small plants into the earth. "Look who's come to visit." Thea brushed the dirt off of her arms.

"What are you planting?" Skylar gazed at the winter garden in wonder. The last of the fat red strawberries were still bunched on short plants. Rosemary, chives, and other herbs she didn't recognize filled half the space. Rows of seedlings stood tall and green. Trays of small plants lined the edge of the plot. Of all the gardens she'd seen, this was the most robust and well-organized.

"Tomatoes," Thea answered. "They're nothing much now, but come summer, there'll be so many we'll have to make tomato jam."

"How can we help?" If she was planning to grow vegetables on her property, she could do worse than learning from Thea.

Thea got them set with tools and demonstrated how to position the small plants in the warm earth. You'd never realize Dani was blind, as deftly as she worked. Logan and Skylar were another matter. Logan clumsily dug the holes, and they patted the plants into the earth the way Thea had demonstrated, completing one to every four the other women planted.

"I'm excited y'all are coming over to help with the horses Saturday," Dani said. "It's our first group coming out."

"We'll be there. And I was wondering if you could recommend a beach. We've gone to the Lake Michigan shore, but it's been almost a year since Logan's played in the sand. She's into her *Moana* movie now, so she's all about the waves, too."

"Why don't y'all come to the beach with us? Jack and I are riding over to Starfish Key on Sunday afternoon. There's a private beach across from this inn where my friend works. On a weekend in March, the parking at the public beaches will be terrible, but we can park at the inn. It's real nice, and we're eating there, too."

"I don't know. I hate to impose." A long day with unfamiliar adults might be too much for Logan.

"Seriously. It'll be fun."

Logan dropped her trowel. "The beach! I want to go to the beach!"

"Not today sweetie." Skylar handed the trowel back to Logan.

Logan stuck out her bottom lip, pouting. "No. The beach."

"In a couple of days, okay? Let's finish helping Thea." Skylar turned to Dani. "The horses can be a trial run. If Logan handles that event okay, we'll join you on Sunday. It would be nice to put the day in someone else's hands for a change."

"It must be hard being a single mom. Even if your little one is as adorable as Logan," Dani continued. "You're such a good helper, Logan."

Logan brightened at Dani's compliment and resumed digging.

Skylar scoffed softly. "There've been some challenges." She held Thea's gaze for a moment but refused to ruin the pleasant morning by talking about her situation. Instead, she focused on the sandy texture of the dirt and the spicy fragrance of the herbs as they warmed in the sunshine.

After a while, they moved inside for coffee and cranberry bread. Thea showed Skylar her quilting projects, and Dani excused herself to go work with the horses.

"How did the tea work last night?" Thea asked.

"Logan slept through. No bad dreams."

"Wonderful. If you want to leave her with me sometime, I'd be happy to babysit. And in addition to the teas...." Thea told her about her healing practice.

"I don't know ...." Herbal tea was one thing.

"You can try the hands-on healing first."

Skylar balked. "I don't have any issues."

Thea gave her an indulgent smile. "Of course not. I was simply offering." Thea pulled a flyer off the shelf. "Here. This is from when I was practicing with a local physician who offered alternative modalities in his office. When he retired, I did too. I wanted to focus on my herbs. But I occasionally get called on by folks who used to come for treatments."

She thanked Thea and accepted the flyer, the polite thing to do. And she'd try the tea.

"Would you like to leave Logan here?"

"What do you think, Logan?" It wasn't that she believed young children should make all their own decisions and run the show like some of the other mothers she'd met, but if Logan had a meltdown, she'd have to drive back to the ranch. She didn't have time for that.

Thea had set out a basket of fabric scraps, and Logan was organizing them by color.

"Do you want to stay here and visit with Thea or ride into town with me?"

"Stay. These are pretty. See! Horses." She held up a scrap of fabric covered with little cowboy hats and brown horses.

Skylar pushed aside the discomfort of leaving Logan after being together round the clock for the past month. She was so preoccupied she almost walked right into Garrick exiting as she opened the door to his house.

"Whoa! You're a woman on a mission."

"Sorry. I don't want to be late for my meeting at the bank." She sidestepped.

Garrick didn't step aside like she assumed he would. He looked down at her, his eyes burning into hers. The previous evening streamed into her mind. For a moment, they stood there, simply breathing together.

"About last night," Garrick started. "That was terrible timing. Sorry, I—"

"It's okay, but—"

"It shouldn't happen again," he finished her sentence.

"No. I was going to say—" she tilted her face up "—I liked it."

But I have so much going on that I can't get involved. My life is complicated, and I have to put Logan first. I can't do a relationship." She searched his face. Before Logan, she'd have fallen for someone like him. Now, after dealing with Alan, having a man wasn't a priority. Perhaps when Logan was older.

Garrick lowered his face and whispered, "So you like this?" He moved his thumb over her lip, the corner of his mouth curving up. "You like me?"

"Yes." That was his takeaway? "But it can't go anywhere. I'm moving out soon and need to focus. It's hard enough being a single mom." She placed a hand on his chest and could feel the heat of his skin through the thin fabric of his shirt. "Now probably isn't the time to talk about this. I'm just saying I can't offer anything serious. Friendship is it."

"Understood," the word came out slowly. "Who said anything about serious?"

She couldn't keep herself from smiling, the excitement of something new, of possibility lighting her up. "Logan can never find out. But while we're here ...."

And then his lips were on hers. She looped her arms around his neck, pulling him closer, molding against him like she was drowning, and he was oxygen. Oh, mama, the man knew how to kiss. He pulled her inside the cottage and pressed her against the wall. They stood there locked at the lips, passion making her skin flame.

"Garrick."

"Yeah," he whispered against her throat.

"I really am late for my appointment."

"Right. I need to go, too." He pulled away, his breathing ragged, but he paused long enough to brush back her hair, his expression fierce, his look scorching, making her want to blow off her appointment.

He stepped back. "Hey. Where's the munchkin?"

"I left Logan with Thea."

"Good choice. She's great." He placed a hand on the doorknob and then glanced over his shoulder. "Later?" His tone was heavy with meaning.

A laugh burst out of her. "We'll see."

He nodded, grinning wickedly.

"Wipe that smug look off of your face, Garrick Stone."

He left.

She smiled as she leaned against the door gathering her wits. Next week, the flooring should arrive, and the roofers come at the end of the month. Soon they'd be leaving. Garrick was a good guy, really handsome and he made her feel attractive and appreciated. As long as she remembered her priorities, what harm would there be in taking advantage of this situation?

CHAPTER TWELVE

Garrick drove into town to meet with Tate, replaying what happened with Skylar, shocked, still high on that kiss he'd stolen on the way out of the house. And the possibility of more. Their discussion hadn't gone how he'd thought it would. Instead, he'd hit the jackpot. She was into him and wanted something casual.

Two weeks in the same house with a hot woman, and he'd only scored a couple of kisses. His younger self would be kicking his ass right now. But this was different. He was different. And there was a child involved. A girl who had him wrapped around her tiny little finger. They'd proceed with caution, and no one would get hurt.

He parked in front of Hudson's, and the door chimed as he entered. "Morning, Lauren."

"Hey, Garrick." Tate's sister flashed her bright smile. She was a beautiful woman, and he'd fantasized about her a few times. But he'd decided right from the get-go that he valued Tate's friendship more than he wanted to mess around with his friend's sister.

"Tate's expecting you. He's in the office going over the books." She arched her eyebrows. "Don't say I didn't warn you."

He veered away from the room where they usually met and entered the office. Until several months ago, this had been the space Tate's father used. He knocked two fast and one slow and was invited inside.

"G-man. What's going on?" Tate turned away from his desktop, the deep crease in his forehead easing as he offered his greeting.

Garrick studied the area beyond Tate. The computer screen displayed columns of numbers. Were they having financial problems? Tate was one of those closed-mouth types who didn't volunteer information unless you were one of his inside circle, and even then, it was on a need-to-know basis. Most people didn't need to know anything. Which is why he liked Tate. A solid guy, similar to a few he served with, Tate could be trusted.

He scanned the office, a room he'd rarely been in. A computer set up, identical to Luke's, sat to Tate's left. Luke's influence? His brother and Tate had connected before Garrick came to the ranch.

He took a seat and laid out the whole situation.

"Huh." Tate opened his other device and tapped. "This guy?" Tate rubbed his thumb and index finger together very slightly, a gesture he did when he was thinking hard.

"That's him." Garrick nodded.

"And he's somewhere near Chicago?"

"For now." He ground his teeth, frustrated. "This needs to be handled. The sooner, the better. Luke's coming up with a few ideas, too."

"You're pretty close to the situation. You and Skylar?"

"No. It's not like that."

Tate huffed. "Right."

"Seriously. Something needs to be done. He's guilty, he's a threat, and he's walking the streets."

"I hear Chicago's nice this time of year. Feel like taking a vacation?"

They both chuckled. The late winter blizzard moving across the Midwest had been all over the news.

"Yeah. We're a little short-handed right now." Tate cocked his head, his gaze a degree too intense, the unspoken invitation hanging there. Garrick grew uncomfortable and wanted to shift his position, but he held still and refused to feel guilty.

"What's the latest on Hawk?" he asked, changing the subject.

"He's facing six months to a year of rehab. Hard to tell until the wound's completely healed." Tate rubbed his chin. "A couple detectives paid Hawk a visit. Wanted to know more about why he and Ron were there, questioned him."

"Are they filing charges?"

"Doubtful. They've got nothing. His weapon wasn't fired. He was pretty out of it on pain meds when I visited, but I gathered he and Ron walked into a trap."

Garrick exhaled sharply. It could've so easily been him.

Tate continued. "It's out of Kurt's hands, but he'll keep me in the loop as much as possible. Thing is, Kurt's feeling skittish, wants to chill. Doesn't want anyone looking his way."

"Gotcha."

"But, G-man, you know Flash and I always got your six."

"Likewise." Disquiet fell over him. They both knew his priorities had changed. He wasn't showing up like he used to. And Tate would have his back, but he had the shop to run and couldn't always drop everything on a dime, even if the situation demanded it.

Tate needed to cover the register for his sister's lunch break, so they walked out front. While Tate helped a customer, Garrick left and headed toward Cedar Bay to spar with his trainer. Steel resolve tightened his gut. He'd helped a lot of people, and a few he hadn't been able to save. Skylar would be one of the ones he helped.

CHAPTER THIRTEEN

This day had been a long time coming. While Wyatt and Avery set up the goat barn as a petting area, Garrick and Striker handled the horses in the corral at the end of the miniature horse barn. Only the gentlest and most predictable of the minis had been selected for the Tall Pines Equine Therapy Program.

Garrick moved the last of the six miniature horses into the ring. Gracie, Avery's favorite, nudged him, expecting a carrot. He stroked the small horse's neck. "Avery's got you completely spoiled, doesn't she?"

"You should've seen that horse when she arrived. Emaciated and scared of her own shadow. This is Avery's work." Striker tied up fat little Peppercorn.

Garrick said, "I hear you had something to do with it." Striker worked with Avery daily, and she'd become quite the horse woman. "I guess we're done here." He was ready to slip away and let the others run the program.

Dani approached, trailing along the fence, and came to a stop at the gate. It was amazing how easily she got around, despite being totally blind. "How's it going over here?"

"All the minis are tied up as ordered," he said. "You're crushing it, Dani. You got this operation up and running."

She grinned. "Thanks Garrick. We did. I can hardly believe this day is here. We're still working with DBS to get a group of blind adults out for a session. Did you, by chance, talk to the people at the veterans' center?"

"I will, for sure." He'd intended to. It was the main reason he'd driven over. But after that emotionally draining session, he'd high-tailed it out of there.

"Promise me you will. Jack and I have been doing research. It may not seem like a big deal, but working outdoors and being with animals can really help some people. We're even thinking of a garden program." She headed back to the main barn where they'd be starting.

His hard-edged brother was reading up on helping people? That was a tough one to wrap his brain around. But they were onto something. Riding Rusty and working the land had to be a huge part of what kept him sane.

The gate at the end of the drive swung open, and a large blue van with a symbol on the side pulled in. Jack guided it to a parking spot then greeted the driver and helped the passengers out. One young person used a service dog like Dani's, two others used wheelchairs, and another had braces on his legs and moved awkwardly. Then four teens, a little rough around the edges, climbed out and assumed postures, likely trying to look cool. In addition to a few young people with disabilities, teens with school attendance issues were helping out today, getting credit for volunteering. They were starting small. In all, eight young people and a few adults were expected.

Dani and Jack accompanied the group into the big barn. Had his brother gone completely soft? Had Dani done that to him? It wasn't bad, but it was like having a duck egg and seeing a long-necked goose hatch out of it.

"Gricky!" Logan's voice came from behind. She ran ahead of Sky and locked her arms around his legs, nearly knocking him off balance.

"Hey, little champ, watch those tackle moves." He ruffled her hair.

"Logan, you shouldn't run away from me like that. I'm so sorry," Sky said.

"—Hey, no worries. If the little charger wants to play tackle football, I'm up for it."

Logan squeezed his leg, threw back her head, and laughed.

"That's how it is—huh?" He picked Logan up and, holding her tight, turned her sideways and swung her gently in the air.

Logan squealed in delight.

Sky's jaw hung open.

"Oops, I'd better put you down. Don't want to worry your mama." He set Logan on the ground.

"No, no. I'm not worried. It's good to see her behave so normally."

Logan took Sky's hand. "Horses, Mommy."

"We're going over to help now. Are you coming?" Sky asked.

"I have stuff to do...." He hadn't planned to get that closely involved. "I'll be back in a while." He was ready to tack up Rusty and get some alone time, ride over toward the McClure acreage, and check on the new water system.

Sky and Logan headed toward the end of the mini horse barn, and he positioned the saddle blanket over Rusty. He lifted the saddle. His ringtone sounded. Jack?

Garrick answered, "Yeah?"

"We need you. Now. Got a hurt kid."

"What's wrong?" He walked as he talked.

"This kid." Jack huffed. "There's blood. A cut, I think. I can't tell how badly he's hurt." Jack's stiff tone barely hid his anger. Someone had messed up.

Every barn had a first aid box, but he preferred his own kit, which was more advanced, always well stocked, and familiar. He retrieved his bag and hustled over to the middle of the commotion in the big barn. Dani and Jack led most of the group away so he could handle the problem. A volunteer stayed back with the kid who clutched one hand over the other. It was bleeding pretty good.

"What happened?" He listened to the kid's story while he cleaned the laceration.

Logan watched in quiet fascination as he bandaged the wound. From what he gathered, the two boys were being your average dumbass kids, and then one pushed the other, and he fell and cut his palm on the edge of the gate. Clumsy, and bad luck for their first event, and Jack was furious.

"Come on, sweetie." Sky tugged Logan's hand. "Don't you want to visit the horses?"

"No." Logan pulled away.

"Logan. Come back here," Sky caught up with her.

"She's not in the way," Garrick said.

The woman volunteer stood to the side, a grim expression on her face, anger coming off her in waves.

"William. You knew better than ...." She caught herself.

Good. Scolding the kid in front of everyone wouldn't change a thing.

"It was an accident." William grimaced, his tone petulant.

The woman probably wanted to throttle the kid.

Garrick suppressed a grin. "All set. His parents may want to take him to a walk-in clinic, but it's clean and bandaged."

"Gricky." Logan held out an index finger. "I have a hurtie."

"A what?"

"A hurt-ie!" Her face screwed up impatiently. She touched her finger.

He raised his brows. "You do?"

Skylar's brows drew together. "This is the first I've heard about it."

He squatted and held Logan's middle finger. A tiny pink scratch, barely breaking the surface, ran across the tip.

"Band-aide?" she asked, her expression intense.

He huffed a soft laugh, dug a bandage from his kit, and cleaned and dressed the nearly invisible wound. Her tiny smile was worth it. "All set, munchkin. You're good to go."

She held her bandaged finger up, effectively flipping everyone the bird. "See?" She jabbed her third finger in the air and showed the volunteer. "See."

The woman's eyes rounded. "Oh my."

He chuckled.

Skylar shook her head. "Come on. We're visiting the horses. That's why we're here." Skylar hiked Logan onto her hip and carried her away.

A funny feeling formed in his chest, like his heart was too big. Now he had to figure out how to get the munchkin to stop calling him Gricky before it caught on with the other guys.

<hr>

Garrick attended the morning meeting for the third day in a row. They didn't even raise an eyebrow anymore when he showed.

There was discussion about the equine program the previous day being a success, despite the boys' roughhousing. Eventually, they divvied the daily tasks, and the others headed out.

Jack cornered him. "So, you'll come with us?"

He groaned. Yesterday, Jack had invited him to ride along to the beach, and he'd immediately declined. Despite living here for a year and a half, he wasn't a beach guy and had managed to stay away. Hadn't he had enough sand for one lifetime? "Not interested. I've got too much to do."

"C'mon, man. Now Skylar's coming. I'm outnumbered. Next, they'll have me putting up a pink beach umbrella and making sandcastles."

"Yeah. Have fun." He started toward the door.

Jack stepped in front of him. "This could rack up some

points with Skylar. Butter her up good, and she'd be more receptive."

"She already said no." After kissing her the other day, he didn't want to upset her. He'd enjoyed it and planned a repeat, but with Logan around the timing was tricky.

"Change her mind. Anyway, there's more."

"What?"

"I heard from the attorney."

"And?"

"And officially, we're leasing the land her house is sitting on. We can evict her. Make her leave. She'd have to go."

"What are you saying?"

Jack shrugged his shoulders in an innocent "sorry, can't help it" expression. "The language in the lease stipulates the acreage and doesn't include omissions. Whoever drew it up hadn't imagined someone would want to live there. They were concerned with getting an income from the property."

A sick feeling washed through him, and he steadied his voice. Provoking Jack was never the best approach. "You're not suggesting we boot her out of her house?" She'd already invested a load of money in repairs.

"It's leverage. We don't have to let her stay."

"It'd be a jerk move to evict her from her own house." He rubbed the back of his neck. It pained him to contemplate the massive hurt this information would cause Skylar.

"Her hanging around, selling off acreage would be a problem for the ranch. I have to think of our bottom line. The programs Dani's started. The horse breeding. Everything here could be affected."

Garrick winced, torn in different directions.

"So, maybe you oughta come to the beach." Jack lifted his hand, palm up. "Work on her. Make sure we don't need to do it. Because if she tries to get out of the lease or lines up developers to buy it when our lease is up, that's throwing down the gauntlet, my man. Makes her the enemy as far as I'm concerned. After all you've done for her. Letting her stay in your cottage. Mighty ungrateful if you ask me."

Jack was still in a pissy mood after yesterday's minor disaster. But the injured kid was okay, and the parents weren't upset. He didn't need to lean into this situation with so much attitude.

Garrick exhaled hard. "I'll ride along. You don't have to blackmail me."

Jack drew back. "Blackmail? I want your company, brother. Besides, I'm just stating facts."

"Yeah. I'll state you a few facts. Bonehead."

"We're leaving in a few hours."

"Copy that." He turned to leave.

"We're staying for dinner at the inn." Jack had a meaningful tone to his voice.

He glanced back over his shoulder. "You're telling me this because?"

"So, you'll know how to dress."

He gestured to his jeans. "This isn't okay?"

Jack scoffed. "No dummy. Bring a change of clothes for the inn, something nicer, less ranch. And wear a swimsuit, flip-flops, or something."

"Flip flops? Seriously?" He stared down at his Tecova ranch boots. Flip flops weren't exactly standard issue in the Army, and he hadn't been to the beach since arriving in Florida. "I don't own a pair."

"I'll loan you some."

Garrick nodded. "Okay." Luke took after their father, long and lean, but he and Jack took after the men on their mom's side and had a similar build. Six feet tall, more muscular, and wore the same size boots.

He stormed away to finish the job he'd started earlier in the tack room. How could he face Skylar knowing what Jack wanted to do? He'd fight it, but if the others sided with Jack, he'd be outvoted. Sky had crap coming at her from all angles. And poor Logan.

He dropped to the stool in the tack room. What in the hell was he doing getting all tangled up in their stuff? But he was. Inextricably. They were in trouble and needed him. He grinned, recalling Logan's bright face when he bandaged her finger and the knowing look he'd exchanged with Sky when Logan was flipping everyone the bird, showing off her bandage. He couldn't turn his back on them and walk away. Not now. Because, temporary or not, his heart was involved.

Skylar sang along with her faves playlist as she packed a tote, adding a few recyclable containers to use as beach toys. What a relief it'll be to have a normal day playing with her daughter in the sand on a March afternoon.

With Logan ready early, she pulled the car seat from her SUV and walked down to the main ranch house where Dani and Jack lived with his father. Black shutters flanked updated windows, and a fresh coat of light gray paint covered the wooden exterior. A large porch ran the length of the front, and while the garden beds needed a little color, the place glowed with down-home charm. Someday, her home would have a porch like this. The houses had to be close to the same age, and this one was a beauty.

Dani greeted her at the door, and Skylar stepped onto old hardwood floors. Dani was visually impaired and lived there with two sighted men, Jack, and his father Bud. It came as no surprise to find the room decorated in wood and leather with a large recliner. The masculine tone of the room was offset by a few soft throws and colorful quilt wall hangings.

"Look who's here," Thea greeted them.

"Hey, Thea. Bud." She nodded, a little surprised to see the old woman sitting beside Garrick's father in the living room.

Dinosaurs lumbered across the screen in a nature program playing on TV. Logan stopped, transfixed.

"Those are Apatosaurus," Thea said.

"Apat...." Logan tried to say it, her eyes wide, staring at the surprisingly realistic creatures.

Thea slowly repeated. "Apat-o-saurus."

"Apat...o...saurus. It has a big neck."

Chills moved over Skylar as she shifted her gaze between the two of them. "Logan, that's great. I like the Apatosaurus, too."

Thea bent forward, getting on Logan's level. "You're a smart girl. Aren't you?"

Logan brightened. "Thank you, Nana Thea."

Skylar blinked. Thea had told Logan she could call her that, but it'd seemed pointless at the time since shyness kept her from warming up to people. What was it about this place? It was as though the cat had let go of Logan's tongue, and the words she'd been saving up for the past year were tumbling out.

"She can sit in here with us and watch the show until you're ready to go." Thea patted the place between her and Bud on the couch, and Logan climbed right up and perched there, looking an awful lot like a kid with their grandparents—something her daughter had never had. It made Skylar's heart squeeze.

What good fortune the ranch was right next door to the farm, and they'd become friends. She followed Dani into the kitchen, and while they loaded drinks and chips, they compared notes about different beach experiences. Dani told her about camping near Driftwood Beach on Jekyll Island and how fun it had been to explore the huge trees that lay all over the sand.

"Lita said she has beach toys for y'all and umbrellas we can use," Dani said.

Jack entered the kitchen. "Everyone ready to head out?" There was something hard in the way he looked at her that made Skylar uncomfortable.

"All set, handsome." Dani, oblivious to her husband's hostile expression, beamed. And Jack gave Dani the kind of embrace that reminded Skylar they were practically newlyweds.

She slung the beach tote over her shoulder, gathered Logan,

and grabbed the car seat as they headed to the car. Why didn't God give parents three arms? You should be given an extra appendage when you become a mom or dad. That, along with an instruction book, would only be fair.

Noticing her struggle, Jack reached for the car seat. "Let me help." After his earlier greeting, she was startled at his kind gesture but handed it over.

Across the driveway, Garrick leaned on Jack's Ram pickup truck, wearing a T-shirt, bathing suit, and flip-flops, his arms folded in front of him. Garrick was coming, too? Her heart lifted. The day just got a whole lot better.

They started over, and he sprang into action, meeting them halfway. "Let me help."

"You said you weren't going to the beach." She offered the heavy tote.

"Changed my mind." Garrick positioned the car seat in the back of Jack's truck like he'd done it a thousand times. A protest died on Skylar's lips when Logan raised her arms, and Garrick lifted her in, his movements sure and strong. At that moment, there was a flash of *this is what it could be*. They were almost like a family, and it felt good. Too good.

Skylar buckled in between Logan and Garrick, and the five of them rode west. It would take about an hour to reach the beach.

"It's nice to be the passenger for a change." She said, enjoying the opportunity to take in the countryside. This was the town she'd call home, and there wasn't much to it. Hudson's Farm and Ranch Supply came into view on the right. "There's that farm supply place. I guess I'll be getting familiar with it."

Jack glanced back from the front seat, something meaningful passing between him and Garrick.

What was going on? She got the uncomfortable sense it had something to do with her. Was this about her being an outsider and not patronizing the local businesses? She'd made most of her purchases at the big home supply store in Heron Park, but she planned to start shopping in Pine Crossing.

Garrick placed a hand over hers and squeezed, but his face hardened enough that she detected tension.

Mac's Diner appeared on the left, followed by Lone Star Pete's Tavern. They drove through the crossroads that marked the heart of Pine Crossing. Too small for a town square, several businesses of the independent, local type spread out from the central intersection. The grocery where she shopped came along next, a small building that also held the post office and pharmacy. The craft store was coming up. Ahead to the right was a coffee shop she'd never tried, and beside it, a couple boarded up businesses with dirty windows. It wasn't exactly a tourist destination.

"There aren't too many stores here," she remarked.

"True." Jack agreed, his tone mild. "Really doesn't offer much. Got to drive all the way to Heron Park or Cedar Bay for most things. I'd imagine most folks coming from a city like you would find it pretty inconvenient."

She drew back at his disdainful tone.

Garrick scoffed.

"Are we almost there?" Logan piped up.

"Pretty soon." Sky gave her daughter's leg a squeeze.

Logan held out her unicorn. "Peg wants a drink."

"When we get there." She whispered to Logan, then raised her voice, "How much farther is the key compared to Heron Park?"

"Not too much," Dani explained. "There's a beach in Heron Park, but we're going out to Starfish Key off Cedar Bay. It's a smaller town than Heron Park. But with the tourists at the public beaches, it'll be good to park at the inn and use their access. They're a B&B, but they have a nice kitchen and they're making us a special dinner. Y'all will be blown away by their food. And they have this amazing bakery. Jack's especially partial to their coconut bars."

"If the bakery's still open, I want to pick up a few," Jack said.

"I beat you to it and already ordered you a dozen." Dani sat a bit taller. "Lita will have them ready."

"You're the best." Jack reached for her hand.

"I know," Dani teased. "I guess you got lucky."

As they approached town, the landscape transformed from oaks and brush bordering fields to lush, well-maintained carpets of green, a variety of palm trees, and bushes covered with flowers.

Turquoise water appeared as they approached the bay. Skylar gasped. "What a view."

Whitecaps dotted the water beneath them as they crossed the bridge and left the mainland. Stately palm trees towered on both sides of the road, welcoming them onto the key. Large homes with gated entrances and yards rivaling botanical gardens alternated with older, smaller homes and jungly wild patches. They passed a pretty lighthouse park, continued down the key, and a short time later, pulled into a shell parking lot.

Tropical landscaping surrounded the inn, a white structure with a wide veranda and gingerbread trim like something from a storybook. A rainbow of flowers, zinnias, and others she didn't recognize, bordered hibiscus bushes with large yellow and pink blossoms. To the right of the entrance, green bananas hung in bunches from wide-leafed trees. Skylar had to keep her mouth from hanging open. "This is amazing. I had no idea it was so beautiful here."

"You might prefer living by the water. Most people do," Jack commented. "It'd be pretty doable. Your land would fetch a good amount in today's market."

"Enough," Garrick huffed as they climbed out of the vehicle.

Jack shrugged off Garrick's warning. "Just stating a fact."

Disquiet settled over her at Jack's not-too-subtle remarks. His comments had to be related to Garrick asking if she wanted to sell her farm to Tall Pines. Since Garrick hadn't brought selling up again, she didn't think it was still an issue. Indignation tightened her jaw, and she wanted to confront Jack but bit back the words. This wasn't the time or place.

Skylar's chest sunk a little. What had started out to be a

wonderful day was tarnished, but she wouldn't let it get to her. What would she tell her clients? Suck it up and remember, she had the power of choice. Her focus would be on what was right with her day. Logan, Garrick, and Dani wanted her here. She had a right to be here—to live on her farm. Jack could go jump in the lake or the Gulf or whatever.

Or perhaps she was imagining his attitude. She'd been so paranoid lately. After hiding out for a couple weeks, coming out in public so boldly, living life normally had her on edge. It'd been over a month, and there'd been no sign of Clive. Wasn't it about time she relaxed?

They unloaded their beach supplies while Dani texted her friend that they'd arrived.

"I love the scent of the Gulf." Dani lifted her face toward the sky. "And all the sea birds. Do you hear the gulls?"

"Yes." Skylar listened to the sea birds and inhaled deeply. "And there's a tree covered with white flowers. Are they what smells so good?"

"Those are orange blossoms," Garrick said. "We can smell them at the ranch too. There's a grove to the north of our properties."

"I knew I recognized that fragrance."

A tall woman with a white cane came down the inn's entrance steps, followed by a woman with pale skin and light red hair.

"Hey, Dani!" the redhead called out.

"Amy?" Dani perked up.

"Sure is. When Lita told me you were coming, I made y'all some sandwiches for snacks. Interested? If not, I'll set them out for guests." Amy's voice had the smooth sound of a central North Carolina accent.

"Are you kidding? We'd love them," Dani replied. "I was in charge of snacks today, so you know they were all gonna starve."

"I'll run get them." Amy darted inside the house. She returned with a cooler, which she handed to Jack and a clunky bag that she offered to Skylar. "We keep these beach toys on hand for guests who have little ones. Y'all have a nice afternoon."

They crossed the beachfront road and headed between sea grapes and clumps of tall grass lining the path. Suddenly, the view opened to a vast expanse of bright, sugar-like sand. Rolling aquamarine surf crashed on the shore. White birds called in the cobalt sky. Had she gone to heaven?

Maybe Jack was right. It was all kinds of beautiful here.

Garrick stared down at the powdery residue on his legs, similar to the dusty sand covering everything back in Afghanistan. A jolt of nerves, a lot like electricity, moved through his arms and legs, buzzing as though someone had plugged him in. He took a moment to get a grip. There was sand, and there was sand. This was sand, true, but that's where the similarity ended. This place was nothing like the desert. For starters, this sand was whiter. And the scenery was so picturesque. The blue-green Gulf of Mexico met the wide blue sky at the horizon, and his lips parted in wonder. To his six, the landscape was like a rainforest with every shape of green plant you'd ever want to see. Even banana trees. It was worth the trip out here. All this was a mere hour and a half away from the ranch. Astounding.

He studied the area, getting the lay of the land and figuring out where the threats were, any dangers to Logan, Sky, or anyone else in their group. It was automatic, part of his personality from the start, but honed to a new level when he'd served. He couldn't *not* do it anymore. Which was part of the problem. Sometimes, there weren't any threats.

Most of the time, there were.

After the meeting this morning, he'd researched what local hazards to expect at this beach. Jellyfish weren't plentiful here, but there could be stingrays. Those things had barbs, and if you stepped on them you could wind up in the hospital. He needed to make sure the area was clear before anyone swam.

Logan screeched, startling him from his thoughts. Wearing a pink and white floaty vest, she ran full out toward a flock of seagulls standing in formation, shrieking as they fluttered into the air.

"Watch her, will you?" Sky called over as she spread out a blanket.

He started toward Logan. The munchkin turned ninety degrees and tore off toward the waves. "Oh no, you don't." He sprinted over and caught her, circling her waist and pulling her back. How was this shy kid so fearless at the water's edge? He picked her up and held her sideways over the surf while she laughed with pure joy, which made him laugh in return, all the while checking the sandy sea floor, making sure there weren't rays. The problem was stingrays buried themselves in the sand, and you were supposed to do a shuffle to scare them off.

Having spent a good chunk of his military service in the southeastern part of the country, he was familiar with the North Carolina beaches. He'd never pondered stingrays. Talking trash and friendly insults were the only barbs back then. But he'd learned that while stingrays lived along the Outer Banks, they preferred shallow, warmer waters, like the beach right here.

"What's down there?" Skylar approached and stood beside him, her hands on her knees, studying the water. "Are there fish?"

"Just noticing how clear it is. And it doesn't hurt to be mindful of stingrays." He set Logan down, and she stood between them, patting the waves rolling over their ankles.

His gaze strayed to Sky, taking a leisurely assessment, and he could've dropped to his knees in worship. The woman was rocking a sweet bathing suit. Yes, it was a one-piece, but it fit her like a second skin. He checked the back, full coverage. He hadn't expected a thong, but you couldn't blame a man for hoping. Considering her personality, he wouldn't have been surprised if she'd worn men's swim trunks and a T-shirt. This was much better.

She stood, and the breeze picked up her hair.

His breath stuck in his throat, and he wanted to kiss her. He wouldn't. Not here. Not in front of Logan. Not unless Sky initiated it.

Sky grinned. "This is great, isn't it?"

Before he answered, she ran through the water and splashed him, and then Logan got in on it. The three of them splashed and laughed like a bunch of kids, the stingrays forgotten.

They walked the hard, wet sand along the shoreline, stepping around the seaweed left behind by the outgoing tide. He kept an eye in the shallows for rays but never saw any.

Logan hunted for shells, finding mostly broken ones, exclaiming over them nonetheless. "Pretty." She handed over a shell with scalloped edges. "It's for you."

"Thank you." He accepted the shell and started to toss it but stuck the thing in his pocket. There was something so pure in her simple gesture that he had to keep it.

She found a stick and poked at a patch of seaweed, then squatted down and started teasing it apart.

"What does she have?" Sky came closer. "Don't touch that. Let me see."

"Hold up." Garrick borrowed Logan's stick and found a small, spiky shape entangled in the seagrass. "It's a sea horse. I think it may be alive." He whispered to Logan. "Want to save it? Help it go home?"

"Yes."

The three of them walked into the shallow water. "Put your hand next to mine, and we'll let it go together."

Logan helped the seahorse slip away. In the clear water, it revived and moved into the surf.

"Wow!" Her voice was filled with wonder.

"Wow is right," he said.

"That was pretty amazing," Skylar agreed.

He laced his fingers through Sky's, and they started back up the beach. After a moment, something brushed the fingertips of his other hand. Logan had offered her hand, too. Which is how he found himself walking back to their spot in the sand, Sky's hand in his left and Logan skipping and jumping while tugging on his right.

He wasn't soft, wasn't a sucker, but it was so unexpected that something in him ached.

As they drew closer, Logan released his hand and ran screaming toward Dani and Jack. "A seahorse. A seahorse."

"Y'all found a seahorse? That's so cool," Dani said.

"Come here, Logan." Sky opened the bag of the beach toys.

"Are you kidding me?" Garrick gestured to the set-up.

"Dani made me do it." Jack shrugged. He'd erected two striped beach umbrellas, one dark pink and white, the other blue and white, both emblazoned with the inn's logo. The things were huge and cast a wide shadow over the blankets and chairs, like an ad in a travel magazine. "But don't knock it. The shade's nice. That sun is hot."

Garrick folded his arms and huffed. "Yesterday, you worked outdoors in jeans. Now it's too hot in swim trunks?"

"Hot is hot." Jack shrugged. "Why do you think I want to hire more hands?"

"C' mon Garrick. You're man enough to sit under the beach umbrella and enjoy the shade," Dani teased. "You've got to be secure in your masculinity, like Jack." Her hand strayed to Jack's arm, and his brother grabbed hold of it and kissed her fingers. Those two were unreal. His brother was forty-four and under some kind of spell like a lovesick teen.

"What's going on?" Skylar positioned Logan in the sand with a plastic shovel and bucket. "Thanks for the shade. It's so warm. I'm ready for a cold drink." She pulled two cold cans from the cooler, plopped down on a beach chair, and patted the one beside her. "Have a seat."

He accepted a can of fizzy lemonade and reclined in the

shade, staring over the water—when he wasn't staring at the better view of Skylar, sitting to his left.

Truth be told, he could get used to this.

They ate lunch.

Garrick unpacked the remaining beach toys.

While the others napped and read, he showed Logan how to build a sandcastle complete with turrets and a moat. She was awed. It was a top-quality feat of engineering. He puffed up with pride and had to fight the urge to tell everyone to check it out. What was he, seven years old?

The afternoon had flown by. They climbed the path back to the inn, pleasantly tired, and changed in the spa house.

Amy, Lita's sister, led them inside. A short woman, gorgeous, with pale skin and light reddish hair, Amy had to be close to his age. "This way to the dining room. Lita's already in there."

The inn's interior exuded what you could only call charm, and Garrick had to admit this wasn't bad at all. When he slipped his fingers through Sky's, she rewarded him with a little squeeze. He leaned closer. "This has been a great day. What do you say we go out for dinner tomorrow, just the two of us?"

"Without Logan?" She cocked her head.

"Didn't Thea offer to watch her anytime you need her?"

Sky's lips pursed thoughtfully. "I'd like that. But can we make it somewhere close, like in Pine Crossing? In case she has a melt-down, and I need to go home?"

"Sure. We can go to Lone Star Pete's."

Jack cut him a sidelong glance and dipped his chin in approval.

Garrick groaned inwardly. He wanted to take Sky out, wanted to get her on the dance floor up close. This had nothing to do with buttering her up or being manipulative, at least not in the way Jack imagined.

They followed Amy down the hall to the dining room, where a buffet awaited. Chilled wine and cold beer sat on ice beside pitchers of tea and lemonade. Crisp, colorful salads, pecan-crusted salmon filets, and chicken in orange sauce were offered with rice and pasta, spears of asparagus with hollandaise sauce, and a basket of mouthwatering croissants and dinner rolls.

Jack helped Dani through the line, explaining the choices to her while he dished them onto her plate.

Garrick focused on them as though watching strangers. He marveled at this tender side of his brother.

"This is a feast," Jack said. It was common knowledge at the ranch that Jack knew his way around the kitchen and did most of the cooking for the household. Garrick wasn't above dropping by at dinner time.

"Thank you. I helped prepare it," Lita said. "It's the least I can do after you grilling dinner every time I come out."

"Hey, I want some credit for those meals," Dani said.

"That's right." Lita laughed. "Your bean salad is very tasty."

"You know I'm great with a can opener, but I have to chop onion, too," Dani said.

He studied the exchange between Dani and Lita, both totally blind. After living with Jack and Dani for a while, between her snark and independence, she'd surprised him a few times.

"I have someone's favorite. Coconut bars," Amy announced as she delivered a tray of desserts. She pulled out a chair and stayed to share the meal with them.

"Are coconut bars your favorite too?" Skylar asked.

"No. I'm a peanut butter man, especially the kind with oatmeal and chocolate chips." Garrick chose a plain peanut butter cookie from the tray, along with orange cupcakes with cream cheese frosting for himself and Sky. After a glance at Logan's excited face, he snagged one for the munchkin.

"That's covering all your bases. Oatmeal, chocolate chip, and peanut butter in one cookie," Sky replied as she peeled Logan's cupcake.

He wagged his brows. "I know a good thing when I see it."

They ate and talked, and Logan took turns sitting on everyone's lap while they swapped stories. Amy told them about some celebrity guests who'd stayed there. One was a famous country singer who'd ended up getting married and staying in the area. Lita told them about some mishaps with an order in the bakery, resulting in a huge overage of cupcakes. They'd delivered four dozen of them to a local shelter. If they were anything like the citrus-flavored cupcake he'd polished off, those people had a treat.

These were good people, easy to be with. For the first time in a long time, since being with his team in the Army, the crew at the firehouse, or with Tate and Flash, he felt a strong bond of connection—here with family and friends. It was odd. But nice.

"Are you goin' to play for us?" Dani asked Lita.

They wrapped up the evening listening to Lita on her flute, not a regular flute, but a large one, alto, unlike he'd ever seen, and the music was rich and low. He draped his arm over the back of Sky's chair. When he moved his thumb over her shoulder, she leaned toward him, the scent of the beach and sunscreen and something feminine filling his nostrils. He planted a kiss on her hair. This was getting real, and he didn't hate it.

Jack caught his eye and held it for a beat, then moved his gaze to Sky, a reminder, sending his meaning crashing over Garrick like a dump truck full of gravel. Jack wanted Sky off her land, and Garrick was supposed to be working on it.

That wasn't happening. It wouldn't happen if he had anything to say about it. Skylar deserved to have her home as much as they deserved theirs. They'd figure something out. He'd talk to them each later—separately.

CHAPTER FOURTEEN

I t was over a week later when Garrick was able to take Skylar out like she was his girlfriend. One thing after another had gotten in the way and he'd been growing frustrated. He'd had to help with calving, and twice, he'd been called in to work extra shifts at the firehouse. Then Sky had a late afternoon at the farmhouse. A couple of days, they were simply too tired. Now their date was happening. They left Logan at Thea's house with a tote full of toys and his woobie.

Garrick glanced over as they drove into town. He'd seen Sky zombie walk into the kitchen for morning coffee, fresh out of bed, hair sticking out all over the place, and she was beautiful then. But tonight, she'd made some effort. She was a knockout.

What happened to his two rules? They weren't dating. No. They were already living together. His rules were toast, and right about now, he didn't care. Despite the plan for this to be a temporary, casual thing, he'd spent every available minute with Sky and Logan, eating, watching movies, talking, and showing them the ranch. The new calves, the baby goats. He'd even convinced Sky to let him set Logan on Rusty, holding onto her while she gripped the saddle horn, her eyes round with wonder. They were playing house, and he may regret it, because, in the near future, she'd take Logan and leave. But he pushed those thoughts aside and vowed to enjoy their evening together.

He placed his hand on the small of Skylar's back as they made their way into Lone Star Pete's. It wasn't crowded, and the hostess led them toward one of the several available seats.

"Garrick, over here," Levi called.

"Levi?"

"Howdy. Pull up a seat." Levi and Janie were seated close to the bar with three drinks in front of them. Levi was grinning like he'd won the lottery, and he gave Skylar a questioning glance. "Kelsey's in the restroom." He said softly.

Garrick didn't want to sit with them, and Kelsey being there sealed it. Having two women he'd gone out with in the same space reminded him why he had his rules in the first place. He had half a mind to take Skylar somewhere else. But the diner wasn't what he'd had in mind, and the rain they'd driven through earlier meant the outdoor place by the river was out.

He talked to Levi for another minute before he lifted his chin toward the booth in the corner. "We're heading over there."

Skylar sat and he slid in beside her, his back to where Kelsey would be sitting.

"You don't want to sit on that side?" Sky asked.

"No. Because if I sit here, it's easier to do this." He leaned down and brushed his lips over hers. It was dark, and they were the only people in this corner of the room, so he kissed her again, deeper.

Sky pulled back, whispering, "The server is coming."

They ordered drinks and food and talked for a while, sipping their beers while they waited for their meal to arrive.

Zac Brown's *Whatever It Is* began playing over the speakers, and Garrick slipped out and extended his hand. "How about a dance?" He led her to the dance floor and pulled her up close. The next number was Toby Keith's *When You Kiss Me Like That.* Perfect. He pulled her tight and enjoyed her body against him, exactly like he'd imagined when he'd planned this evening.

The third song was a two-step.

Sky winced, glanced over at the booth. "I don't know how to do this one."

"I'll show you. Follow my lead." It went well until the turn, and she messed it up and came slamming against him.

"I don't think that move is in the dance." She laughed nervously. So damn cute.

"Maybe it should be." He stole a kiss right there on the dance floor.

They returned to their seats.

"It's been really nice of you to have us." Skylar looked up from her drink. "Seriously, I don't know what we would've done."

"No need for thanks." He held her gaze, conveying intention, silently asking a question.

Sky bit her lip, her expression making him tremble inside.

He drew a path up her arm with his finger as heat pooled low in his belly. "How about we get our food to go?"

"I'd like that. Thea said she'd put Logan down to bed at her house."

"Perfect."

The server returned, and they waited a few excruciating minutes while she ran his card and boxed their meal. Garrick took Sky's hand and blazed past Levi, sitting with the two women.

They rode back to his cottage, the air between them crackling with possibility. Before he got her through the door, he claimed her mouth, kissing her long and hard right there on the porch.

He fumbled with the keys, got her inside and kicked the door shut, never taking his lips from hers, moving his hands over her back, around her hips, drawing her close, pressing her up against the wall, he slid his hand under her shirt. Her skin was so soft, warm. He smiled against her neck, taking her earlobe between his teeth before returning to kiss her lips.

"Hold on." She pulled her top off over her head.

The breath went right out of him. She was so beautiful, he ached with need for her.

In an instant she ripped open the snaps on his shirt and her hands were on his chest before circling around him, digging her fingertips into his back.

A bonfire ignited inside him. He growled as he planted open mouth kisses down her bare shoulder and cupped her breast. He moved his open palm around the front of her belly and slid it down to the waist of her jeans, then undid the button. She gasped.

He brought his hand back up to her breast, memorizing her curves and backed her across the room kissing her as they undressed. By the time they made it through the living room, a trail of clothing lay on the floor. He hiked her legs up around him and carried her into his room.

Skylar was sleeping hard. Garrick had gone to the bathroom, and when he'd returned, she was out like a light. He didn't have it in him to wake her. Pale light poured through the window hitting her back while he studied her peaceful features.

He ran his hand over her hair, and she shifted but didn't wake. This woman, who'd come into his life so unexpectedly was so damn perfect. He wanted her. She answered a call from deep inside of him, filled a place he hadn't known was empty. In that moment he knew. He loved her. He loved her and Logan and could see this being a regular on-going thing.

But did she feel that way about him? It didn't seem like it. She'd flat out said this needed to be temporary. He was all for seizing the day, it's how he'd lived for decades. But now he found himself wanting more. It was the damnedest thing.

He groaned. She couldn't stay overnight in his bed. Not because they needed to retrieve Logan from Thea's house but because he wasn't up to sleeping with her all night. It might not be safe. Thrashing and swinging out in his sleep, he was dangerous when he had nightmares, and had bruises to show for it. He'd stopped setting a glass of water on his nightstand, having shattered a few. It tore him apart to wake Sky and send her to her room.

He opened the app on his phone, but instead of scrolling to the sleep meditation, which he might want later, he clicked on Doc Austin's home page and booked an appointment. It was time to double down on getting better. Facing what needed to be faced and leveling up to where he needed to be. While he'd had no problem continuing PT for his body, he'd neglected his mental health. He might not be capable of showing up in a relationship with her. And never, in a million years, did he want to pose a risk to Logan.

A lot of guys he knew were getting divorced if they weren't already. Adapting to civilian life had been difficult. Since he'd never married, that wasn't his issue. Until now, the nightmares had only been an inconvenience to him, but with Sky here, everything had changed. He was motivated.

This was uncharted territory and put a twisty feeling in his gut, made his nerves buzz. But when he watched her sleep, he knew—she was worth it.

He pulled on his pants and fetched their carry-out dinner, heated it up, and carried it into the bedroom using a shallow box from a recent delivery. A tray would've been nice, but he'd never needed one before. "Hey, Sky, sweetheart. I've got dinner here."

She stretched and came up on one arm. "A bed picnic? My favorite."

They ate and talked until it was embarrassingly late to pick up Logan. "I'll get the munchkin," he offered.

"You will?"

"Sure. No reason for both of us to go. And when I get back, and she's settled...." He tipped her face up and claimed her mouth again, letting her know he was up for a longer evening.

Garrick left Skylar and started along the path to Thea's house.

"What are you up to?" Jack's voice startled him.

"I'm getting Logan." There weren't many exterior lights in the ranch, but he could make out Jack's puzzled expression in the moonlight. Dani's yellow lab waved a friendly tail at Jack's side. "What are you doing?" It was obvious, and his question was meant to be a distraction. He'd seen Jack take Dani's service dog on many a late-night walk. But he didn't want to get into it with Jack—not after the stellar evening that wasn't over yet.

"I'm walking Lucky." Jack didn't say dummy, but it was implied. "How'd your date go?" The way Jack said date, full of meaning, irked him.

"Fine. I need to be going because it's getting late, and I'm fetching Logan from Thea's."

"Did you talk to Skylar about selling, about our—leverage?"

"No." He shoved a palm over his scalp. "I'm not having that discussion with her."

Jack drilled into him. "Want to explain why not? Or has she got you so whipped you can't remember where your loyalty is?"

Tension shot up his spine and into his arms. "What'd you say?"

Jack scoffed. "Do you want that land, or are you okay with a neighborhood going where our cattle are grazing?"

He grimaced. "It's complicated. I don't want to upset her. It's better if she's here, close by. There's this jerk up in Chicago. Killed her sister. Might be coming for her."

"Are you kidding me? That's the situation you were talking about? It's not resolved?"

"No. I'll check tomorrow. Give you an update."

Jack was silent a beat. "Is Luke involved in the update?"

"Possibly."

Jack exhaled forcefully. "Unbelievable. Don't you think you oughta let the ranch manager know there's an issue?"

Jack said *manager* like it meant something, but they owned

equal shares of the business. Jack was probably more upset about being left out of something he and Luke were doing. His older brothers had been rivals as far back as he remembered, and he'd refused to take sides. "I have to get Logan. Let's talk tomorrow."

"You're getting mighty close to that kid. Just remember, you're not her dad. And Skylar's not your woman. How do you know she isn't using you to get you to break the lease?"

Fury propelled him toward Jack, grabbing his shirt, and with exquisite self-control, he stopped short of throwing a punch or taking his brother to the ground. "Take that back." He released Jack and forced himself to step away. It wasn't like him to get into a fight or lose his cool when provoked.

Surprisingly, Jack didn't take a swing at him.

Instead, Jack, who was never one to shy away from a fight, chuckled. "Yep. The truth hurts. Keep in mind, this using thing works both ways."

"You don't know what you're talking about."

"You've been offering her and the kid a free place to stay. Maybe you ought to start thinking with your brain and remember what matters." Jack turned and walked away with the dog.

Garrick stood there a moment, fuming, his jaw tight, and fought back the urge to tackle Jack from behind. Instead, he closed the distance between himself and Thea's house.

"I heard all about the sea horse." Thea led him inside, and he scooped up Logan from the couch. Bundled in his woobie, she smelled like baby shampoo and the familiar scent of his poncho liner—still her favorite blanket.

"Gricky," Logan whispered as she stirred and nestled into him, her body heavy with sleep.

"Thank you," he whispered to Thea. It occurred to him he might oughta pay her. "How much do I owe you?"

"Nothing. Don't be silly. But Garrick take this." Thea pressed something into his hand.

He glanced at the bag of sticks and leaves before jamming it into his pocket. "What is it?"

"Make tea. It will help calm your mind. It's not cannabis, but it will help you deal with ... whatever. Help you get through therapy."

His gaze sharpened. How could she know? He'd just now scheduled it.

She smiled the way she did when she knew something she wasn't saying, using her intuition. It was kind of creepy and astonishing all at once. But the old woman had worked wonders with his dad. Bud moved easier, spoke more clearly, and his mood was better.

Thea walked him to the door. "You know, she's crazy about you."

He chuckled. "She's pretty cute."

"I mean Skylar. But Logan, too. They're good medicine."

"What does that mean?"

"Her love. Both of them. Whatever you need to do to hold on to this, to convince yourself you deserve it, do it. It's worth it. You're strong enough." She narrowed her gaze, and it drilled into him, making him feel exposed and uncomfortable. "Now go. An old woman needs her rest." She patted his shoulder and shut the door behind him.

He carried Logan home, untangling his thoughts, wanting to believe Thea, but his experiences with Melody were enough for Jack's seed of doubt to take root. The porch steps creaked as he climbed. Inside, a warm woman awaited him, and he wasn't about to waste the night. He'd think about Jack's words later.

Skylar had gotten up and was now asleep on the couch.

He carried Logan into her bedroom and laid her tiny body in the twin bed. Tucking her in, with his blanket snug around her, he pressed a kiss to the top of her hair. "Night night, munchkin."

"Night, Daddy."

You could have zapped him with a stun gun. Had he heard right?

Logan turned to her side and snuggled her unicorn.

He waited for the urge to run, to shut down. Instead, his chest ached with tenderness. He covered Skylar and took himself to bed. Alone.

CHAPTER FIFTEEN

After spending a good chunk of the day hacking back the jungle landscaping surrounding the farmhouse, Skylar was beat. But the finish line was in sight. She rinsed the dirt and sand from her arms and splashed cool water on her face. Visions of colorful flower beds surrounding a screened-in porch formed in her mind. Of course, she'd plant a great big vegetable garden full of tomatoes and green beans.

Perhaps they'd get a chicken coop and even a dairy cow. She could churn butter and they'd eat fresh eggs. She chuckled. Logan would absolutely love collecting the eggs. It always helped to have an end in mind, a mental equivalent of what she wanted. This was a huge project and different from anything she'd ever done before. There was a lot to learn, but between online research and her friends at Tall Pines, she could make it happen.

A car door slammed shut, startling her from her fantasies.

The electrician and his assistant headed over and they walked through the house together. Filled with bubbly anticipation, she asked questions about the timeline, went over the work that had been done, and they discussed what still needed to be completed. There were fans and fixtures to install but she'd planned to do some of those herself to save money. Over the past seven weeks, the subfloor had been replaced, the termite treatment was done, and the house had a new roof. She was deep in debt, but the interior was ready for painting and then she'd install the laminate floor. Before long, this house would be back to its original glory, probably better.

The electricians left.

Not in the mood to prime the walls, she wandered from room to room, visualizing the finished space. After staying with Garrick for almost two months, the thought of moving in had lost its luster. Evenings after Logan was in bed were incredible, but they were coming to an end. That was the understanding. They'd already stayed with Garrick longer than she'd planned. Just because it was good now, when there was an expiration date, didn't mean it would continue working long-term.

Garrick was excellent with Logan, but it'd been a mistake to let her daughter get so close to him. Since she hadn't dated anyone since adopting Logan, this situation had crept up on her and taken on a life of its own.

She sat and rubbed her face. What had she been thinking? Her own stepmother went through a series of men Skylar and her sisters had called "uncles", and she'd known the disappointment of getting attached to people who would leave. Had she done the same to Logan? Maybe not. Tall Pines was their neighbor. They could still visit.

The materials for doing the floors needed to be organized and inventoried. She opened the top box of laminate flooring stacked in the center of the room and frowned. The cherry brown was beautiful but didn't match the gray she'd ordered. She checked the other boxes. Gray, white, mahogany. How had she not caught this sooner? None of them matched. That's what she got for ordering online and requesting delivery. Most of this would have to go back.

One by one, she lugged ten thirty-five-pound boxes out to

her car. She was leaving when the mail truck stopped at the end of the driveway. What? Bills already?

She hiked to the gate, checked the box, and found a single lavender envelope. A smile sprung to her face. Aunt Janice was one of the few people who knew where she lived. Even though she and her aunt emailed, the occasional snail mail card she got from Janice was a special treat. She tucked it into her purse to enjoy later.

At the home store in Heron Park, she presented her invoice to the customer service clerk and explained the problem. Pain from loading and unloading the boxes of flooring tightened her muscles, and she arched backward, pressing her thumbs into the area above her hips. "Do you have someone who can help me load the correct flooring?"

The woman at the register cracked her gum as she tapped on the computer. "Sorry, we don't have any of that in stock."

"Really?" She thought fast. "What if I didn't get the gray?"

"No. I mean, we've got none of that in stock. Supply chain issues."

Are you kidding me? After spending too long listening to why she wouldn't have flooring until sometime next week, Skylar trudged from the store, pushing a cart with twelve one-gallon cans of paint. Five-gallon buckets would've been cheaper, but her back couldn't take it. On the bright side, now she could work on the walls. But her schedule was seriously messed up.

Needing a lift, she drove to the shop to get her cell phone screen replaced. There was a line. It took two hours and she was ready to pull her hair out by the time she got back in the car. But it was finally repaired. She ran her thumb over the smooth on her phone and tapped out a text to Thea.

Skylar: *Can you keep Logan a while longer? I'm running to the grocery.*

Thea: *Sure. I love having her.*

Something inside Skylar relaxed as she read Thea's reply.

She'd been getting close to the older woman. It was almost like having a mother for herself and a grandmother for Logan. She'd really gotten lucky. They had Garrick to thank for these wonderful connections.

Garrick had worked at the firehouse the previous two days, then he'd headed out that morning to help with the new calves—without even going to bed. He deserved a treat and she was in the mood to bake away her stress.

Garrick ducked off the ranch midafternoon and headed into Heron Park. Originally, he'd booked the appointment so Sky could safely sleep with him. But, bottom line, he wanted to be able to sleep, period. He needed rest. So even if what Jack said was true, and Sky was using him, he needed to be here.

With some trepidation, he strolled into the back hall of the veterans' center, where Doc Austin would be waiting for him. The three sessions he'd had when he first came to town played through his mind. Honestly, he'd felt like crap a couple of times after he'd left. Therapy wasn't like having a one-and-done filling drilled. It was an ongoing thing, like having multiple surgeries back-to-back without anesthetic—with the promise of better at the end.

Doc directed him to the small couch.

"New couch." He took a seat. It was more comfortable than it appeared. "I figured we'd do this virtually."

"We can do some of it virtually," the doc said. "But certain modalities are better in person. First, catch me up. How are things?"

He gave the doc a brief summary, mentioning Sky and Logan but glossing over the details. They talked a bit about work, he mentioned Jack, and eventually, the topic came to the main issue —nightmares. There were fewer with Sky in the house. But he still had them.

"Are you using the VA meditation app?"

"No."

"Those mindfulness drills on my website?"

"Once or twice."

"Regular is better. Think of it like PT for the brain."

He nodded but was still subjected to a long list of statistics related to mindfulness and resilience. "Is this what we're doing today? Because I was hoping for—" He shrugged.

"—a magic pill to eliminate the nightmares." The doc chuckled.

"Something like that."

"Fresh out of magic pills, but I do have a tool." Doc explained EMDR nightmare protocol. "You game?" The doc gestured toward a device. "But I'd want you to commit to several sessions, come in once or twice a week."

He drew down his brows. This wasn't at all how he'd pictured therapy.

"It takes courage to go into combat like you did. Jump into the unknown. Courage to be a medic and put yourself at risk trying to save others and still have to fight. It takes courage to do this, too. But I wouldn't offer if I didn't think you could handle it." Dr. Austin sat calmly as if whatever Garrick chose would be okay.

Could he make that commitment? Was today a day he could willingly call up the dream about the incident that wouldn't leave him alone? The one with that girl—a shitstorm. He'd taken a round to the chest. Two of his brothers-in-arms had fallen that night. And Brad.

He didn't have to do this. He was here by choice.

The clock ticked.

He studied his hands, glanced at the door, then met the doc's gaze. Doc Austin faced the world every day with his scars on the outside for the whole world to see.

Garrick exhaled hard. At least he was alive. He was alive, and he wouldn't waste it, wouldn't live one more day letting the crap he'd been through dictate his future. He'd always considered himself brave. Surely, he was brave enough to handle this.

"I'm ready."

After a long day, arriving at the house to find a homemade dinner was a treat he could get used to, but today, the aroma was different and enveloped him like a hug. Garrick intended to make this the night he had a serious conversation with Skylar. With Jack on his back, they needed to talk. But after seeing the doc, and then getting hit with the mouthwatering scent of peanut butter cookies, he decided to back-burner all that and embrace the now. How's that for mindfulness, doc?

He headed into the kitchen, where he found Sky washing a baking sheet, which she must've bought, because he owned nothing like that. A couple of dozen golden cookies lay on paper towels. "Are those oatmeal peanut butter?"

"Yes. With chocolate chips, except for those few at the end. They're plain."

He snagged a large warm cookie and consumed it in two bites, then grabbed another. "Who'd eat plain when you can have chips?"

"I would. I happen to like them plain."

"Do you have a fever? Seriously, I know a coach who might be able to help you with the errors in your thinking."

She chuckled. It was a beautiful sound.

He ate a second cookie. "What's in the pot?"

"Chicken and dumplings."

"For real?" He lifted the lid and sniffed. The best memories of his mother and grandmother streamed into his brain.

"There's also kale-strawberry salad ... because we still have to be healthy."

"I can handle that." He placed the lid back on the pot and

paused. His favorite cookies. His favorite dinner. "What's going on?"

"Nothing. I always cook."

"What happened at the house today?"

Sky groaned. "The flooring won't be here for over a week. The delivery was all messed up."

"Huh. That's a shame." Not. He'd pay the store to delay delivery if it meant she'd remain in his house a little longer.

"It is because it means we may need to stay a few more weeks. If that's okay with you."

He moved his gaze from the hot meal to the cookies, to Skylar. "You made this, so I'd say yes?" He could tell her he liked her, that she didn't need to sweeten the deal.

"I figured it wouldn't hurt." A sheepish grin lifted the corners of her mouth.

Something inside him shifted. He was torn. He didn't want her to leave. And she was cooking for him, all his favorites, but she wanted something. She wanted to stay longer. Jack's words filtered through his mind. Was Skylar using him?

Ordinarily, he didn't mind being used by a woman. It was sometimes a mutually beneficial arrangement. No strings. These weren't strings. What they had was a huge, tangled knot. He hadn't minded until now, but after the intense session with the doc, he felt off tonight, like on Star Trek when the Enterprise's shields were down, and they couldn't seem to get them back up. He needed to get away and clear his head. "I've got a headache. I'm taking a nap."

"But dinner is ready." Her brows cleaved together.

"I'll eat later."

He slipped into his room and paced, felt caged. No. He needed to get outdoors. While Sky was settling Logan at the table, he slipped outside, saddled Rusty, and, in the fading light, rode the fence line, something he was supposed to do earlier.

Luke was in the barn when he returned. "Got a minute to come to my place? There's something I want you to see."

They headed up to Luke's house and sat in front of the computer. After tapping a few keys, Luke gestured to the monitor.

Garrick leaned forward and studied the screen. "Is this what I think it is?"

"We're in. That's the inside of the pawn shop. And wait ... there's more." Luke turned up the volume, and voices came through the speaker. "We have sound. It took me a minute to get through his firewall. The man's not an idiot. But now we have eyes and ears in his shop."

"And?"

"They've been talking about Skylar. I have this set to record the voices. Clive's making plans, not sure what yet."

"What are they doing?" He scrutinized the image on the screen.

"He's got some book. I think it belonged to Skylar's sister. And he said something about going to Tennessee."

"Tennessee is a long way from here." Garrick squeezed his forehead. Did he need to be concerned about the aunt, the previous owner?

"True." Luke nodded thoughtfully. "But I have a hunch there's more."

"Text me right away if you hear something else." He stood, then sat back down. "The old woman who owned the farm lives in Chattanooga."

"Right. But Skylar's here."

"True." Still, it bothered him.

Instead of needing space away from Sky, he had the sudden urge to get home.

Sky was in Logan's room reading her a story when Garrick leaned through the doorway and said, "Thanks for dinner. It was excellent."

"Enjoy your nap?" Her arched brows told him she was aware he'd slipped out instead of taking a nap.

"I remembered something I needed to do." He headed into the shower. By the time he was finished, Sky was on the couch with her coffee, watching that new show with a female CIA operator. He watched the remainder of the episode with her before turning off the TV.

"You don't want to find out what happens?"

They typically watched a few episodes of something before moving on to more important things. He was all for moving into those other activities, but this conversation needed to happen before the ranch shareholders held a vote. It tore him apart, not only because it would inspire her ire and revive the sleeping honey badger, but because he cared about this woman and her child. He didn't want the land issue to come between them. Talk about a conflict of interest. What was good for her was bad for the ranch, bad for the entire area.

Garrick set aside his attraction and got down to business. "There's something we need to discuss." He leaned forward, kept his tone even, and started on friendly territory. "How's the house coming?"

"Like I said earlier, we may need to stay here a while longer." She took a moment to tell him more than he wanted to know about her flooring. "I didn't think you'd mind." Her head tilted in question.

"I don't. That's fine."

"And, aside from wanting to stay here a few more weeks, I have to revisit selling off more land. Pablo can get me a good price for that back piece. With the road there, it might be desirable enough to entice a buyer in spite of the lease."

He groaned softly. Jack's words, "throwing down the gauntlet," played through his mind.

Sky winced a little. "I know it's not optimal, but I really need the money."

"The thing is, there's a tradition, an honor. We don't parcel off our land and sell. I may be a newcomer, but I'd never do that to Tall Pines. And our ranch is only part of what it used to be. That piece on the south side of the road used to be four times as large. But the previous owner sold part of it. Have you seen that new subdivision towards town? All those houses close together and bringing traffic."

The muscles in her face hardened. "So?"

He was on thin ice here. "You're a McClure, right? Didn't you say your kin built that farmhouse?"

"Yes. Why?"

"That land is in your blood."

"I don't have a choice." Her face pinched. "My finances are a mess right now, and the potential is right there to straighten it out."

"Sell it to us."

"I can get three times as much if I parcel it smaller." She scoffed.

Sky had a point. All of her points were valid. And the ace up his sleeve was that they could send her packing. And she'd probably sell half the damn place to developers if they played their ace. It might get really ugly. "We'll match what he promised."

"Why? That's stupid. You need grazing land that bad?"

"I need no subdivision there that bad." And they needed the grazing land. To be honest, it was both.

"Oh." She was quiet a beat.

Was she finally coming around, seeing his angle?

"I don't like being told what I can and can't do with my property." Her chin lifted. "But I'll think about it."

His stomach dropped. It was like seeing two trains on a collision course. Jack and Skylar. And there was little he could do to stop it. "Thanks. Think kind of fast, okay?" If Wes got wind of her plans and told his brothers, Jack was sure to go on a rampage. Whatever he and Sky were doing here may be collateral damage.

Her expression softened. "I'd like to figure out a win-win, but my options are limited."

He studied her face. Guileless, concerned, a devoted mother and a woman trying to survive even though she'd been dealt a crappy hand. "Thank you."

"I'm not making any promises."

"But you'll think about it?" He studied her mouth, her lips were captivating.

"Yes."

"Good." He leaned in for a kiss and she was right there with him, parting her lips, inviting him in. It must've been his lack of shields, because a tide of emotion filled his chest making it ache with tenderness.

This time, when he led Sky to his room, it was lovemaking, pure and simple—at least for him.

They laced their fingers together and talked. They always did afterward, but tonight, he was different, more open.

"What's with your pinky finger?" Sky asked. "I noticed you shake your hand; sometimes you rub it."

He looked at her sharply. She was the first person to comment on his hand. "I had frostbite. Damaged the nerve in the tip of that finger."

"Because it was so cold in Montana?"

"That, and I rescued my friend's kid brother. It's not as heroic as it sounds. He fell through the ice, but the water wasn't even chest deep." It'd been horrible at the time. "I had to build a fire to warm us up and dry out. But we were mostly okay in the end." He'd been terrified the kid would die from exposure. But so many awful memories had been laid on top of this one that he hardly gave that event a second thought anymore.

"You got hurt." She brought his hand to her lips and kissed his finger.

"Keep doing that and—" He offered her a wolfish grin.

Skylar traced a scar on the side of his shoulder, ignoring his innuendo. "What's this from?"

"Shrapnel. IED." That'd been a bad day. But not the worst.

"Oh. Ouch. But you were okay?"

"Mostly. I lost some hearing in this ear." He gestured.

"And this?" She grazed her finger over the stubble on his chin.

Shivers raced over his skin. "Bar fight."

"Seriously?" She drew back. "What happened?"

"It was my twenty-first birthday. Jack took me out for a beer. There were these guys throwing their weight around. Bothering his friend. This woman he threw darts with. Jack was a bruiser, but mostly on the side of what he thought was right. It was over pretty fast. I walked away with a split chin."

"Did you learn your lesson about fighting?"

He scoffed. "I learned I needed to improve my moves."'

Her hand strayed to his lower rib cage. "What about this one?"

"Bullet." His stomach tightened, and he decided to tell her. "That was, possibly, the worst day of my life." He'd said that earlier to the doc and now to Sky. Saying it hadn't killed him. Hadn't bothered him nearly as much as he'd thought it might.

Her face pinched up. "That had to hurt."

"Wasn't a picnic. Two other guys, who were like brothers, died that day. My cousin, too."

"I...I don't know what to say. I'm sorry. That's horrendous." A long moment of silence stretched between them before she spoke again. "When I was a kid, I lost both my parents, then two and a half years ago, my sister, so I understand a little bit about how it feels to lose someone close. I don't know if that pain ever completely goes away." They lay there in each other's arms, holding one another, just breathing together.

After a while, she traced her finger in circles over the scar near his lower ribs. "I hate..." she kissed his collar bone, then kissed a path down his chest sending shockwaves of heat through him, "that you went through that." She trailed feather-light kisses down to the scar on his side. "Is it better now?"

"I'll show you better." He rolled toward her, pulled her up, and pinned her below him, claiming her mouth, enjoying the feeling of her beneath him, her hands on his back, her soft sighs.

Later, when she fell asleep, he was overcome with the urge to do something, to fix the messed-up situation. If she was serious about listing that parcel, he'd find a way to buy it. Build her a big new house over there if he had to. He had money, not only ample savings from when he'd been in the Army but also a trust he'd inherited from his mother. Sitting there, untouched. One thing he knew for sure. He wanted Sky here, and there was no way the others could leverage her completely off of the farm. He'd figure it out.

Garrick hit his arm on the nightstand and called out, jerking awake as he bolted upright. It was one-thirty. He'd let himself fall asleep with Sky there. She was unhurt, still sleeping. Thank God. The same couldn't be said for the flattened tissue box lying on the floor beside the bed. If he'd struck Sky instead of the night-stand.... The thought made him sick.

He rubbed his face, his heart still hammering, the anxiety fading, and waited for the rush of angst but detected only disquiet and unease. The session earlier that day might've actually helped. It was good he was going back to the doc. He wasn't taking any chances.

"What's going on?' Sky sat up.

"Nothing. Bad dream."

She rubbed his back. It felt odd, comforting, but unfamiliar. "Does that happen often?"

"Often enough."

"Logan sometimes gets those. I think it's from seeing her mom and Clive fighting." She brought her hand around and laced her fingers through his. "Should I sleep in here?"

"No." He jerked away.

"Okay." She sounded hurt.

"No, Sky. It's not like that. I love it when you're next to me. It's just. It's probably not safe." He cupped her face in his two hands. "I'm getting help." He kissed her forehead. "There's nothing I'd like more than to sleep all night beside you." He kissed her mouth. And in that moment, he knew, without a doubt, he meant it. She was the first woman since Melody he'd wanted to wake up next to.

Skylar turned her face sideways and kissed the palm of his hand. "And you will. I believe in you." She pulled on her shirt. "I'd better go."

He let her walk to her room. He felt like the biggest jerk, sending his woman away in the middle of the night.

Resolve brought him clarity. Now he had to do it. He wouldn't let her down.

Doc Austin leaned back, listening, as Garrick finished explaining the equine therapy operation at the ranch. "Sounds like a decent program." Doc steepled his fingers and pushed up his chin like he was thinking.

"So far, we've had one group out, but another is scheduled next week. And my sister-in-law is all gung-ho to expand the program to other populations."

"Equine therapy is on the rise."

"She's also talking about agri-therapy. Gardens for veterans. There's property we can set aside. And we have a master gardener on board to help." Garrick had eaten lunch with his dad and Thea the previous day, and she was excited about the prospect.

"You seem really interested in this."

Garrick shrugged. "I'm only the messenger."

The doc leveled his Yoda gaze.

He chuckled. "It was pretty cool seeing how excited those

kids got. And bottom line, when I'm on Rusty, even when I'm brushing him, it's good. I get it about horses."

"I'll check on what the interest level is. Now, are you ready to dive in? Or is this a stall tactic?"

"No stalling. Bring it." Garrick lifted the buzzing devices. This was their third session. He was getting pretty good at it and feeling better, which was astonishing. But mostly, he was ready to have Sky sleep beside him.

CHAPTER SIXTEEN

It was rare he and his two brothers fed and groomed their horses at the same time. This was good. Garrick enjoyed the sense of being a team, the three brothers of Tall Pines. The scent of horseflesh relaxed him, and they'd been tossing around insults. It'd been going well until he brought up his idea.

Jack stepped away from his latest purchase, a beautiful roan mare, and scowled. "You're thinking of what?"

Garrick increased his grip on the hoof knife, fighting back his ire, breathing in chill. Jack's reaction was expected. He met his brother's gaze. "I can buy that parcel. I've got the funds. It's the best option. If we make Skylar leave, she could retaliate by selling more. She won't stand for being pushed around." It was all true. Which is why they ought to believe he was doing it for the ranch.

Luke leaned an arm on the stall beside Jack. Being a half-brother, he hadn't inherited the same wealth as Garrick and Jack but was making up for it with his tech business. "You could buy that section. Spend your money that way. But what's to stop her from selling another? And if she sells something between that parcel and her house, that messes things up worse. It's no solution—if helping the ranch is the objective ... Unless you give her a reason to stay."

Jack scoffed and shook his head. "She's been here, what? Less than three months? Now she's collecting rent and getting us to pay through the nose to buy land we were happy leasing for a reasonable rate a few months ago. She's crazy like a fox, and you look a lot like poultry, bro."

He replaced his pick and grabbed the curry comb, beating back the urge to knock Jack upside the head. His brother had reason to be distrustful. His second wife had used him to make her ex jealous, then dropped Jack like a sack of rotten potatoes.

"She's not like that." He started brushing Rusty a little too hard, and his horse swung his head around. He stopped and patted his buddy in silent apology.

Luke stepped closer, his tone conciliatory. "Give her a reason to be loyal to the ranch."

Something inside him tightened. He'd thought about what Luke was suggesting. But he wasn't good at talking about that stuff and wasn't clear what he wanted anyway. Every time the conversation headed in that direction, things got weird. It seemed like neither he nor Sky liked having a relationship talk. With women in the past, that was a plus.

Jack continued, "I meant it when I said it was a declaration of—"

"Gotcha." Garrick lifted a palm, stopping him. "But she...." He wasn't sure what he wanted to say. He wasn't about to declare his love for Sky to his brothers. This wasn't some chick flick. They weren't having a Hallmark moment. This was business, and his feelings for Sky were muddying the waters. The fact was, he was on her side—in direct opposition to his self-interest.

Jack walked over to the desk at the end of the barn, pulled out an envelope, and made a show of handing it over. "Here." He shoved it at Garrick. "Show her this contract. Hiram drew it up. She can see for herself. Be the good guy. Tell her you're preventing her from being evicted. She can live there, but she can't sell. Not until the lease is up, and then we have the option to buy first or sooner if she prefers to cut and run. She can sign it, and all will be cool. You won't have to spend your savings on that parcel of land."

He practically spat. "You moved forward with this?"

Jack stood feet apart, hands in his pockets, all confident and smug.

Garrick studied the paper. There was no scenario where this would go over well. "I'll have to wait for the right time."

"Sooner rather than—"

"—later. Got it."

Jack's phone buzzed. "It's Dad. I'll be back shortly."

Jack left, but Luke hung back. "You got my text?"

"About?" He instinctively pulled his phone out of his pocket.

"Clive and one of his brothers left for Tennessee. Chattanooga. I can't think why they'd go there unless...." He shrugged. "You may want to warn Skylar or her aunt."

"Thanks." He'd do one better. He'd fly up and meet them after he made a couple stops. He needed to change his schedule.

CHAPTER SEVENTEEN

Garrick found Zeke in the firehouse office and requested his schedule change.

Zeke's brow furrowed. "That won't work. This is Cody's week off. He left on vacation. Molly and Levi are out on a transport, but tomorrow she's heading to Miami until Friday. We've got a couple volunteers on call to cover. You can try contacting her later, but she's staying with her sister, who just had a baby, and Walt's already put in overtime. Aside from the volunteers, you and Levi are it this week.

Garrick exhaled sharply. He'd driven to the firehouse for nothing.

"You said you wanted the hours." Zeke lifted his shoulder. "Now we need you here."

Frustrated, he raked a hand over his head. He couldn't leave everything to Levi, but he had to do something. He headed to Hudson's.

Garrick entered the farm and ranch supply and looked for Tate.

Flash stood at the checkout counter, ringing up a customer. He waited for the man to leave. "You work here now?"

Flash puffed a laugh. "I'm holding down the fort until Tate's finished meeting with someone. Lauren's out with the flu, and the new guy quit."

Garrick's stomach dropped. He had to work, and Tate wouldn't be able to get away.

"What's the problem?" Flash asked.

"I need to get to Chattanooga, but I have to work tomorrow at eight a.m., and I'm guessing Tate's busy."

"What's in Chattanooga?"

He lowered his voice and explained the situation.

Flash nodded slowly. "I have a buddy who has a plane. Owes me a favor."

He rubbed his forehead. "Clive and his brother have a good head start."

"Let me call someone in Atlanta."

Garrick studied Flash. They'd worked together, and from what he could tell, these jobs were Flash's full-time work. The man had connections everywhere. "What will I owe you for this?"

Flash dismissed the question with a wave of the hand. "You saved Hawk. Watch the register." He stepped outside and got on the phone.

Garrick had a brief experience of déjà vu. Flash, standing on the deck behind Tate's house before everything had gone to hell, was seared into his mind. He folded his arms in front of his chest and frowned, a knot forming in his gut. He wanted to get this handled but hated relinquishing control.

Voices came from the aisle. He watched, listening hard for the customers, hoping nobody approached since he couldn't even ring up a sale.

No such luck.

The squeaky wheels of a shopping cart approached, and Kelsey, from the hospital, rounded the corner. An odd expression crossed her face. "Hello, Garrick," she said tightly. "I haven't seen you around. Is this your new job?" She set packets of seeds and a flat of tomato plants on the counter.

"Just helping out." He stared at the merchandise and glanced at the cash register. How hard could this be?

Kelsey's mouth took a determined set. "And I want two hundred pounds of good black dirt."

"A delivery?" he asked as though she were any other customer. Tate stocked topsoil, but most people drove to the store in Heron Park for their mulch and soil needs.

"No. Bags. Big ones. I'll want it loaded in my car." A slight smile tugged at the corner of her mouth. "On second thought, make it three hundred pounds."

Kelsey knew his back bothered him. He groaned inwardly at the slight dig.

An elderly man, possibly the guy with the pig farm, came up behind Kelsey with a basket full of hardware. Great. Now he had a line going. He picked up the hand scanner and started ringing up the seeds.

Flash ended the call, returned, and took over at the register.

"Who's loading my topsoil?" Kelsey asked.

Flash gestured to Garrick.

What could he say? He followed Kelsey out and around back and, in heavy silence, loaded her SUV. He should say something. "I didn't know you lived out this way."

"I don't." She shut her door and drove away with no further explanation.

He scratched his head. Yep. She was angry. And rightly so. Like a jerk, he'd ghosted her. This is why he had rules number one and two.

By the time he rounded the corner and entered the store, the lot was empty except for the motorcycle that'd been there when he'd arrived. Flash was leaning on the counter. "Someone will be at that Chattanooga address shortly. We can fly up and back in time for you to work."

"What about the store?" Garrick asked.

"I don't work here." Flash drew back. "Tate's got it covered. His meeting ended. He was talking to someone who might be interested in joining the team. Meet me at the Heron Park South Airfield in ninety minutes."

That was enough time to drive home and pack or head to the diner for lunch. They should be up and back in twenty-four hours. Years of experience had taught him that if you're hungry, you'd better eat while you can. He drove to the diner, powered through a good-sized meal, and sped toward the airport.

The Tennessee air was crisp and cool as they deplaned and headed to a black SUV waiting for them at the private airfield south of Chattanooga. Big Joe, five-feet-two and built like a bull, waved them over before climbing into the driver's side. They drove toward Aunt Janice's community.

"TJ's already there," Big Joe explained. "Word is, there's a car with Illinois tags in the driveway."

Garrick drummed his fingers on his thigh and beat back his anxiety. Clive and his brother would have no issue with hurting Sky's aunt. A variety of possible scenarios played out in his head, none of them good. He called up the calm that had served him in the past, the breathing technique in his mindfulness drills. It was always easier when he took point, but like it or not, Flash had assumed command since these men were his guys.

They approached the aunt's community, drove right through the unmanned guard gate, found the house, and parked a short distance down the road.

Flash pulled radios and earpieces out of a gear bag, and they checked their comms. Once they were set, they crept toward the house, assumed positions, and waited.

TJ had a slim mic threaded into the window. "I only hear one guy." His hushed voice came through the earpiece. "There doesn't seem to be a problem."

The front door opened, and the man stepped out. Clive's brother, Cletus.

Garrick instinctively gripped his Glock.

"No Clive?" he asked.

"That's the only guy inside," TJ replied. "Stay in position."

Janice stood on the porch as if saying goodbye to a friend, and Cletus walked back to his vehicle.

Garrick's brows drew down tight. This didn't add up.

TJ and Big Joe slipped into a grey Accord, and when Cletus drove off, they tailed him.

Flash and Garrick returned to the rented black SUV, waited for Janice to go inside, and watched the house for a long moment.

"What do we do now?" Garrick asked.

Flash glanced up from his phone. "Wait."

"Where's Clive?"

"We'll know in a few minutes."

Garrick's heart wouldn't settle. Flying to another state and getting involved with these unknown men put him on edge. Could he count on them? Were they dragging him into something bigger than he'd planned for? Flash could go rogue in a heartbeat.

Flash closed his phone. "Clive caught a ride share to the airport."

Garrick's heart jumped to his throat. "She told them where Sky was?"

"Negative. Cletus posed as an old boyfriend and went in solo. When he found out Skylar's address in Florida, he texted Clive, who was waiting outside."

"I can't believe her aunt would tell some old boyfriend where Sky was."

"She didn't. He saw a card addressed to her. He took a photo and sent Clive the address."

His jaw just about unhinged from his face. "How did your guys find all this out?

"They're pros."

"As in?"

"As in, you didn't hear this from me, and I'm only telling you because you're part of the team—and Hawk's alive because of you. They're undercover US Marshalls. Clive and his associates have been on their radar. I alerted them to your situation, and they were more than happy to move in."

"And they were okay with us being here?"

The corner of Flash's mouth edged up. "We have a symbiotic working relationship."

"Are your guys heading south?"

"Unsure. They took Cletus in. The photo of Skylar's address is incriminating, and they have other stuff on these lowlifes, racketeering, drugs...."

"Any reason to stick around?" Garrick asked.

"You need to visit her aunt?"

"No. Let's head back."

"We need to make a stop first. I have to drop something off with a friend."

He texted Sky as they rode but didn't want to panic her.

Garrick: *We need to talk. Soon. Stay away from the farmhouse.*

Her notifications were silenced.

He tried calling. It went to voice mail.

Dammit.

Buzzing, fidgety energy filled him as he opened his browser and scoured the internet, checking the departing flights on their drive back to the airfield. Which one would Clive be on? Would it be faster to fly commercial?

The sooner he got back to Sky, the better.

CHAPTER EIGHTEEN

I t was four a.m., and he'd only caught a nap on the plane.
Garrick had enough time for a pit stop at home before
heading to the firehouse.

Before he showered, he texted: *I'm home.*

A short time later, his brother arrived. Luke opened an app
on his phone. "Surveillance shows the youngest brother running
the shop. Cletus is still in jail, and the other brother left town,
but not sure where he went. Clive's gone dark." Luke had
researched flights, but there'd been no Clive Warwick on any of
them. Miami International seemed the most likely airport, but
when Flash's guy checked it out, he'd come up empty. There'd
been no word, not a sign.

Garrick sat, resting his arms on his thighs, and hung his head,
exhausted. "Now what?"

"Keep listening," Luke said matter-of-factly. "Watching.
Someone will say something, see something."

"Hey, you," Skylar said, rubbing her eyes on the way to the
coffee maker.

His heart leaped at the sight of her, safe and in his house.
"We didn't mean to wake you."

"It's okay. I have an early client." She leaned on the edge of the counter and held her coffee like it was a lifeline. "I got your text. Is that what you're talking about? Did you find him?"

"Not yet. You need to be extra careful. Keep alert," Garrick stressed.

Her brows furrowed. "Is he here?"

Garrick hated scaring her, but a healthy dose of reality was in order. "We're not sure, but it's likely he'll come."

"Or he found out they arrested his brother, and he's hiding somewhere." Sky said.

"Possibly," Garrick had to agree. But it didn't sound like the Clive she'd described.

"I have alerts in place," Luke said. "If I pick up anything on him. If he uses a credit card, if his name appears anywhere, I'll text you."

Garrick directed his gaze to Sky. "I only want you at the farmhouse when someone else is there."

"I can't halt everything again because he might be in the state. What if he flew to some island to lay low? Or went back home?" She rubbed her cheek. "I have work to do, and we don't even know if he's in Florida."

Sky was right. But he didn't like it. "Keep an eye out. Be extra careful. Lock doors." It sounded feeble. It was feeble.

"She's pretty safe here on the ranch," Luke said. "I can put cameras up at the farmhouse."

"That's good," Skylar agreed. "And I can text you when I arrive and leave the farmhouse."

Garrick scratched his chin. "I'll ask Wyatt and Brick to work that part of the ranch for the next few days. They'll be around if you need them."

"Sounds like a plan. I'll order the cameras. Let's keep in touch." Luke held up his phone. "I'll start a thread with the two of you."

When Luke left, Garrick pulled Sky in for a smooch. "Be careful."

"I will."

"You'd better." He squeezed Sky against him in a tight hug. Despite her logical argument, his intuition pushed his anxiety meter into the red zone.

Skylar picked at a spot of paint on her arm as she walked the property with Pablo. After spending the morning in town, she'd worked the entire afternoon painting the interior of the house and welcomed the break. She studied the landscape next to the road on the north side. Cattle grazed among large oaks, and tall herons waded in the ditch.

"This will fetch a good amount." Pablo gestured to the parcel of land. "The fifteen acres can be divided a few different ways."

"Whatever will bring me the most income." As she said it, a wave of unease moved through her. The quiet, the long view, and the wildlife were things she liked about it here. A neighborhood may change all that. But if she was careful, income from the sale of this land, combined with what she was getting already, would supply her with seed money to start a business down here and cover living expenses. She'd visited an in-home daycare in town and toured the primary school Logan would attend in the fall. She was digging in and making a life—and would do whatever it took.

"Chica." Pablo sounded weary. "Wes Blankenship has approached me once again."

Tension moved into her shoulders. "On behalf of Tall Pines?"

"Of course. And once again, I must ask. Would you sell it as one parcel to the ranch?"

"But you said Seaside Development will pay more."

"It's true. But it is also true you want to get along with your neighbors." He raised his forehead in an expression that could only be called a warning.

She ignored it. "I need the best price you can get me." Would this come between her and Dani? Her and Garrick? Surely, they'd understand it was business. She'd have a conversation with Dani and feel her out. Garrick's position was clear. But he'd eventually get over it, and they'd remain friends. They'd gotten pretty close.

They walked to Pablo's car and drove back to her farmhouse. She waved to Brick and Wyatt, who were working on the fence, then locked the farmhouse and returned to the ranch. It was time to collect Logan from Thea's.

"Look!" Logan said excitedly. A horse puppet pieced from red and orange calico fabrics, with yarn for a mane and buttons for eyes, covered Logan's hand up to the elbow. "His name is Rusty."

"Like Rusty that Garrick rides?"

"Yes. Daddy's horse." Logan gathered cloth scraps with her free hand while galloping the puppet over the table.

Skylar's brows jumped together. "No—"

Thea laid a hand on her arm. "She's been calling him that. I didn't stop her."

She whispered, "But he's not her dad."

Thea gazed at Logan thoughtfully. "I didn't see the harm in letting her have it. What she feels inside is the same, whether she calls him that or not."

Skylar's heart pinched. True, Logan would feel hurt and miss Garrick either way when they moved out. But what would happen if Garrick heard her call him that? If he corrected Logan, it would tear her to pieces. Would he think she told Logan to call him dad? She hadn't. This was getting sticky.

"Do you need me to watch Logan tomorrow?" Thea asked. "We're planting zinnias."

"I'd love that. Can it be later in the afternoon? I have a class tomorrow morning and want to try her at the daycare for a few hours."

She and Logan headed home for a quiet evening since Garrick was working a twenty-four-hour shift.

While Logan was in the bath, she glanced at her phone and saw she'd missed a call from Aunt Janice.

"Hi, Skylar. I thought you'd want to know that a man named Cletus stopped by looking for you. He was very polite and quite friendly and said he was an old boyfriend. I remembered because it was so unusual, and I got a strange feeling from him. Anyway, I told him I don't know where you are. But he kept looking around my house as if he thought you were there. It was quite odd. I wanted to tell you. I didn't tell anyone where you were. Be safe. Love you."

Cletus? The name meant nothing to her. A chill climbed up her spine. This felt connected to Clive. Perhaps Luke or Garrick could check on the names of Clive's brothers.

After his shift at the firehouse, Garrick met Flash, Tate, and Bear at the diner. The biker was the latest addition to their group. Bear resembled his name—a hulking dude with a black beard and sleeves of tattoos over beefy arms. He'd served in the Army for four years, did a couple tours, and they knew some people in common. The man was their go-to mechanic for any equipment that broke.

Garrick opened the photo Luke had texted. Clive was standing with his three brothers. He pointed to the screen. "This one, Cletus, is in jail, and this one's at the pawn shop. This other one may be working with Clive."

"I'll keep an eye and an ear out," Bear said. The auto repair shop was attached to the one service station in town and across from the coffee shop—another hub of local gossip.

They discussed the situation in Chattanooga.

"So, Clive is nowhere?" Bear drew his bushy black brows into a flat ledge resembling a hedge that needed trimming.

"And there's the other brother." Garrick had that edgy sensation like someone was watching him. He scanned the room. Just a few ranchers. It appeared safe enough.

"They'd best stay up north." Flash stirred a third of a packet of sugar into his heavily creamed coffee.

"I can't believe you drink that." Tate fake-coughed, "Wuss."

"I can drink it black. But any chance you get to stock up on nourishment, you should take it." Flash nodded sagely.

"I can't believe Clive gave the Feds the slip," Garrick said.

"He's no dummy." Flash drained his coffee in an instant and caught the server's eye for more.

Tate raised his chin toward a man leaving the diner. "Do any of you know that old guy?"

Garrick studied the man as he climbed into a car. With a hat pulled low over his face, old wranglers, and a denim jacket, he resembled a hundred guys around here. But his shoes. There was something off. The guy glanced back before pulling out of the parking lot. Most men in those clothes would be getting into a pickup truck, not a rented white Accord.

Garrick came to alert. "That could be our man."

"That old dude?" Bear set down his cup and stared in the direction the car had driven.

"Not old," Garrick said. "I'd bet my left nut that guy's wearing a wig."

Flash stood. "I don't know how we missed him, but I'm going for a ride."

"I'm coming along." Garrick stood.

"No, bro. I have somewhere to be. I'm flying solo this morning. And we aren't sure that's him. I'll text you what I find." Flash left his half-eaten meal and was out the door.

Garrick glanced at the other two men.

Tate lifted his palm. "Go home and crash, bro. Flash can handle it."

"Yeah, maybe I will." He dropped a couple bills on the table, hustled to his Jeep, and followed Tate. At the red light, a semi-truck pulled in front of him.

He lost them.

CHAPTER NINETEEN

Skylar had hardly seen Garrick for two days, so she took extra time with dinner, knowing how much it meant to him. She'd bought tiny, yellow key limes and found a recipe for Key Lime pie with homemade whipped cream.

While it chilled, she cooked the orange chicken recipe from the inn, wild rice, and salad, assembled with vegetables and fresh pineapple from the garden.

Garrick trudged in, dead on his feet. He'd worked another hard shift at the firehouse before coming home and helping work cattle. She handed him a tall tea and lemonade mix and he went to change.

Garrick came out in fresh clothes. "What's this?" He lifted the card from Aunt Janice.

"Oh. My aunt sends me cards. She's old school. But I like it. There's a thing about holding an actual card in your hand." The card, displayed on the counter, gave her a comforting sense of connection.

"She has your correct address? Did this come here?"

"No. It came to the farmhouse last week. She sends me cards or letters pretty regularly. Of course, she has the correct address.

She sold me the property. Well, for a few dollars. It was supposed to go to my father."

"That's how you got it." He bowed the card in his hands.

"When my dad died, I got nothing. My stepmother took it all, and my stepsister and half-sister became like my kids. I was basically the parent and cook and housekeeper for several years while Vera did whatever she wanted."

"What? You were a servant in your own home?"

"Pretty much. Which is why it feels like poetic justice, or karma for me to get the farm." Sky sighed loudly. "Living with Vera never felt like home. It was a roof. And food. And I loved my younger sisters even if they only thought of me as someone to meet their needs. That's how I learned, early on, who I could rely on."

"Who?"

"Me. Myself, and I." She huffed. "That's why it's so important for me to be there for Logan. She'll always know I have her back." She kissed Logan's head. "And her front." She kissed her daughter's forehead. "And everything in between." She tickled Logan before lifting her into her seat. "Take that off, sweetie. You can't wear it to eat."

"Whatcha got, munchkin?" Garrick focused on the horse puppet covering Logan's hand.

"Rusty." Logan's eyes sparkled.

"Like my horse?" He sat at the place across from her and beamed in return.

Skylar watched their exchange, amused. Garrick would make a good dad someday. A wave of sadness edged out the warmth. How would it be when he brought another woman here and had children, and she became superfluous? It was likely. She'd noticed the exchange between him and that woman at Lone Star Pete's. He'd tried to minimize it, but she'd caught the way the woman had looked at him. They had a history.

Garrick was a handsome man. A good man. A man she could love.

"We both have Rusty horses." Logan grasped the fork in her free hand and began eating. "Rusty likes pineapple. Miss Terri says horses like apples."

"Who's Miss Terri?" Garrick buttered a chunk of crusty peasant bread.

"I found an in-home daycare in town. Logan's going there while I go to classes."

"Classes? What classes are you taking?"

"It's a self-defense series. Over at the boxing club outside Cedar Bay."

"For real? That's where I train. Jack too. But we go at different times. He's more into straight boxing. I have some sparring partners and do Krav Maga."

She held his gaze a beat. "I guess we have something in common."

"If you want to practice, I'm available. I know a few moves."

"You certainly do." She gave him a smile that promised fun later.

Garrick's phone buzzed, and he glanced at the screen. "Sorry, babe. I have to take this."

Logan's forehead wrinkled. "Where did Gricky go?"

"Logan," Skylar started. "That's not his name."

Logan offered a tiny smile. "Daddy?"

She groaned inwardly. There was no winning this one.

Garrick glanced back at the house, lowered his voice, and took the call. It was their family real estate agent.

"You told me to let you know," Wes Blankenship said through the speaker. "Pablo got in touch with me."

"If I don't put in a bid, the property goes to Seaside?"

"Yes. You or Tall Pines needs to make a bid," Wes said.

He exhaled hard. "Put in an offer. Whatever Seaside offers, make mine a little more."

"You sure? A bidding war might get pricey."

Garrick could practically hear Wes rubbing his palms together. "I'm sure."

He ended the call and returned inside to eat with the two women who lifted his heart. Now, to navigate the situation. Did he find a builder and surprise Sky? Did he sit her down and have a talk? Did he wait for this Clive situation to be resolved? He was getting ahead of himself. What they had was good, but would she even consider long-term?

"There's Key Lime pie for dessert." Skylar cleared Logan's place while he finished his food.

"Woman, I do love your cooking. I could get used to it."

"Thanks. But don't. My flooring should be here next week. But, if you're very good, I'll bring my nice neighbor dinners occasionally."

He grabbed her arm and pulled her closer. "How about we eat together every night?"

She met his gaze, a parade of emotions moving over her face: distress, sadness, perhaps real caring. It wasn't the reaction he'd been hoping for.

"Occasionally. Friend." Sky pulled away and cut the pie.

He fought the disbelief, making his head spin. She'd understood his implication. He'd lay money on it. This never happened. Usually, it was the other way around. Sky was keeping him in the friend zone? Dinner had lost its appeal, but there was pie, and he'd eat it. Because, after all, it was pie. And he'd still meet with Wes and the attorney in the morning. He wasn't giving up that easily.

CHAPTER TWENTY

"GSL is the name you want on the deed?" Hiram Goldsmith, the family attorney, sat with Wes and Garrick, going over the contract for the parcel of land at the north edge of Sky's property. He was paying too much, but knowing it was going to Sky sweetened the bitter taste of being backed into a corner. There's no way he'd show her the contract Hiram had drawn up. This was the best solution.

"You don't want Skylar to know you're the buyer?" Hiram asked.

"Not yet."

"Or your brothers—"

"In due time. For now, it will appear as though nothing has changed."

Hiram seemed to consider his words. "This is irregular, but since you're part owner Tall Pines it works. You're already leasing the land."

"Works for me." Wes leaned on the dark wood of the table, probably figuring his next stop would be paying off his Mercedes. Tall Pines kept this man in business.

They finished their meeting, and Garrick walked out of the room decidedly less wealthy. But he now was the sole owner of twelve prime acres. Which was strange. He was leasing the land back to his business. At least a development wouldn't go on that property. And he'd bought Sky some time.

His phone buzzed.

Tate: *Come by the shop.*

That was more succinct than usual and likely meant he had news about Clive.

Orange monarch butterflies flitted among the shrubs, and the spring sunshine warmed her face. Skylar stepped lightly as she and Logan walked the path to Thea's Garden. She'd gotten the asking price for that land.

The buyer wasn't Seaside Development but some other group. It didn't matter. Life was moving forward. Pablo was helping her find a fixer-upper to flip. She could cover living expenses, reduce her client load, and focus on Logan. For the first time in years, she was putting down roots.

Lately, she'd been taking Logan to daycare, but this morning, her daughter was bubbling with excitement over helping Thea.

They found Dani in the garden, filling a basket with beans.

"Hey, Dani. I've got Logan here. Where's Thea? Logan's supposed to pick tomatoes with her."

"Bud needed to go to the doctor for his foot. Her friend drove them to the clinic in Heron Park in a while ago. She said she'll do it when she gets back."

"I was planning to go to my class while Logan helped her."

"If you want, y'all can help me in the garden. But I can't babysit. I'm working at the produce stand today."

"Thank you." This wasn't optimal, but she'd take Logan to the daycare and along on errands afterward. Maybe they'd get an ice cream. It would be fun. She found a basket and Dani demonstrated how to tell if the tomatoes were ripe.

Skylar guided her daughter's hand. "Gentle. Only pick the ones that come off easily."

They talked while they worked. Dani explained the properties of the herbs and told her about the healing creams she made. They discussed the horses. Their conversation meandered, easy, in that relaxed way it was with friends.

"I sure do like you and Logan being here," Dani said. "And you'll be right next door. I'm glad you and Jack came to an agreement. I don't ordinarily get involved in the business end of things, but I'm sure glad you're staying."

"What are you talking about?"

"You staying. Some letter or contract the attorney drew up."

"A contract from an attorney?"

"The one that says you can stay if ... you really don't know what I'm talking about?"

"No." Skylar drew out the syllable. "I have no idea."

"Oh, dang. I'm sorry. I thought you knew. Jack gave the letter to Garrick a while back. He was supposed to have you sign it. You know, so you can stay in the house. Since it's on the leased property and all."

"What?"

"The Tall Pines lease includes the land the house sits on. But the contract says if you don't sell, you can stay. Win-win."

The breath whooshed out of her. Win-win? "I need to discuss this with Garrick."

Stay in her house? On leased land? Was her house part of the lease deal? The house has a fence around it. The cattle were in the pastures. That made no sense, and she'd already sold that parcel.

She gathered the spilled tomatoes and carried the basket to the bench. "Thanks Dani. We're heading out now."

"Dang. I didn't mean to upset you. Do me a favor. Please don't mention what I said to anyone. I probably shouldn't have said ... I could've been confused."

No. She couldn't promise that. "Don't worry, Dani. It'll be

okay. We're friends." But she'd call Pablo as soon as she got in the car, and the next time she saw Garrick, he needed to explain.

She strapped Logan into her car seat with her Pegasus, pressed Pablo's cell number, and got his voicemail. "Call me. Please."

Discomfort niggled at the back of her mind as she drove into town.

CHAPTER TWENTY-ONE

Garrick and Tate rode to a house in an old neighborhood with mature landscaping, pulled next to a thicket, and prepared to surveil the property. Flash had tracked Clive to a vacation rental outside Pine Crossing. Bear would meet up with them when he finished repairing a tractor. Garrick understood. He prioritized his work at the firehouse and was damn grateful the guys still had his back. Apparently, his quick work with Hawk gave him credibility, even though he'd have done the same for anybody. Anybody, except for the scum-suit staying in the house they were watching.

He rubbed his eyes. After a twenty-four-hour shift with three middle-of-the-night transports, he could've used more coffee before heading over here.

A rented white Accord was parked in the driveway, but the dead quiet gave the house an empty vibe. They waited in position and kept eyes and ears on the house.

Flash signaled for them to meet in the secluded area around the back. "He's not here." Despite the mic planted inside the window and the tracker Flash had installed in the car, this operation was a bust.

Garrick rubbed his forehead, frustrated. His phone buzzed. It was the group text.

Bear: *It'll be a while. Are you still over by Big Pine Dr?*

Tate: *Neg. we're heading back to the shop.*

Garrick's phone buzzed with a text from Luke: *Heads up—one of the brothers flew down last night and good news about the other plan.*

He showed his screen to the guys. "Clive's brother's here. They're likely together. But where?"

They climbed back into Tate's truck.

"If they have her address, they may be at her farmhouse," Flash said. "Let's head that way."

"What other plan?" Tate started the truck and made a U-turn. "Do you want to stop and get your car?"

"I've got a bad feeling. Let's head straight out to her farm." He took a moment to explain what he and his brother had been doing online. "Luke's talking about messing with Clive virtually."

"Luke's got some skills," Tate commented as he passed the center of town and headed east. "You ought to convince him to come work with us."

"Right." Garrick huffed.

"I'm serious."

"He has his hands full between his business and the ranch."

A determined calm settled over Garrick, even as he drummed his fingers on his thigh. His senses sharpened, like the eagle before diving for that snake. His number one priority was stopping Clive before he could find Skylar.

He texted her: *What are you up to? Location?*

———————

After Krav Maga class, her sensei had her doing extra work on the bag to level up her cardio fitness. Skylar's earlier conversation with Dani kept circling in her brain, and she used her anger to fuel her workout.

"Whoa. Tiger. You're going at it today." Sensei widened his eyes.

She stopped for water. "As hard as I work on my renovation projects, you'd think I'd be in better shape."

"We don't count that as fitness training. But, because you train, it should be easier."

"Y'all are tough. At least, now I'll know some self-defense techniques."

"You've completed one series," Sensei said. "Sign up for the next one and the one after that. Then we'll talk about real life."

"But the moves I've learned should work?"

"Keep working. Practicing. You're doing good for a beginner."

"Thanks?" Skylar blotted sweat dripping from her face, disappointment washing through her. Soon she'd be moving into the farmhouse alone and Clive was still out there. "I'd better get going. I'm expecting a delivery today." She grabbed her phone. Darn. The battery was dead. The daycare wouldn't have been able to reach her. As soon as she got in the car, she plugged it in.

Skylar drove to the daycare to pick up Logan and run a couple errands before meeting the flooring delivery man at the farmhouse. Despite what Dani had said, she was still determined to make it her home. "Quitter" wasn't in her vocabulary.

On leaving the daycare, Miss Terri handed Skylar two large paintings. Mostly pink and purple splashes of color. "These are the ones she did last week. The ones from today aren't dry yet."

"Wow. Logan, they're pretty. You're my little artist." Skylar buckled Logan into the car seat.

Logan was exceptionally bright today, playing with Peg as they drove and talking about a toy horse at the daycare.

"We can find some horse fabric for your pillows." Thea was making pillows, and Skylar had promised she'd buy the material.

"We're heading to the craft store, then we'll get lunch and ice cream."

"Can we get paints?"

They carried paint at the craft store, but she wasn't ready to introduce that mess into Garrick's house. "Not today. We're getting more fabric."

Skylar steered onto the road leading to the craft store and glanced in the rear-view mirror. Was that the same car that had been behind her in Cedar Bay? What were the chances it would be taking the same route with a detour by the daycare?

She struggled to see. Between the glare and window tint, she couldn't make out the driver.

"Mommy, Peg's hurt. Look. Look!" Logan screeched, swinging her Pegasus forward, trying to position it so Skylar could take it.

"Wait." She split her attention between the road, Logan's talking, and trying to monitor the car in her rear-view mirror. "Wait until I stop. I'll check it. If it's ripped, we'll get something to mend it at the craft store."

"It's broken." Logan began crying. "Peg's wing."

"Hold on sweetie. We'll be there in a just second."

Logan wailed.

Her cell phone began pinging with messages, but she couldn't read them while she drove. She was already distracted enough.

"Peg!" Logan screamed. She must be hungry.

"Okay." With one hand on the wheel, she reached back. "Hand it up here. I promise it will be okay. We'll fix it."

Logan jabbed Pegasus toward her.

She reached behind and grabbed the stuffed animal. When she glanced in the mirror again, the car behind her was gone. Where was it? Had she imagined it was following her?

Skylar hadn't replied. There were no cars in front of her farmhouse. To be sure, Garrick and Flash checked around back.

No Skylar. Cattle grazed beyond the fence.

Tension had his temple throbbing as they hustled around the front. He rubbed his forehead.

"Let's go to the shop and work on a plan." Tate said as Garrick and Flash climbed back in the truck. "Bear's finished with his job. He's coming over."

"Can you make a quick stop at the ranch?" Garrick asked. "Sky might be there."

"Sure." Tate slowed as they approached the gate.

"You can't track her phone?" Flash's brows wove, perplexed.

Garrick's defenses came up. "I guess I could. But I haven't set it up. Privacy and all."

"How's that working out?" Flash scoffed softly. "I'd always know where my woman was."

Tate huffed. "Probably why you don't have one."

Garrick clenched his jaw. He had something with Skylar, but she'd be irked if he called her his woman. Right about now, with that tight knot in his gut, there was no other way to describe her. He'd never felt like this before. She had to be okay.

They pulled into the ranch and drove toward his cottage. Her car wasn't anywhere in the area. Dammit!

On the way out, he spotted Thea and Bud near the main house. "Hold on a second." He leaped from the passenger seat. "Hey. Do either of you know where Skylar and Logan are?"

"That's a fine way to greet your old man." Bud scowled.

"You look worried." Thea narrowed her gaze. "Is everything okay?"

"I need to talk to her."

"She's stopping by the fabric store after class today," Thea replied. "Then meeting the flooring man later. That's all I know."

"Thanks. Call me right away if she comes home or if any strange cars show up."

"What?" Bud asked.

"Just call me. Okay?" He hustled back to the truck, checking the phone as he walked. Still no reply.

Skylar helped her weeping daughter out of the car seat and headed into the store. "Don't worry. We'll fix Peg. It'll be as good as new." Thea likely had every thread you could imagine, but as long as they were here, they'd find something to mend the stuffed animal.

Holding Logan's hand, she pushed through the entrance. Music and laughter drifted out of the classroom in the rear of the shop. From the sounds of it, they were having a lively class. The modest-sized store held a huge inventory. Arts and crafts supplies filled rows down one side, and sewing supplies were on the other. Bolts of fabric in tempting colors crowded the aisles like a thick forest. She scanned the room to find a salesperson for help.

"I'll be with you in a moment." The employee waved from the far end of the store before ducking into the classroom.

Skylar reached into her tote for her phone. It had buzzed several times in the car. Darn. It wasn't in the zippered pocket. She dug around the bottom of her tote.

Logan ran toward a bolt of shimmery fabric resembling the wings on her Pegasus. "Look!"

"Stay right there, Logan." Ugh. In her hurry to comfort Logan, had she left her phone in the car? No matter. She should be in and out of here fast enough. She glanced up in time to see Logan running down the aisle. "Logan, wait."

Logan scampered to another fabric bolt farther away. "Look! Horses."

"Logan. Stop." What had gotten into her? Skylar scrambled to catch up.

Logan laughed. She actually laughed.

"We don't run around indoors." She glanced toward the classroom. The sales lady hadn't come back out, and it was unlikely she heard her scolding. "Logan, we aren't playing."

Logan stopped near the entrance, frozen, as though realizing she might be in trouble.

"Logan, come here. Right now." Angry, she strode over.

Behind Logan, two figures appeared in the glass doors.

Men.

Clive?

Skylar sprinted toward Logan.

The door opened.

Clive stepped inside. "What do we have here?" He nodded toward Logan, and the other man stepped forward and scooped her up.

Logan shrieked. "Mommy!"

"Be quiet, Lizzie," Clive said. "Your uncle has candy for you in the car. You like candy, don't you? And toys."

Logan stopped squirming as though considering his offer.

Skylar approached. "Put her down. Now."

She didn't remember Clive being so tall.

———

Tate drove closer to the craft store.

Skylar's car sat in the parking lot.

A car with Illinois tags sat beside it.

"Shit!" Garrick said. "That's Clive and his brother."

The two men were right inside.

Tate pulled up to the side of the entrance, out of view. Flash and Tate exchanged a nod. "Flash will be over by the shrubs in case they try to leave. I'll take point."

Flash dug into his gear bag and pulled out a thick blade. "They won't be driving anywhere." He stole around the back of the shop to circle over to their car.

"I'm taking point," Garrick argued, pulling his Glock from his boot, and sticking it in his back pocket.

"No." Tate glanced over. "You're too close."

"No. I will." His tone left no argument. They had a brief stare-down.

"Go on." Tate laid his hand on the weapon he kept holstered under his belt.

They made a quick plan.

Inside the shop, the two men continued arguing with Sky, unaware of their arrival.

Clive's brother held Logan.

Garrick's heart pinched. He inhaled calm and found the clear, focused thinking that served him in dicey situations. There'd be time to feel later. Now, he needed to think, act, and rely on instincts and skills honed on other missions.

Calling forth his best dumb cowboy persona, he pushed open the door, stepping quickly inside. "Howdy fellas."

Tate entered right on his heels.

That was enough to startle the men and cause four sets of eyes to glance their way.

"Gricky!" Logan reached out.

Everything seemed to happen at once. Garrick grabbed Logan while sweeping the legs out from under the man holding her, landing a brutal kick to the man's knee as he pulled her away.

The jerk grasped his leg, screaming.

Clive lurched forward, grabbing Sky.

Skylar landed a backward punch to Clive's groin. Tate threw Clive to the floor.

Clive went down hard, groaning.

Garrick shoved Logan at Sky. "Go."

She grabbed Logan and ran to the back of the store.

He turned to the still-moaning man scooting away and aimed his Glock. "Hands out at your sides where I can see them."

Still wincing, Clive was going for his weapon.

"Don't even try." Tate aimed his Sig at Clive and disarmed him.

They had the two men spreadeagle on the linoleum floor of the shop.

That's when Garrick noticed the voices at the end of the room. And sirens outside.

"We called the sheriff," one of the women said. Two sheriff's cruisers abruptly halted outside the glass entrance doors. Flash approached the entrance, speaking with Deputies Kurt and Evans.

Evans spoke first, handcuffs in one hand and sidearm in the other. "Put down the weapons. What do we have here?"

"Tate and Garrick are okay." Kurt shook his head and mumbled, "Are you trying to put me out of a job?"

The other two deputies Mirandized Clive and his brother while Kurt and Evans took their statements. The group of women in the back, wearing smocks and wielding paintbrushes, fussed over Logan and Sky.

Garrick waved Sky up to the front of the shop to give Kurt her statement. He didn't give a damn if they were in public or if he was in the friend zone. He circled his arms around the woman he loved. "Sky," was all he could say. He held her, breathing in her scent. Something tight inside of him let go as he kissed the side of her head. "I've got you, sweetheart, I've got you."

"Thank you." She raised her face and kissed him. Right there in front of everyone. That had to be a good sign.

While she finished talking to the deputy, he strode to the back of the room. The grannies were fussing over Logan, distracting her, making the ordeal sound like an adventure.

Logan grinned at him and raised her arms.

He lifted her up and held her tight.

"Oh, are you her father?" asked the pink-haired lady with a tattoo on her arm.

"Not yet." He kissed the top of Logan's hair, and she laid her little cheek on his shoulder.

He carried her back to Sky.

CHAPTER TWENTY-TWO

After their ordeal at the craft store, a group of them went to the diner. Logan was cranky and needed food. Skylar ordered a meal because everyone else did, but she was still too upset to eat. While Logan devoured her grilled cheese, Skylar only picked at her wrap. The server brought her a box.

Clive was in custody. That was good. She should feel relieved, but a sense of surreal had settled over her. Her hands were cold and she felt shaky inside, her mind swirling. Memories of Tessa, the sneer on Clive's face, and that moment his brother grabbed Logan, mixed with Dani's news that the rancher's at Tall Pines were scheming to control her land. It was impossible for her to process it all. She needed space. Alone time.

She and Logan sat in the u-shaped corner booth with Garrick, Tate, and Kurt.

"I can't do my job if you don't keep me in the loop." Kurt laid his napkin on his empty plate.

"We only recently learned about the brother," Tate said.

Garrick reached below the table and laced his fingers through hers.

She pulled her hand away. As much as she loved the feeling of his warm hand, it made her uncomfortable. She'd been relieved to see him, and had even kissed him at the craft store, but the things Dani had said earlier played in her mind. She needed to have a talk with Garrick, later, when she could think more clearly.

When they left the diner, Garrick asked. "Ready to go home?"

"If by home you mean the farmhouse, yes. They're delivering the flooring this afternoon, and I thought I'd get started."

"Are you sure you want to do that today?"

"Yes. Thea is babysitting. I need to work." Keeping to her plans seemed like a good choice. Hard labor would be grounding and give her time to calm down.

Over the last few days, Skylar had prepared the floor and needed to lay the laminate over the sub-flooring. The rectangular shape of the room made it easier, and the job should go fast, but her heavy heart made it difficult to concentrate.

Outside, a car door closed.

The front door opened, and Garrick stepped in, wearing jeans and a work shirt.

"Do you need something?" she asked, not ready to talk to him. "Is Logan okay?"

"Logan's fine. And she'll be even better when her mom gets home. I thought the job would go faster if I gave you a hand."

"Why would you do that?" She sounded snippy, and she didn't care. She'd had time to think. If what Dani had said was true, Garrick wasn't being honest with her. Tall Pines wanted her gone. It hurt. Why hadn't he said anything about this situation? Hadn't they been getting close?

She continued arranging the floor panels.

Garrick squatted beside her. "Tell me how to help."

She sighed hard. "You can help by telling me what sneaky

thing you have planned. Do you have some kind of contract for me to sign?"

He rubbed his face, looking guilty.

"You want to tell me what's up with that? Something about me not being able to stay in my own house?"

"It's complicated." He exhaled hard.

"Give me the short version."

"The Tall Pines lease on your land includes the property your house sits on."

"No. That's not how I read it. The cattle don't graze here."

He lifted a shoulder. "Our attorney looked into it. Legally, we could make you move. The contract allows you to stay here if you agree not to sell any of the land while you occupy the house, as long as the lease is in place."

Pain tightened her throat and gripped her chest. The day had already been horrible, and now this? She stared at Garrick wanting to see the man she might love, but instead she saw him as a part of Tall Pines, a business that might evict her from her home.

"I can show you the document." Garrick lifted his brows. "But maybe we can—"

"You need to leave. I have to think."

"What?" Shock registered on his face. "I can explain."

She stood and folded her arms across her chest, unwavering. "Please go. Now."

"Why don't we—"

"Just go." She turned away, unable to stand the look on his face.

When Garrick left, she sat on the floor and leaned on the wall, her stomach in knots. Her mind was spinning. Everything that had happened over the last twenty-four hours had her feeling raw, had brought up the horrible few years Tessa had been involved with Clive, and all of Skylar's efforts, in vain, to help. Her sister's death, and all of the sickening court proceedings. And Clive's threats. She felt like she'd been terrorized.

She was a life coach, and she had tools. She had skills. And she used them. But it still hurt, so bad. It was all ... too much. Tears stung her eyes and flowed down her cheeks. She wiped at them with her palms until she was forced to search for a paper towel.

Garrick had saved her. And Logan too. She wasn't supposed to love him. That wasn't their deal. They were supposed to be friends, and she could've imagined them becoming more someday. Her chest ached. She loved him now, as much as she loved Logan, and as much as she'd loved Tessa.

But, there was the contract. Garrick had lied. A lie of omission. It was a big deal. A friend wouldn't do that. She rubbed her head. Her brain hurt.

What could she do? Why finish her house? When they found out she'd sold that parcel—and they would—they'd make her leave.

She texted Max and waited. No reply.

CHAPTER TWENTY-THREE

Garrick was desperate enough to brew that foul tea Thea had given him. It tasted like dirt in a glass, but drinking it had helped him log a few hours of rest.

Zero four hundred came, and he couldn't get back to sleep. His gut burned, and his head throbbed. He paced the house.

Logan and Sky's beds were still made from the day before. She hadn't come home. That's how it felt to him. Home. She belonged with him.

The sun hadn't cracked the horizon when he stepped outside. Sky's car was pulled up to Thea's house.

She hadn't acknowledged his texts.

He forced himself to continue to the daily meeting. The five men were already sitting around the table.

Jack and Luke exchanged a meaningful glance. Right. He probably looked like hell and still wore yesterday's clothes.

After a few minutes of rehashing what had gone down with Clive, it was time for him to make a statement. He pulled out the contract Hiram had created, held it up, and ripped it in two.

Jack raised a brow. "Is that what I think it is?'

The corner of Luke's mouth tugged up. He could guess what was coming.

"You know we can print another one." Jack turned up a palm.

"We're not evicting Skylar." Garrick set his jaw.

"We can't buy every parcel she lists for sale." Jack shook his head, exasperated. "Especially at the prices she's asking."

"Tall Pines can't evict the woman I plan to marry. She'll be part of the ranch. It'll all work out."

Jack appeared genuinely shocked. "You asked her to marry you?"

"I'm planning to. If she'd talk to me."

Jack scoffed. "Like I said."

"She's not the enemy, and she's not using me." He ran a hand over his head, wanting it to be true.

It'd been two days. Garrick stared at Thea's house wanting to storm over and demand Sky come out and talk to him. When he'd gone over last night, Thea had sent him away. His stomach clenched. This was his ranch, she was here, and he couldn't see her.

He marched over to the barn and tacked up Rusty, ready to lose himself in a day of hard work.

Boots thudded on the floor behind him. Striker and Luke approached.

"How's the whole getting married thing going?" Luke raised a brow.

Why had he spilled that at the meeting? Damn, his big mouth. "Don't ask."

Striker asked anyway. "Have you got a plan?"

He shrugged. "Talk to her I guess."

Luke leaned on the stall beside him. "Sometimes it takes more than talk."

He snorted. "You came over here to give me that expert advice?"

Undaunted, Luke asked, "Did MaryAnn ever tell you about the love languages?"

He winced. "No." His sister, eight years older, was closer to Luke. "We don't talk that much. If we did, it wouldn't be about that."

"When it looked like me and Ellie weren't happening, MaryAnn explained it. You have to show Skylar how you feel. Not just tell her." Luke glanced at Striker.

"Talk is cheap." Striker shrugged.

"I never told her."

"Seriously, man," Luke said, shaking his head.

Garrick regretted that now. And he would tell her if he could get her to talk to him. "So, flowers?" he asked.

"Yeah. Maybe. At least. Or—do something. Or do what she wants to do. I don't know." Luke grimaced. "The thing is, it has to be more than words. Unless hearing words is her thing."

He squinted at his brother. "You been watching therapy TV?"

Luke scoffed. "Yeah. Right after my tea party."

Garrick huffed.

"There's a website, dummy. A book, too." Luke said.

"I'll check it out." Garrick nodded slowly. "And I've got an idea. I might need some help. You two up for a project?"

Garrick wasn't a wimp. The appointment had been on his calendar anyway, and he may as well talk to Doc about Skylar.

"You weren't honest with her?" Doc hiked the brow over his prosthetic eye, which stretched the main scar on his face.

Garrick tried not to stare. After all, he'd seen a lot worse. And the doc was such a regular guy when he wasn't channeling an interrogator version of Yoda.

"Not dishonest." He gripped the arms of the chair, released, and stretched his fingers. Why was this so hard? "More like stalling, buying time until I figured something out."

"Like?"

He squeezed his forehead. Yeah, like what? The fact was, she'd gotten under his skin right from the start, and he'd been torn. Being a part of the Tall Pines team had become important to him. "I didn't want her to go."

The corner of Doc's mouth curved up almost imperceptibly. "Because...."

He gave the doctor an exasperated look. "I care. I'm feeling ... it." He nodded slowly. They sat in silence for a long moment. "I'm ready for more."

"More?"

"More with Sky. More..."

"Are you doing the meditations?"

"Yes." He hated to admit it, but they made him feel calmer overall, helped him deal with the boatload of crap he was dredging up.

"Ready to work?" Doc dipped his chin toward the device.

For the next hour he dealt with his shit, made connections. Landed a few insights. Remembered an innocent kid. The one who shouldn't have been there. He hadn't known she was hiding. He'd been the one to call the room clear. It made his gut clench. He'd carried the guilt for so long. He'd seen her the day before, playing. Then....

"It's not all about the kid in Kandahar," he whispered.

"I know," Doc said.

"But some of it is."

They were quiet for a moment.

A wave of pain moved up from his belly, thick and heavy, like a dark fog. It pushed up through his chest. It ached, constricted his throat. Lodged in his head. And of all friggin' things, his eyes watered.

Dammit!

He leaned forward, stared at the floor, arms on his thighs,

and tried like hell to pull it together. He never cried. Nobody at home had ever cared when he cried, so he'd given it up. It was a stupid waste of time. He palmed his damp cheek.

Then he broke down. And tears flowed. It was probably a minute. Maybe two. But it felt like a damn hour.

He leaned back into the couch and used his bandana to wipe his face. "Sorry Doc—"

Doc huffed. "Do not apologize for having the capacity to feel. You're human. A real warrior has a heart. You've got heart."

They sat in quiet for a minute before the doc spoke again. "It's okay if you care about Logan. It's okay if you care about Skylar. Every relationship is unique. Sky's not Melody, and Logan's not that girl. And if they somehow fill a place and it makes you happy, what's the harm? You deserve happiness too." Doc paused, probably to let it sink in. "You've been working hard in therapy. You say the nightmares are less frequent?"

"They are."

They wrapped up the session talking, and when Garrick walked out, he felt spent—and a little lighter.

Skylar set down her phone, groaning. Max's voicemail had done nothing to improve her mood. Now that Clive was in custody, other charges had surfaced: credit card fraud, phishing scams, extortion, and more. He was facing a long sentence, and she was free to go anywhere.

Off the grid, Max wouldn't return from his annual fishing trip for another week. He'd cut back on residential flips to focus on a commercial property. Instead of remodeling the second house she'd planned to renovate, he'd rented it for a year, recovering barely enough to break even. If she went back north and stayed with him and his wife, that meant living with his four teenage boys. How could she subject Logan to that chaos when she was doing so well? Nadine was an option, but only for a couple of weeks. She had her hands full helping her mom. Staying there felt like an imposition.

"I saw Garrick drive off this morning." Thea placed a bowl of oatmeal in front of Logan. "He's probably going to work at the firehouse today."

"Good." Skylar glanced at her shirt. "I'll go over there and get our stuff." They'd worn the same clothes for three days, washing them in the evenings. She hadn't been back to the farmhouse. It hurt too bad. But twice, she'd allowed Thea to give her healing sessions to help her release grief. She had to admit she felt lighter, as though there was extra room in her chest.

Thea had been keeping her busy too, needing her help packaging herbs, weeding the garden, and assisting with some quilting projects. Thea said her arthritic hands bothered her. Which was odd, since she had all those healing creams and teas. Could Thea be intentionally delaying her?

The Wizard of Oz played in the background while Logan ate.

"While she finishes breakfast, I'll pack. I guess we'll be on our way." She'd head north, stay with Aunt Janice for a couple of nights, and start looking for another property in Elmwood Park. A pang of regret hit her. She'd miss the sweet scent of Pine Crossing, the palm trees, the horses, and the people. Perhaps she'd return in five years and live on her farm.

Thea took the seat beside her at the counter. "You can stay with me as long as you like. Besides, I can use more help."

"Thanks." She glanced toward Garrick's house. "But it's too difficult staying here."

"Does he know how you feel?"

A familiar ache formed in her chest. "It doesn't matter how I feel. I work late, and there's Logan. Alan gave me a hard time about it. People are demanding. They always need something. I can't split myself apart like that."

"It seems to me Garrick enjoyed making Logan a priority."

"True."

"Here on a ranch, work hours can be long and unpredictable.

Dealing with nature, calving, and livestock, we have to adapt to their schedule. Garrick might be more understanding than other men." Thea huffed. "Look at his schedule. He never knows when he'll have a call. Even when he's not working, he gets called in."

She turned her mug in her hand, feeling ... backed into a corner. "He may understand, but we had this agreement, and then there's this contract thing."

"I don't know anything about a contract. But I do know that agreements can be modified. As the seasons change, so do our needs. We figure it out as we go along sort of like being a parent. Logan keeps changing. You keep adapting. It's always like that. I was married, then widowed. I worked as a holistic practitioner. Now, I sell things at the produce stand. Life keeps unfolding. That's the journey."

"But I need to be a good mom. Lord knows I understand the difference. I had a wonderful mom for a while. Then I had Vera. It was awful. I need to make sure Logan has better."

"Don't you deserve something good, too? You've been giving to others your entire life. Sometimes, when we give ourselves what we need, we can show up better for those we love."

"True. But I'm still getting my things from Garrick's." And she did. Yes, she was a coward, but she couldn't face running into him. Even though he'd made her feel welcome in his home, she felt used. He'd misled her.

Once the car was loaded, she and Logan wandered over to the ring where several mini horses were wandering around. Her heart ached. She'd miss them. "Hey, Dani. Need a little help?"

"Is Logan ready to brush Angel?"

Logan jumped in place. "Yes."

Skylar walked her over, and together, they ran the brush down the miniature horse's coat.

While Logan worked on Angel, Skylar whispered to Dani, "We love it here, but today is our last day."

"Oh, sugar, no way. Why?"

"I think you know why." She pressed on her eyelids unwilling to break down. Dani wouldn't be able to see her cry, but she'd be able to tell. "I sold a piece of the land. When they find out, they may kick me out of here anyway."

"But they might not."

"I can't live with that hanging over my head. I'll stay with my aunt while I figure it out."

"Up in Tennessee?" Dani sounded genuinely distressed.

"Yes."

"What about Garrick. I got the feeling—"

"Garrick and I had an agreement about how this thing between us would work."

"I get the sense he really cares about you."

"That's not enough. Feelings, actions, words. They all need to line up. We're leaving after lunch."

"No. Dang. I'll miss you." They worked on Angel's mane for a few minutes before Dani asked, "Have you talked to Garrick?"

"What would be the point?"

Dani came closer. "Why not spend one more night here? We can have a girl's night, a goodbye dinner. I'll give Ellie a call. We can probably go over there."

"I don't know."

"What's your hurry? Do you have something waiting for you?"

She laughed, a bitter, mirthless sound. "No. Nothing. Nothing at all."

"Alright then..."

"Okay. One more night."

"Logan and Thea too. All the ranch women. And we'll handle the food. Y'all just come."

Ellie greeted them at the door. "You're leaving. I've hardly had a chance to get to know you."

Thea walked Logan into the kitchen while Ellie gave Skylar the grand tour.

Ellie said. "I'm sorry. I've been wildly busy with my new business and teaching online."

"No worries. I've been busy, too. Your home is amazing."

"Thank you. We designed it ourselves."

They spent a few minutes discussing the architectural details. Ellie was so happy, so at ease in her home, that something small and hard inside Skylar ached with longing, with envy. They had a beautiful home and each other. She had a farmhouse she couldn't use for five years.

She followed Dani's sister to the kitchen where Avery and her friend Emma, Dani, Thea, and Logan were seated around a large farmhouse-style table, eating snacks, and talking. As Garrick would say, they were good people. These wonderful women were her neighbors—if she were staying.

Garrick balanced a squirmy pup and a tote full of dog supplies in one arm, and opened the door to his cottage, excited. Now, to get Logan and Sky back over here. He released the puppy and scanned the area. It was different—empty. He moved from room to room, his stomach dropping. All of their things were gone, and his woobie lay spread over the bed. He frowned. Logan would miss it.

He glanced out the window. Sky's car was still parked in front of Thea's house.

Acting fast, he stormed over and pounded on Thea's door.

No answer.

He texted: *Where are you?*

Sky: *Why?*

Garrick: *We need to talk.*

Dots appeared on his cell phone screen—then stopped. She'd read the text but hadn't replied. Where was she?

He texted Luke: *Have you seen Sky?*

Luke: *She's over here.*

He snapped the leash on the pup's harness and barreled outside. Colonel leaped and pulled like a wild bronc. "At ease, Colonel." The headstrong little beast still thought he was the boss. He snatched up the critter and carried it.

Luke opened the door. Sadie and Scout, the puppy's elders, crowded around him. "Is that thing housebroken?"

Garrick huffed. "Probably not."

"Great. Hold onto it, okay? They're in the kitchen." Luke gestured. Voices rose and fell, and laughter spilled out of the room.

"What's going on in there?"

"They're having a going-away gathering for Skylar."

"They?" He hesitated. This plan wasn't well thought out. "You want to tell her I'm here?"

Luke shook his head with a wide, closed-mouth grin. "Nope. You're on your own."

He carried the pup into the kitchen.

The women stopped talking, and he stood in uncomfortable silence for a beat before Logan saw the dog.

"Puppy!" She leaped from the chair, hurling herself forward and reaching up. "It's Boots."

"*Colonel* Boots." He had no choice but to set Colonel down with Logan.

"He's so cute." Avery and Emma joined Logan and Colonel Boots on the floor.

The puppy licked Logan's face, and she laughed, raising her chin. It was a love match, for sure.

Despite all the commotion, he locked eyes with Sky.

She glanced away.

His stomach tightened. "Hey Sky, can I talk to you a sec?" He gestured toward the hall.

She remained seated and glanced at Thea, who nodded.

After a moment, she stood grudgingly. "Okay."

"Watch the dog?" he asked Luke.

Luke's two dogs entered the room, all wagging tails, and Colonel peed on the floor. "Thanks a lot," his brother said.

"I've got this." Avery took charge of the dogs. "Scout, sit."

Sky stood several feet from him in the foyer, arms locked in front of her chest.

"Come for a ride with me?" he asked.

She tilted her head. "Why would I do that?"

"Because." He took a step closer. "Because I love you. Because I have something to show you. Because what we have could be good, really good. I want you to stay. Come back to my house. Come home."

Her expression softened for a moment, then she scoffed. "Are you kidding me? What about your ranch kicking me off of my land? You have this contract, but you say you love me? How do you connect those dots?"

He pulled the contract out of his pocket and showed her the pieces. "I tore it up. I tried to tell you that the other day. Yes. Jack wanted you to sign it to prevent you from chopping up your land and selling it for residential. But I have a better idea."

"What?"

"Come and see."

She exhaled sharply. "Garrick, I had a reason for wanting to keep things casual. My schedule can be all over the place. In my experience, that's an issue."

"Have you seen my schedule?"

"And there's Logan."

"Haven't I shown you I care for Logan? Damn, Sky. I love that kid. Don't you think we can have an understanding and make it work? Between the two of us, Logan would always have someone around, and then there's Thea. And Avery and everyone else here who loves her, who loves you."

Her forehead gathered, but she didn't say no.

Hope bloomed inside of him. "Come for a ride with me."

She glanced toward the kitchen.

"We'll be back in a half-hour."

She stared at the floor as though debating, then slipped into the kitchen for a moment and spoke to Thea. "Watch Logan, okay?"

They rode over in quiet.

When they approached her gate, he slowed. "Close your eyes. It's a surprise." He pulled up to the farmhouse. There, in the tree at the front of her property the two bald eagles basked in the long rays of afternoon light. His heart lifted. It had to be a good sign. He opened her door and helped her out of his Jeep. "Okay. You can open them."

Her lips parted. "The porch? How did—"

"Me and the guys built it yesterday. And there's more."

They climbed the steps and went inside.

"The floor! It's beautiful." She scanned the room, wonder filling her face. "You finished painting and installed the floor—and those fixtures."

"Is this how you wanted it?"

"Exactly."

"Then it's ready for you. But I wondered if there's something else you might want here?"

"What?"

"Colonel and I were thinking about living on a farm. With a beautiful woman and little girl who I'd like to adopt."

"You're serious?" Her expression squeezed his heart.

"I've gotta adopt her if I'm marrying her mother. Do you love me?"

She bit her lips and nodded. "Like you wouldn't believe."

He pulled her close and kissed her thoroughly, kissed her like she was the last woman on earth because, to him, she was.

"Let's make this real." He dug the well-worn leather box from his pocket and offered her the ring. Platinum, with a ring of tiny diamonds surrounding a central diamond. "This was my grand-mother's. It's probably too old-fashioned. Will you accept it as a placeholder until you pick the one you like? Let's get this house furnished and move in."

"What, exactly, are you asking me?"

"I'm asking you to marry me."

Sky's smile hit him straight in his heart. "Then I'll say yes." She facepalmed her forehead, "Now I wish I hadn't told Pablo to accept that offer. Some company, GSL Enterprises, bought those acres."

He fought back a smile. "GLS? As in Garrick, Logan, Skylar?"

Awareness lit her face. "It's you?"

"Garrick Lyle Stone. My initials are the first letters of our names. It's meant to be. It's us. A piece separate from the ranch. That we'll make our own."

CHAPTER TWENTY-FOUR

Skylar wiped Logan's sticky hands. "I don't know why I let you have pancakes this morning. You've got syrup everywhere."

"Munchkin deserves a pancake breakfast on her special day." Garrick winked at Logan.

Logan grinned in return. "Peg likes pancakes." She held up her unicorn, its already scraggly fur matted with maple syrup.

"Me too." Tate rubbed his belly. He was Uncle Tate now and, officially, Logan's godfather. He'd been Garrick's best man at their wedding.

There were eight of them left in the large booth, the one in the side room of Mac's Diner. Bud and Thea had ridden in with Dani and Jack. Levi had eaten and hustled out early since he was on duty at the firehouse that day.

"This is too much to handle at the table." Skylar slid out of the booth and led Logan to the restroom to get her cleaned up. "We need to hurry. We don't want to be late for your first day of school."

After practically bathing Logan in the ladies' room, they were heading back to the table and nearly ran into Jack standing in the center of the hall.

"Oops. Excuse us." She stepped to the side.

"Hey, Skylar." Jack glanced away and back, looking uncomfortable.

Was he just going to stand there? "Hey, Jack. Can we get by?"

He rubbed his neck and frowned as though gathering his thoughts but didn't step aside.

This was awkward.

Hold on. Was he ... waiting for her?

Jack shoved his hands in his pockets. "We kind of got off on the wrong foot."

"True. But we're okay." They had to be since Dani was her closest friend in addition to being her sister-in-law.

"What I'm saying is—" Jack winced a little. "I'm glad you're here."

Oh my God. Was this ... he wanted some kind of heart-to-heart? Now? Logan needed to get to school.

Jack continued. "You're good for my brother. He's like his old self, maybe better."

"Thanks. But it's not all me." Garrick had been seeing Dr. Austin and told her about the group. The guys from the Veterans' Center had come out for an unofficial equine therapy day. He took them riding and showed them how to groom the horses. It might become a regular thing.

"I know," Jack said, "but some of it is you and Logan. I think you gave him a reason to get better. I just wanted to say...." Jack lifted a shoulder. "Thanks for sticking around when I didn't make it easy on you. I was a real bonehead ... a jerk ... a ... aren't you gonna stop me?"

"I thought you were doing pretty good there."

"I deserve that."

A small knot inside her unraveled as she understood. Jack was apologizing. "We're good." She raised her hand for a fist bump, but he pulled her in for a hug.

"You're good for Dani, too. Thanks. Sis." He chuckled softly.

"Okay, brother." She gave his arm a squeeze.

With all this tender talk, Logan sensed an opportunity. "Uncle Jack, can I ride on your shoulders?"

"Sure, pumpkin, but only for a minute. You have somewhere important to be." Jack hoisted Logan onto his shoulders, and the three of them strolled back to the group.

"Hey," Garrick gave Jack a stink eye. "Don't you be moving in on both of my girls."

Luke strode into the room, so late he'd missed the breakfast. "I just left Wyatt and Striker at Wren's. A pipe busted. Water's everywhere. It's a huge mess."

"Oh, no. Where?" Dani asked. "Not in the honey house, I hope. She was having problems with the plumbing."

"No. It's in her house." Luke pulled his cell phone from his pocket.

"I should go help. I can evaluate the situation. I've handled some real plumbing disasters." Skylar said.

"You have enough to do." Garrick gave her a nudge.

Luke took a seat at the end of the booth. "Check out what hit the news. Clive's been sentenced." He turned his phone and flashed them the headline. "And they got him and his brothers on the fraud charges."

"Couldn't happen to a nicer family." Garrick's eyes sparkled with mirth as he met Luke's gaze. "Send me the link."

Sky followed their conversation. "What are you two up to?" Based on their body language, it almost seemed like they were taking the credit.

Garrick gave her a look of exaggerated innocence.

"You'd better not be doing anything that gets you into trouble." She swung her gaze from Luke to Garrick to Tate.

They laughed.

They settled the check and made their way out of the diner.

She and Garrick drove Logan to school.

Garrick couldn't be prouder if Logan was his own. He opened his camera app and motioned. "Stand over there, out of the sun." He snapped a photo and then, for good measure, took about two dozen more.

"Daddy, Peg's hot." Logan's face was getting red.

"Okay, that's all, munchkin. Why don't you let me hold Peg, and I'll take care of her while you're at school?" He gave his daughter a big hug and accepted her toy. Ten months ago, if you'd told him he'd willingly carry around a sticky, beat-up stuffed Pegasus, he'd have said you'd mistaken him for someone else.

They escorted Logan to her kindergarten teacher.

"Wait!" Logan said as they turned to leave. She kissed her hand and blew on it.

He made a fist, kissed his hand, and right there, in front of God and all creation, blew a kiss back to Logan.

She grinned. "Magic."

"Magic." His chest just about burst with love.

Back at the Jeep, Skylar wiped a tear from her cheek.

He pulled her over, his beautiful wife, and stroked her hair. "Hey, sweetheart, she'll be okay."

"I know. I'm just emotional. Maybe it's hormones." She climbed into his Jeep, and he drove them to their next appointment.

As clinic rooms go, it was comfortable, light yellow with clean, gleaming stainless steel. Garrick sat in the upholstered chair beside the exam table. The doctor moved the transducer over Skylar's belly and glanced over. "You wanted to know, didn't you?" At twenty weeks, they could tell with great certainty.

He met Skylar's gaze. They'd debated this, and ultimately, she'd said it was up to him.

He nodded.

"Well, Dad, Mom. It looks like you two are having a boy."

He wanted to leap right out of his seat. A boy! A son. Now, it was his turn to blink back tears. Somehow, by the grace of God, he had Logan, and now she'd have a brother. He laced his fingers through Sky's and kissed her hand. The doc wiped the gel from her belly and reviewed the list of what Skylar needed to be thinking about at this stage of pregnancy. At forty-three, Sky's pregnancy was considered high risk, but she was in excellent shape, and the doctor didn't see any problems with her or the baby.

When the doc left the room, he moved in for a hug and held Sky close, enjoying the feeling of the bump holding his son. Warmth filled his chest. This was the woman he wanted to wake up next to every morning, to live out his days with. They were a family. "I love you."

"I love you too." Sky kissed him.

They scheduled another appointment and walked into the sunny morning.

A familiar truck had pulled up right in front.

"Dad? What are you doing here?"

Jack, Dani, Bud, and Thea approached.

Bud gave him a sheepish grin. "I had to find out."

"I could've texted you," Garrick said.

"I couldn't wait." Bud lifted his chin. "Well, are you telling us, or is your old man going to his grave without knowing?"

"Don't even say, that Bud." Thea's forehead wrinkled.

Garrick had the urge to shout it from the rooftops, but he checked with his wife.

Sky nodded. "I guess this is our gender reveal party."

"It's a boy," he choked up as the words came out.

Jack clapped him on the shoulder, then pulled him in for a hug. "Way to go, bro."

His father's eyes shone. Bud had embraced his adopted granddaughters, but this new baby touched his dad in a way that

Garrick had never witnessed before. "A son." Bud's voice broke. "We're having another boy in the family."

Garrick's chest puffed out like it was his doing. And it was, in part. He'd take some of the credit for passing along the family name.

"I'll have some tips for you on raising boys." Bud nodded sagely.

Garrick had to keep from scoffing. His marriage would be nothing like his parents' if he had any say in it.

"Well, come over here." Bud opened his arms to Skylar. "Let me hug the woman who's making me a grandfather again. And giving me a grandson."

Skylar collected hugs from everyone, and all Garrick could do was stand there grinning like a happy fool. "Where's Luke?" he asked.

"He's helping Wyatt and Striker at Wren's house," Thea answered as they turned to leave.

Garrick laced his fingers through Sky's and gave them a squeeze. "I'll take you home, then I'm lending a hand at Wren's."

"No way." Sky said with that determined set to her chin. "I feel great. I'm coming with you. We're a team now."

"You've got that right." He opened the door to the Jeep for her and stole a kiss before shutting it.

They drove east, happiness and ease filling him despite the messy job ahead at Wren's. He didn't have to do it. He wasn't duty-bound to do it. He chose to do it. Because he cared and he was showing up. Everywhere he looked in his life, there were teams of people he was connected to, groups bound together by choice, commitment, and love. He was connected to all of these people. It wasn't that there was no place he fit. It's that he fit many places. He saw that now.

Dear Reader,

Thank you for reading this book. Reviews are important. If you enjoyed the story, please take the time to leave a review. It will help others find and enjoy the book as well.

Warmly,

Juliet

If you enjoyed the virtual trip to the beach and the Sea Star Inn, read on for a sample of Beachside Bakery, a second chance romance with a dash of suspense.

Kathryn Hart adjusted the batter crusted twenty-quart stainless-steel bowl in the commercial sink. It tilted. She jumped back. Soapy water splashed over the top and soaked her arm. Shocked, her hand slipped, and the nozzle sprayed the white fabric of her shirt. It clung to her arms. *Great*. She scowled.

This day was not starting out well. If the food critic showed, she'd look like she'd been bathing in the kitchen sink. She pushed damp hair off her wet cheek. At least the baker's apron she wore gave her some protection. She finished scrubbing the bowl and groaned at the other pots waiting beneath it. Why was water pooling in the sink to the right? Was the drain clogged again?

Dishwashing was not her job, but they were running behind. As owner and manager of Sugar Star Bakery and Deli, she'd do whatever it took to keep the bakery going. If she wanted things done right, she had to stay on top of everything herself. But some things she couldn't do. Like bi-locate or clone herself. Or fix plumbing. She wiped her forehead on her sleeve and made a mental note to call a plumber and place another help wanted ad in the online classifieds.

Memorial Day weekend at the Sea Star Inn and Cottages on the southwest coast of Florida was fully booked. Sugar Star Bakery, along the road between the cottages and the main building of the inn, was already doing brisk business, and it was only Thursday. But a steady stream of customers had filtered through since she turned the bakery sign to *OPEN* an hour ago.

Where were Ashlee and Celine? It wasn't like either of them to run late...and on the same morning? It was past the time for her to deliver breakfast to Aunt Caroline who, diabetic and seventy-five years old, needed to eat on schedule.

The entrance to the bakery chimed. "Raldo? Can you get that?" She'd been running back and forth between the kitchen and front counter since opening.

"These cream puffs won't fill themselves." Raldo, her pastry chef, glanced up from the flakey delicacies and scowled. "I work the kitchen. You go."

He had a point, and there was no time to argue with her prima-donna pâtissier. Kathryn sighed, slipped out of the drenched apron, and tied on a fresh one as she walked to the front. Her phone buzzed with a text.

Ashlee: *woke up late, be there asap, leaving now*

Kathryn groaned and stuck her phone in her apron pocket. Ashlee, her primary counter help, wouldn't be in for at least a half hour, and her other baker hadn't called or texted.

As she headed from the kitchen to the front of the shop, she toyed with the ring on her finger, rubbing the gold band with her thumb. It was an old habit, but it comforted her. On the other side of the bakery case stood the tall dark-haired man, who'd checked into the inn a few days earlier. He'd swapped his cowboy hat for a Dallas Cowboys cap. Despite the early hour, perspiration dampened his gray T-shirt and dark jeans covered his legs. He had the solid build of a football player and walked like he was in pain. Was he a ball player? No. Probably a fan.

"Howdy. Did I interrupt your shower?" The edge of his mouth tilted up and his eyes sparkled in amusement.

"Just normal chaos." She forced a laugh and glanced down at her still wet shirt and pants, now covered by a dry apron with the bakery's sea star logo embroidered on the top. "We're a little short-handed. You don't want a kitchen job while you're on vacation, do you?"

"What? And ruin my manicure?" He raised his scarred, calloused hands and chuckled, deep and throaty. "I'm better at eating cookies than baking them." Despite his easy banter, he had the sharp focus of someone memorizing details. As if, at any moment, he could be called upon to remember them. It was a little unsettling, but Kathryn brushed the feeling aside. She got all kinds of guests coming in and took people's idiosyncrasies in stride.

"What can I get you?"

He pointed to a shelf of pastries. "Those churros look mighty fine. I'll take a few of them, and a dozen of the chocolate chip cookies."

"Did you see the buffet set up at the Inn? It's part of the B&B package. We put snacks out."

"I've been for an early walk. I'll make sure to check, though. This is for my private stash." He winked, then surveyed the room and whistled softly. "I guess I've come to the right place."

She followed his gaze to the wall where she displayed framed awards, letters of gratitude for donations, and crayon drawings by local schoolchildren. "Yes. Well, I'd like to think we're the best in the area. We use fresh local and organic ingredients, and many of our recipes have been in my family for generations." She assembled and filled a cardboard bakery box with his selections. "I'm sorry we didn't have a cabin available for you. By the middle of next week, we'll have a vacancy."

"Not a problem. The view from my room's not too shabby. I'll enjoy the wait."

Kathryn rang up the Texan gentleman then followed him to the bakery entrance. She scanned the area out front, as if checking the parking lot would materialize her missing employees.

Patches of blue across the island road hinted at the Gulf. The water was there, even if obscured by palm trees, bird of paradise, and sea grapes. If you followed the sandy path between the dunes, the beach across the street was excellent for shelling.

Kathryn's phone buzzed again.

Aunt Caroline texted: *Are you on your way?*

Darn. She couldn't leave Raldo alone.

She replied: *Soon. What do you want for breakfast?*

Caroline: *blueberry muffin and a cheddar-spinach square*

A familiar car pulled into the lot. Moments later, Celine swept in the back entrance. "Sorry, sorry, sorry. The south bridge was stuck. I sat there for nearly an hour. Of all days, I left my phone at home. Can I use yours to text Philippe to bring mine?"

"Sure." Tension melted from her shoulders. She handed Celine her personal phone. "Ashlee's running late. Can you watch the counter while I bring Aunt Caroline breakfast?"

Kathryn assembled a to-go tray and headed out the back door of the bakery, a freestanding wooden building, painted periwinkle blue and pale yellow, built by Kathryn's mother when she'd been pregnant with her. To the left was the Sea Star Inn. Her mother and two aunts established the inn, and it was where Kathryn grew up.

Besides the owners' apartment, the two-story, Key West style building had eleven bedrooms. Upper rooms afforded guests a sweeping view of the key and the Gulf of Mexico. The rooms downstairs had plentiful windows providing a cross breeze. Guests enjoyed the wrap around veranda with rocking chairs and hanging pots of magenta impatiens. Lush tropical landscaping, yellow hibiscus, and pink knockout rose bushes hugged the house, giving it an enchanting garden vibe.

Rental cottages, painted in island style pastels, formed an L-shape to the south and along the bay to the east. Aunt Caroline's cottage was a buttery yellow and thankfully the first one along the canal side. She balanced the tray and knocked. "I'm here."

"It's open."

Kathryn sighed. "You're supposed to keep it locked."

A full-size cardboard cutout of Captain Picard from *Star Trek* greeted her as she stepped into the cottage. Without Aunt Sylvie to keep Caroline in check, her aunt's eccentric ways threatened to take over. "You need to lock your door. The Captain won't protect you, even if he sets his PHASER to kill."

"No, but Jean Luc's so handsome. He might stun them with his charm." Her aunt chuckled.

Beau, a ten-pound Affenpinscher, who thought he was a St. Bernard, scampered over to investigate when she carried in breakfast and set it on the counter.

"Don't worry about me. I have my guard dog." Aunt Caroline tossed her a smug smile.

"Sure, you do. As long as the intruder doesn't have a bakery bag." Wild hair jutted out in every direction around Beau's little monkey face. He sniffed the air and jumped on her legs. "No. Beau, off."

Caroline clapped her hands. "Come here, you little beast."

The small black dog bounded and leaped onto Caroline's lap, then peered out the window at a large gray bird. All the cottages had a sliding glass door leading to a back patio overlooking either the canal or the bay.

"You have to see this heron." Caroline wheeled her chair closer to the window.

"What happened to the walker you were using last week?" Her aunt's recovery from surgery had been two steps forward and one step back.

"My knee's been bothering me again. Come and sit."

"I don't really have time to visit."

"If you're that busy, you don't have to feed me. I can get my own breakfast," Caroline huffed.

"I can't have you doing that when we have so much food in

the bakery." It was the least she could do for the woman who'd been there for her since her mom died. "But I need a spot on the table to set down your breakfast." Why hadn't Caroline cleared a place? "I'll just move these—"

"No. Let me do it." Her aunt wheeled over with Beau balanced on her ample lap. "I have a delicate system and I know where everything is." The delicate system looked like an office supply store vomited on the table. Not that Kathryn could talk. There was a similar messy desk in her apartment.

Caroline closed her laptop and stacked the papers covering the dining table that served as her workspace. Her aunt had authored a best-selling series of science-fiction books full of shifters and aliens. Somehow, her aunt had been able to live her dream of being a successful writer and had still helped run the inn. Since she'd handed management of the inn to Kathryn and her cousins, she was more prolific than ever. "How's your writing going, dear?" Aunt Caroline narrowed her eyes.

"Slowly." Kathryn had the additional responsibility of a bakery to run, and wasn't in the mood for a lecture about balancing her life. Five stars for her bakery had to come first. Regret tightened like a coil in her chest. Her unfinished manuscript and article for a local magazine sat waiting in her apartment

"That's the heron who made the nest in the tree." Caroline went on as though Kathryn had all day.

Kathryn tapped her foot on the floor, fighting back her impatience. This was the week the reviewer from *Coastal Travels* was supposed to be in town and Kathryn needed the bakery to shine. There was more at stake than a write up. If he liked her, he'd be back to film for their national affiliate cooking show *Secret Eats*. Sure, she wanted to hang out with Aunt Caroline. They didn't get enough time to catch up, but it was imperative she return to the bakery.

"The chick is almost ready to launch. I love the view here, but now that Sylvie's gone, Beau and I don't need the three-bedroom cottage. Why don't I take a smaller cabin?" Caroline asked.

"That would be a big job." Kathryn scanned the room. Now that Aunt Sylvie's things were packed away, it was roomier. Her aunts had shared the largest of the cottages for several years, but Sylvie had passed away the previous year. It made sense for Caroline to downsize but having her close to the bakery was a plus. And they'd built an enclosed space off the patio especially for the dog. So, for now, her aunt was staying right there.

"You seem harried, dear. Why not join me for a cup of coffee?"

"I can't. Lita will be there soon, and Ashlee's running late. We're still down staff."

"I told you Raldo was a diva. He's running them all off." Caroline shook her head. "I thought Yolanda was a wonderful baker."

Her chest tightened. Yes, she regretted Yolanda's leaving and perhaps she could've done more to keep her. "Raldo's staying. I need him."

Find <u>Beachside Bakery on Amazon.</u>

JULIET BRILEE BOOKS

Scan the QR code above using the camera on your smartphone and get a free e-book, an e-book cookbook, author updates, bad jokes, and more in my newsletter.

Find Juliet Brilee books on Amazon.

The Sea Stars and Second Chances series

Beachside Bakery a second chance, single father romance with suspense
  Tea Leaves and the Texan a romance with suspense
  Bayside Cottage a later in life, suspenseful romance
  Sugar Star Christmas a second chance romance
  Peppermint Cocoa Christmas a single dad sweet romance

The Pine Crossing Cowboys Series

Born Ready: Luke a fake marriage ranch romance with suspense
  Born Tough: Jack an off-limits romance with suspense

Born Brave: Garrick romantic suspense at the ranch

Born Strong: Striker a friends to lovers romantic suspense

The Valencia Cove Series

Salt Bay Sunrise: a brother's best friend, wounded veteran, tropical romantic adventure

Second Chance Rescue: Tender Hearts Get a Second Chance at South Paws Dog Rescue, an opposites attract suspense romance

Christmas Cake Day a heartwarming holiday romance full of traditions, family, and holiday baking

Shell Point Secrets: a tropical romance with a dash of mystery.

Salt Bay Summer Dance: a friends to lovers romance

Salt Bay Sanctuary: a friends to lovers second chance romance with suspense

Lemon Cookie Christmas a second chance for love, clean and wholesome holiday romance

ABOUT THE AUTHOR

Juliet Brilee has a master's degree in math and science education and has been writing, making art, and teaching for most of her life. Inspired by her tech nerd husband who gardens, and her son who's blind, Brilee creates brainy characters who often work outdoors, in the arts, technology, or science fields. The people in her books overcome challenging obstacles, deal with the unexpected, find love, and create the life they want.

Her visually impaired son, and his friends who are blind or have other disabilities, help her portray individuals with disabilities more accurately. It is her intention to be respectful and compassionate.

Take a virtual vacation through stories at the intersection of romance, women's fiction, and suspense.

When she's not writing, making art, or coaching, she's enjoying the beaches and woods of Florida, or hiking in North Carolina with her bossy dog.

Join the newsletter and get a free novella: A Second Chance for Bronson and other freebies and updates.